Praise for

THE CALLAHANS

"Leigh continues to do what she does best: write steamy hot love scenes, dangerous enemies, and deadly revenge."

—*RT Book Reviews* on *Ultimate Sins*

"*Midnight Sins* has everything a good book should have: suspense, murder, betrayal, mystery, and lots of sensuality . . . Lora Leigh is a talented author with the ability to create magnificent characters and captivating plots."

—*Romance Junkies*

"[An] erotically charged tale woven tightly around a chilling suspense about love and betrayal. *Midnight Sins* features some outstanding characterization and a plot that unfolds to reveal a horrific tangle of events that lead to the unthinkable. You won't want to put this book down until you have read the very last page."

—*Fresh Fiction*

ELITE OPS

"Leigh delivers . . . erotic passion. This is a hot one for the bookshelf!"　　—*RT Book Reviews* on *Renegade*

"Overflowing with escalating danger, while pent-up sexual cravings practically burst into flames."

—*Sensual Reads* on *Black Jack*

Also By
Lora Leigh

WICKED LIES

LORA LEIGH

St. Martin's Paperbacks

This is a work of fiction. All of the characters, organizations, and events portrayed in this novel are either products of the author's imagination or are used fictitiously.

WICKED LIES

Copyright © 2015 by Lora Leigh.

All rights reserved.

For information address St. Martin's Press, 175 Fifth Avenue, New York, NY 10010.

ISBN: 978-0-312-38911-6

Printed in the United States of America

St. Martin's Paperbacks edition / September 2015

St. Martin's Paperbacks are published by St. Martin's Press, 175 Fifth Avenue, New York, NY 10010.

10 9 8 7 6 5 4 3 2 1

For dear friends who understood that some things take a while to figure out, get used to, and find your place within. Thank you for understanding, for giving me that chance to figure it out, get used to, and settle in. I couldn't have survived without you.

CHAPTER 1

Loudoun, Tennessee

Damn, he could feel her watching him.

It wasn't the itch a man got when he was being hunted; he knew that feeling well. This was different. It was an awareness he'd only felt once in his life, with one other person. And if her ghost were going to haunt him, it would have started long before now.

No, the ghost of that young woman wasn't tracking every move he made. A ghost hadn't been tracking him for the past three months, either.

As he moved through the crowded clearing next to the lake where the summer weekend gatherings were held, he scanned the tree line covertly, searching for a certain shadow or movement that would identify her hiding place.

What the hell was she up to?

He'd given her plenty of time to come to him and let him know what was going on. More than enough time to stop with the games and mysterious familiarity he glimpsed in her eyes sometimes.

He was better at this game. Most of his life had been spent playing it in the mountains surrounding his home, and often winning had simply meant living another day. And he was still there to prove he knew what he was doing.

The hunter always knew when he was being hunted, though.

Jazz Lancing knew that feeling well. The question was, what exactly did the pretty little thing stalking him want?

The thought sent a chill racing through him, tearing aside any amusement. There was always the chance that some part of his or his adopted brothers' pasts could be returning to haunt them. But that particular option just didn't feel right. No, she was just a woman, one with an agenda, one playing a very dangerous game.

"Hey, Jazz, what's up?" The question had his head turning, his gaze slicing to the other man where he stood against the side of his pickup.

Caine Manning had only been in Loudoun about a year and a half now. He'd bought an old farm outside of town and spent most of his time trying to pull it into shape. The rest of the time he was part of the Maddox family security force known as Kin. But hell, just about every able-bodied, well-trained male in the area with the right mind-set was part of that force.

"Nothin' much, Caine. You?"

Reaching into the back of the truck and pulling a chilled glass bottle from the tub of ice sitting against the cab, he tossed it Jazz's way.

Catching it, Jazz glanced at the beer then back to Caine.

"Stay a minute and have a drink." The other man's lips quirked with a hard edge as his gaze scanned the crowd. "We're friends, right?"

Hell, he didn't need this.

"Yeah, we're friends." Twisting the top of the bottle off, he tossed the cap into the back of the truck before leaning against the side. "What does that asshole want now?"

The asshole in question, Cord Maddox, had been noticeably absent when Jazz had needed him the year before. These days Jazz wasn't in the mood for any favors the other man might need.

"Just a meet," Caine murmured. "Said to expect him in a few hours. He has a few things he has to take care of first."

Jazz grunted at the information and took a drink of the beer, his gaze once again scanning the area.

"We'll see," he finally answered, catching the surprise that flickered in Caine's gray eyes. "Tell him I'd like to know where he was when Slade was in New York and we needed his help. He was nowhere to be found."

Slade was one of Jazz's brothers, the eldest, the one who had nearly lost his life and the life of his young son while working in DC. Jazz hadn't appreciated the lack of help when he'd called for it, and he'd sworn then that should Cord need him, then it would just suck for the other man.

Caine nodded slowly. "He said you'd be pissed over that. Said to tell you he was chasing a ghost, and he owes you. The meet isn't for him, it's to repay that debt."

Chasing a ghost.

Jazz froze for a heartbeat of time, some warning sensation rushing through his senses. There was only one ghost he and Cord Maddox could have had in common, and chasing after her was impossible. Unless Cord had figured out how to visit the dead.

The information that this meeting was repayment for being unavailable when he'd been needed was interesting, though. What could the other man have that Jazz would consider valuable enough to cancel *that* debt?

"I'll be around," Jazz told the other man shortly. "Tell him to find me. That's not an agreement, just a willingness to listen, you hear?"

"I hear ya." Caine nodded.

Finishing the beer, Jazz tossed the bottle in the trash can tucked into the corner of the pickup's bed. "If he's playing games, though, he'll regret it."

"I'll pass the message along," Caine assured him. "Take it easy, Jazz."

"Yeah, I'll do my best." Turning, Jazz made his way back into the crowd.

Jazz wasn't in the mood for more games. He'd already forgone his normal weekend attire of cutoff jeans and bare feet for boots, denim, a dark T-shirt, and a knife tucked in his boot. There was a warning brewing in his senses, one he'd become acquainted with years ago and never ignored.

He was ready if trouble came, but trouble hadn't entered the scene yet, just the awareness of it, the certainty that it was headed his way, in the form of the slight shadow he barely glimpsed that followed him from the side of the hill rising above the clearing.

Using the trees for cover, shielding herself in darkness, she was making her way to him.

And he was waiting for her.

The little schoolteacher was no slouch, either. She'd had practice and she'd obviously had a good teacher at one time. There were several occasions over the past weeks that she'd reminded him of—

The past.

She reminded him of the past and that was something he didn't want to delve into at the moment. So much so that he had half a mind to ditch Cord's meeting and just go the hell home.

Right after he confronted his little schoolteacher.

He couldn't just stay in one place and let all those simpering, flirting women come to him, could he? Oh hell no, Romeo Lancing had to be in the middle of the crowd where those simpering little twits had an excuse to rub all over him.

She'd heard the rumors that he was a hound dog when she returned to Loudoun, but believing it was something else. You would think watching those women rub over him like cats in heat would be enough proof. The fact that her best friend, Jessie Colter, had told her more than once about Jazz's inability to form a lasting relationship with a woman was just further proof.

But she remembered the twenty-three-year-old he had been ten summers before, the year she turned seventeen. Popular, wild as the wind, and as charming as any rogue could hope to be. He'd been at her parents' New Year's party, and after that he'd become a regular visitor.

Her brothers were at first amused, then irritated.

She'd heard of the warnings Jazz had been given where she was concerned. But he'd only had eyes for her. He'd flirted, smiled; he'd lie for her when she hid from her brothers at the gatherings and laugh if they became angry over it.

Once, long ago and far away, she'd been out there, dancing and laughing, secure and certain of her place.

Long ago and far away—

So long ago.

Now Kenni moved in the shadows, watching Jazz, tracking him. Once, she'd attended these weekend get-togethers with her brothers and cousins.

Kenni remembered laughing, flirting, being the social butterfly everyone called her that last summer she'd been home. And as she did all those things, Jazz had watched. He'd smiled when she caught him watching, winking and laughing at her brothers' wrath.

She would have smiled at the memory if it didn't hurt so bad.

She hadn't flirted or danced just for the joy of it, and in the two years since she'd been back in Loudoun she'd learned nothing had changed really. She was still far too attracted to the man who had held such fascination for her when she was younger.

She avoided him, but that didn't keep her from watching him now as he strode slowly past the bonfire in the center of the clearing. Like a conqueror, a warrior from centuries long gone, he strode past the flames, fierce and unconquerable. Untamed, sexy as hell, sexually renowned, and far too dominant for any woman to ever completely control.

Firelight flickered over his hard features, loved the broad planes and angles and shadowed them perfectly. He looked brooding, intent, and dangerous.

Jazz.

She'd watched him over the past two summers, trying to decide how closely he was tied to her family. Watched as he moved through the gatherings like a panther while everyone else mistook him for an overgrown tomcat. It was almost funny how they missed the animal that lurked around them, always watching, listening, waiting—determined to strike if an enemy showed itself.

At sixteen, almost seventeen, she'd been completely mesmerized by the twenty-three-year-old Jazz. Six and a half feet tall, neon-blue eyes, and rich, thick black hair. He was every girl's dream, including hers.

She wasn't a girl anymore. She was an adult and she'd learned just how dangerous it was to need anyone. Jazz was a weakness she simply couldn't afford. No matter how intent he was on seducing her. But she knew she needed him. And she needed him for something far different from any physical desire that might torment her.

It actually surprised her that he'd stayed in Loudoun though. At thirty-three he'd never married, had no children. The young man had matured into a powerful, dangerously honed adult male cleverly disguised by laughter, jokes, and a facade of innocent, seductive fun.

He'd changed, though. He barely resembled the young man she had known in her teens.

Regret burned inside her chest at the knowledge that she had no idea what had caused those changes in him. She'd been away for eight years with no contact with friends or family and no way of knowing why the Jazz she had known, the one she'd been certain would one day be hers, had lost the gentle softness in his gaze.

Even after her return two years before there was no catching up, no asking why or how or when, because no one knew who she was. The identity she'd returned with would have no cause to know how he'd changed, or why. If anyone here knew who she had been, it would be a death sentence.

The fear of being detected was so strong—and growing stronger by the month now—that she sometimes felt she was becoming paranoid. That the sense of someone watching, waiting, had to be fear rather than fact.

This was the feeling that had her tracking Jazz, had her finally admitting she may need help, despite the terror the thought of revealing herself brought.

She'd been watching him for nearly three months, trying to learn how closely connected he was to her family and the mountain militia group known as the Kin. A group very few people who weren't a part of were actually aware of.

She'd been back in Loudoun two years and still she hadn't done what she'd come here to do. She was still hiding, still watching, still wishing . . .

Still searching for the reason her life had been destroyed. Admitting she couldn't do it by herself hadn't been easy. The thought of going to Jazz, or even Jessie's husband, a former FBI agent, for help, never failed to send panic tearing through her.

She had no idea if these men, adults now, hardened and obviously far stronger than they had been when she'd actually known them, could still be trusted.

Their ties to the Kin had been strong, and those ties were apparent now, but they'd changed. She just couldn't be certain how.

Jazz chose that moment to stop, laughing at something one of his friends called out to him, distracting her from her thoughts. He was amused, cheerful, and seemed to be as immersed in having fun as everyone else. But there was a tension in his shoulders, a tightness she'd glimpsed in the curve of his lips earlier.

He wasn't having fun.

As she watched his head turned, his gaze raking along the crowd and the trees that bordered the clearing as though searching for someone, or something. He didn't look long enough for her to determine who he was searching for, before returning his attention to the conversation. Of course, he knew she was watching him, she'd figured that out months before. Jazz was too well trained by the Kin not to be aware of it. And though she had been trained as well, she hadn't spent nearly as much time being tutored as he had in the past.

The instincts he'd learned to use in the mountains were so well honed now that there was no way to watch him with anything other than lust and he not be well aware of it. Following him without him knowing it would be all but impossible, even for someone well versed in doing so. She was much better at running than hunting though. The prey rather than the predator.

Admitting she knew how to be no more than the prey was enough to piss her off, too. So much so that the decision to go to Jazz for help still had the power to rake her pride. The damned alley cat.

He was a wild man. He always had been. So tall and muscular and so savagely handsome, like some hero in those crazy romance books. He made a woman feel far too feminine and hungry inside. Her legs weakened, her stomach did all those jumpy acrobatics, and her mouth went dry while another part of her part became so damp and heated it was embarrassing.

Kenni was no different from the throng of lovers he'd had over the years when it came to her fascination with him. He was playful, teasing, seductive. And she was as drawn to him now as she had been that summer. Just as drawn to him as every other woman in his vicinity it seemed. And no woman had a chance at holding his attention, let alone stealing his heart.

No one woman lasted long in his bed, but none left it with a broken heart. Regretful, yes, but they all loved Jazz. He was their best friend and their secret crush, their confidant and their greatest sexual fantasy.

She would never be able to leave his bed and his life without a broken heart, Kenni knew. If she ever became weak enough to allow him to seduce her, then walking away without the agony ripping her apart would be impossible.

Then she'd just have to kill him.

And all that was moot if she didn't first finish what began ten years ago.

She wasn't going to do that until she could prove to herself that he wouldn't betray her. She had little reason to trust the Kin. But then, it was impossible to trust a group that had been trying to kill her for ten years.

As Jazz disappeared into Slade's RV moments later she stepped from the tree line and began picking her way along the darkened edge of the lake, around the parked RVs, and back toward the parking lot.

Long minutes later, as she slid around the white-and-tan RV belonging to Slade and Jessie Colter, the sound of cartoons and low laughter had her chest clenching in envy.

Jessie Colter had befriended her when she'd first arrived in Loudoun as the new kindergarten teacher, Annie Mayes. Had it not been for Jessie, no doubt she wouldn't have really made friends. The other woman had insisted Kenni go to dinner with her after school, or have lunch with her occasionally on the weekends.

When Jessie had married her lost love, Slade Colter, the other woman had become an instant mother to Slade's little boy, Cody. That child was a precocious, sweet-natured little handful. Innocent of face, sincere of speech, and as charming as any six-year-old male could be. He stole hearts right and left.

She did smile then. Just a bit of a curve of her lips before it was quickly pulled back.

"Now, was that a smile on our little schoolteacher's lips?"

The voice, as dark as the night, as sexy as the man himself, and as dangerous as any male ever born, drew her to a sudden and complete stop as she passed the corner of the Colter RV.

Dammit. Not tonight. Not now. Resisting him now, when she was so weak, would be so much harder.

Jazz had pulled his own RV about five feet past the bumper of his friends' vehicle at a slight angle that protected the back of Slade and Jessie's home on wheels. It was from there that he stepped, the bottle of beer held loosely in one hand.

"Jazz . . ." She stepped back, wondering if it was too late to run.

"Still running scared?" The amusement in his voice pricked her at her pride more now than it usually did.

"Still determined to seduce someone who's not interested?" she sniffed disdainfully.

God help her. She'd known he was suspicious, but she hadn't expected him to actually surprise her quite this way.

His brows lowered.

Leaning against the side of his RV, he watched her with that low, brooding frown while he scratched at his chest negligently.

"Not interested, huh?" His lips curved into a grin that didn't quite reach those brilliant-blue eyes, though a hint of bitterness might have gleamed there. "You wouldn't lie to me, would you, sweetheart?"

Straight to his face? Well, it wasn't easy, but of course she would.

"What reason would I have to lie to you, Jazz?"

She could think of a page full of reasons.

"Because you think you can get away with it." He sighed his own answer.

She could get away with it, for a few minutes at least. It wouldn't be easy, but she'd manage it if she had to. No doubt she was going to have to if his expression was anything to go by.

"Personally, I think you're a little paranoid," she informed him with an air of pity. "Such a shame, too. Jessie seems rather certain you're a very intelligent man. Paranoia could be quite detrimental to that."

He'd always been fun to play with, too. That hadn't changed, he still enjoyed a few word games as well as his more sexual pastimes.

"Jessie likes to fuck with your head, baby," he chuckled, the low, rough sound far too sexy.

"Or perhaps you're still in denial. That's never a good thing, Jazz," she assured him, enjoying the exchange far too much. "Talk to Jessie. She'll explain it all to you."

Or actually manage to screw his head up completely, she thought, amused. Jessie had learned how to play those games as well.

He sniffed at the advice, never taking his eyes off her. He wasn't stripping her with his eyes, he was warming her with them. But Jazz had a way of doing that, of making a woman feel like she was the only female on the face of the earth. He charmed and seduced and led them along a path of sultry kisses and dominating caresses—and at the end of that path they were left with the memory of something they would never know again. He'd seduced them so well that getting angry at him was impossible.

Kenni begged to claim otherwise. She was furious with him over every former lover he'd ever had. She wanted to claw their eyes out, then claw his out for being such a damned Romeo.

"You're a pretty little thing aren't you?" The statement had her heart nearly stopping before it began racing in her chest with a speed that made it difficult to breathe properly.

"Th . . . thank you." Damn him, now he was making

her stutter? Just because he thought she was pretty? And why had he waited two years to say that?

His head tilted to the side, his sapphire-blue eyes watching her for another silent moment. Sometimes she wondered what he saw and what he thought when he did that. He had a tendency to watch her as though she were some puzzle he needed to put together. If that was the case then she was in trouble. Once Jazz decided to figure something or someone out, he was just as tenacious as the most stubborn men she'd ever met.

Well, probably more.

When he looked at her like that he did things to her that no other man had even come close to doing. She tingled and could feel herself flushing. Her knees went weak. The tingles raced over her body, detoured to the peaks of her breasts, and then went decidedly south with a surge of energy that had her shifting on her feet to dislodge the ache.

Sweet merciful heaven. This was just wrong. This was not why she was here, and she didn't have time for the distraction. She couldn't let him draw her in yet, not until she was certain where his loyalties lay.

"I should go . . ."

"Something about you just makes me hard as hell." He sighed, causing a laugh of pure disbelief to slip past her lips.

Well, he was rather blunt tonight. She normally steered clear of him, so she'd never really seen him like this. Heard of it, but hadn't seen it. It frankly terrified her. If he kept this up, she might have to let him seduce her and that would simply defeat the purpose.

"Something about me, huh?" She lifted a brow at the

phrasing, crossed her arms beneath her breasts, hoped she was hiding her hardened nipples, and tried for a doubtful expression as she watched him. "Perhaps it's because I'm female."

He seemed to pause for a moment. Maybe he was thinking about the accusation. It wasn't possible to deny it, that was for damned sure.

"Well, I am known for my love of females." He nodded seriously before lifting the beer for another drink.

"Yes, Jazz, you are known for your love of females." Damned alley cat. "Healer of broken hearts, seducer of weeping divorcées, and all-around charming rogue," she pointed out. "Never been married and not so much as a chip taken from your heart. Lucky man." The mockery wasn't nearly as subtle as she was trying for.

He glanced down. Kenni stilled at the flash of dark emotion that swept across his face for just a moment as he stared at the bottle in his hand.

He'd been in love? Oh, that wasn't fair. Damn him, she'd never had a chance to give herself to the man she loved as a young woman, no chance to tell him how much she'd ached for him or to see if she could make this far-too-dangerous man fall in love with her. And he'd dared to fall in love while she was gone.

Bastard.

Double bastard.

"Yeah, lucky man." But he didn't sound as though he agreed with her. "What about you? Ever been married? In love?"

"I'm twenty-six years old, Jazz, what do you think?" She would be twenty-seven soon, but she couldn't tell him that. She was tired, lonely, starving for his touch in ways she hadn't in all the years before coming home, and certain that if she allowed herself to taste the pleasure he could give her, he wouldn't just break her heart. No, Jazz wouldn't do anything by half measures. He'd shatter her soul into a million pieces.

She hadn't had a chance to fall in love because she compared every damned man she met with Jazz Lancing. She was terribly afraid what she'd thought was a crush when she was seventeen went far deeper and ruined her for any other man.

He chose that moment to set the now empty beer bottle on the front bumper of his RV and stepped farther into the shadows, closer to her.

She should leave, right now. Kenni knew she should leave. She should run from him so fast and hard that she left dust in her wake. Instead she stood there like some foolish twit too stupid to get out of the path of danger.

She had so thought she had better control of herself than this.

"Are you frightened of me, darlin'?"

Oh God, he was so close.

Kenni stared up at him, his gaze holding hers as his fingers settled at her hip, drawing her slowly closer until she was flush against his much larger body.

"Frightened of you? No, Jazz, I'm not frightened of you." Fear was the last thing she felt, but what she did feel was more dangerous than fear.

It was hunger. It was the overpowering need for touch. For his touch.

His hold tightened further on her as his head lowered, his lips brushing over her jaw.

Instantly sensation shot across her flesh. Like fingers

of incredible pleasure sinking beneath her skin to nerve endings she'd never known could be so sensitive. The slightest brush of those well-molded, sensual male lips had her lashes fluttering in helpless, hopeless need.

Helpless. She couldn't allow herself to be helpless. Helpless meant dying. And she wasn't ready to die.

"What is with this need of yours to seduce every single female you come in contact with?" she questioned him desperately. "Find another playmate, Jazz. I'm unavailable." It nearly killed her to step back and place several feet between them.

"You're always running away," he drawled, the slight curve of a grin at the corner of his lips. "Keep doing that, you'll hurt my feelings something awful."

Really?

She simply couldn't believe that the statement, no matter how teasing, had actually fallen from his lips. There was a hint of frustration there as well. She could see it in the narrowing of his gaze, the way the muscles ticked sexily at the side of his jaw.

"Poor baby." The patently false sympathy she offered him wasn't helping if his glare was any indication. "I'm sure you can find someone to soothe your poor hurt feelings. I hear you could actually start your own harem."

Oversexed ass!

He was so damned powerful, her fascination for him far too strong—yet she had to deny herself. Where was the fairness in that?

"There's an opening if you'd like to apply for a position," he offered teasingly. "Tryouts could start now if you like?"

Kenni could sense far more than just amusement and

irritation now. There was something deeper in his gaze. Darker. Something that made those tingles start playing through her body again.

She really needed to get the hell away from him.

"You're obviously far drunker than I suspected to actually try that one," she accused him as her fingers dug against her palms to keep from smacking the daylights out of his smug face.

"Or not drunk enough," he grunted, watching her closely now. "Hell, I should have known better, right? You have to be the most irritable woman I've come across in years."

Irritable?

Kenni glared back at him, her ire beginning to heat to anger at the accusation. "If I'm irritable then it's because you can't help being an ass. Besides, no one's holding a gun to your head and forcing you to make such idiotic offers."

"Did I say you were irritable?" he questioned. "I'm sorry, I meant irritating. You're damned irritating."

"Because I won't sleep with you?" Disbelief whipped through her senses like a storm. This man was completely unreal. "What? No one's ever turned you down before, Jazz?"

The smug, too-knowing expression on his face made her teeth grit.

"Nope, not till you," he shot back, the growl in his voice matching the irritated look he shot her.

"Then you're far overdue for the experience, aren't you?" Kenni kept her voice sweet as she stepped back to the path leading to the parking lot, and escape. "Rejection can ultimately be a wonderful character builder, I hear."

The way he looked at her then sent a rush of warmth spreading through her body. The reaction was surprising. As angry as she was, her body shouldn't be reacting to him with such sexual warmth. Then again, Jazz had a way of making a woman just want to melt with a look. The lowered lashes, so thick and long they should be illegal on a man. The sexy smirk that tugged at the corners of his lips and the wicked sensuality that filled his expression were simply, almost, irresistible.

"Then again, I haven't actually been rejected by you, have I?" he pointed out before she could escape, his tone resonating with complete, sensual confidence.

That was Jazz, he couldn't help himself, she decided. For all his confidence and arrogant certainty in himself, he was also right. She had yet to truly reject him. She couldn't seem to make herself do it.

"If that's what you have to convince yourself of, then you go right ahead." She had to force the amusement into her voice as she forced the hunger out of it. "I won't argue with you. Besides, it's time I head home."

She turned her back on him.

She should have known better. The second she actually did it she remembered what a bad idea it could be.

Kenni had barely taken that first step when she found herself hauled around, lifted to her tiptoes, and her back pressed against the side of Jazz's RV.

Neon-blue eyes snared hers, refusing to allow her to escape his gaze or his hold.

Perhaps *bad idea* was the wrong description. Not a

good idea, but definitely a move that showed her exactly why fighting Jazz was going to be so damned hard now.

Her fingers curled against his shoulders, nails pressing into the dark material of his T-shirt as he gripped her rear with both hands, lifted her, and pushed one hard thigh between hers.

Kenni's breath caught. Oh God, that wasn't fair. It wasn't right that she get weak like this, that her flesh betrayed her common sense and gloried in his touch. Need surged through her with catastrophic results. The feel of him, hard, aroused, pressing into tender flesh far too sensitive and aching for touch, nearly destroyed any hope she had of resistance. Let alone control.

"You're not rejecting me, darlin'," he stated, his voice deeper, darker than ever. "Say it now. Tell me you don't want me."

He was so warm, so powerful. For just a moment she wanted to relax against him, to allow that heat to just sink inside her and ease the awful chill that filled her, kept her cold no matter the heat surrounding her.

She had to get away from him before he made it impossible for her to escape the need she could feel building. Because he made her feel safe, heated, and oh so hungry for his touch.

"Why do you keep running, Annie? You want me. I can see it, feel it. You want me until you hurt for it. Almost as bad as I hurt for it."

Annie.

He had to call her Annie. He just had to remind her of who she wasn't, and in doing so emphasize that she couldn't allow anyone to know who she was.

"Enough . . ."

"Jazz, let the little teacher go for a minute so we can talk."

Kenni froze, the shock of the voice behind her sending fear racing through her. She hadn't even known anyone was there. For the first time in years her senses had betrayed her at a time when it was most important. With someone far more dangerous to her than any other could hope to be.

"Let me go." Hissing at his ear, Kenni pushed demandingly at Jazz's shoulders. "Dammit, I knew not to let you catch me in the dark."

He grunted at that, but lowered her to her feet and slowly released her, allowing her to step away from him.

She glimpsed the shadow of a man hidden within the dark copse of trees that grew to the water's edge. And she had to walk past him. Dammit, her luck was starting to suck. It was completely ridiculous that Jazz could affect her to this extent. That he could captivate her senses to the point that she was completely unaware this man had slipped up behind them.

"I'm going home," she muttered. "Remind me to stay away from lake parties in the future."

Neither man answered, though she could feel Jazz's eyes on her as she stomped past the hulking intruder, following the path to the well-lit parking area where she'd left her small tan sedan.

Within seconds the motor was humming. She backed quickly from her parking spot and headed for the exit to the main road.

She was going to have to stay away from Jazz for a long time. Long enough to rebuild her defenses and find a way to make certain this never, ever happened again.

She was in Loudoun to finish a game that had begun ten years before. One so deadly, so filled with evil purpose that it had destroyed everything she cared for. She was safe nowhere. No one was safe caring for her, or attempting to protect her. And now there was no way in hell she could actually be honest with Jazz. How could she catch a killer if all she could think about was touching Jazz, and how he would touch her?

Maybe it was better that way. She was so completely alone that her enemies had no one to use against her, or take from her. She had to be alone to face the enemy from a position of strength, she reminded herself. Loved ones were a weakness. Caring was a weakness. And Kenni had already learned the punishment for caring far more than she could bear.

Another lesson just might destroy her.

Now she had to figure out how to complete what she hadn't been able to complete in two years.

Find a killer.

At this rate, she might manage that task before she was a senior citizen. She doubted it, though . . .

CHAPTER 2

Well, didn't it just figure, Jazz thought as Annie escaped, resigned to the fact that this night had just been screwed to hell and back. And just his damned luck.

He would never figure out why she'd been tracking him so often for the past few months at this rate. It wasn't just here at the weekend gatherings. He knew she'd been watching him in town as well, not that he'd ever glimpsed her doing so.

It was that feeling. A feeling he attributed directly to her.

Besides, seducing her was damned hard this way. She was so busy watching him or trying to follow him, catching her face-to-face was becoming more and more difficult. When he did manage it, she was so wary that she ran as soon as she found an excuse.

He'd been trying to get the little schoolteacher in his arms and in his bed for next to two years now. Fat lot of good it had done him. The minute he had her melting against him Cord Maddox showed up like a harbinger of doom.

He should have expected it. Cord always showed up at the most inopportune times.

"Pretty girl," Cord remarked as he stepped farther from the shadows, his gaze moving slowly from the direction of the parking lot. "What do you know about her?"

What the hell did he care?

Jazz's brows arched. "What should I know about her?"

Cord didn't ask useless questions. The fact that he was supposedly there to do Jazz a favor only made him more wary of Cord's interest.

Emerald eyes sliced to Jazz, thoughtful, suspicious. The ex–Navy SEAL didn't have a whole lot of trust in him. Hell, Jazz had always sworn Cord and his brothers had been born distrustful.

"What do you want, Cord?" Running his hand along the back of his neck, Jazz rubbed at the tense muscles there. Dammit, he had a bad feeling about this.

"Can we talk inside?" Cord nodded to the RV. "It's important."

"Must be for you to show up at a gathering," Jazz bit out as he pushed his fingers through his hair, turned on his heel, and made his way to the narrow door on the back side of the RV.

Moving into the home on wheels his gaze swept over the area, subconsciously prepared for intruders while hoping no one was dumb enough to piss him off tonight. It wouldn't go well for them.

"The gatherings hold too many memories, Jazz, you know that," Cord remarked as they moved to the front of the RV.

Opening the fridge and pulling free two bottles of beer, he tossed one to Colt while opening his own.

For the Maddox family, the memories the gatherings held were all about one bright, flirty young woman-child they'd gathered around to watch out for. Cord's baby sister had begun attending the gatherings when she was thirteen. Each of her three older brothers, often her parents, and a multitude of cousins turned out as well to make certain she was protected.

The Maddox Princess.

She would often laugh at her big brothers and their friends for their protectiveness, Jazz remembered. She'd slip away from them when it seemed there was no way possible to do so. She would do it just to make them crazy as they searched for her. Just to show the big bad Navy SEALs that they weren't all that, she'd claim.

God, how many times had she convinced him to help her even when he'd known better?

Far too many, he remembered. And each time Cord, Deacon, or Sawyer Maddox had planted a fist in Jazz's face for his efforts. Never once had Jazz not considered it worth it just to watch her effectively escape three men trained to keep her in sight.

God help him, he still fucking missed her, still ached so deep inside that the sensation was a constant companion, a constant reminder to never let it happen again.

Finishing his beer in one long drink Jazz tossed the bottle to the trash, uncaring of the reverberation of sound that crashed through the RV.

Cord didn't flinch; he barely blinked, though his gaze sliced to the can and held there for long moments as though considering the move.

"Yeah," he breathed out, the sound both saddened and resigned. "Damned hard to forget that summer, isn't it?"

Impossible. Especially with Cord or one of his brothers reminding him of her every chance they had. Damn them. It had been long enough, far too long.

"Just get to the fucking point," Jazz snapped. "I don't have all night to waste."

Cord just stared back at him, the somber memories in his eyes more than Jazz wanted to confront.

"Tell me, Jazz," he asked then. "If I hadn't threatened to kill you over her that summer, if I'd given you the go-ahead to court her, would you have been with her when she left?"

He would have shadowed her like a fucking lovesick dog, desperate to be by her side. But that weight was one Cord didn't need to carry. He carried enough guilt as it was.

His jaw clenched. "I don't want to talk about this, Cord. It's ten years old, let it go."

"Answer me." The banked fury in Cord's voice didn't intimidate him, it simply emphasized the importance of the question.

He'd asked himself that question far too often and the answer always pissed him right off.

"That was her and her mother's trip. I wouldn't have gone with her unless she'd asked and your mother agreed. And that's assuming she'd even wanted anything to do with me."

It was their girl time.

He'd have stayed close, but he would have never interfered. Hell, he'd nearly done it anyway. That one was his fault.

"She would have asked." Grief still lined Cord's face. "And she would have had you, Jazz." He ran his hand over his face wearily then. "She would have had you."

Ten years. Almost ten years to the day that Cord's mother and sister had died, supposedly in a fiery explosion that swept the upper floors of their hotel.

"Why are you here, Cord?" he finally asked. "What the hell do you want that's so damned important that you came here tonight?"

As far as he was concerned, the discussion, like the past, was over. Just because he remembered, just because he still dreamed of her occasionally, didn't mean he wanted to talk about it now, any more than he'd been able to talk about it then."

"You may as well call Slade and have him hear this as well," Cord said after taking another sip of his beer. "I didn't see Zack outside but if he's here, call him in. I don't have time to wait for him otherwise."

Jazz paused in the act of reaching inside the refrigerator for another beer. Grabbing the bottle he turned on the other man slowly, closing the door absently as he twisted the cap free and tossed it to the trash as well.

"I already warned them you were showing up. They have a few minutes before arriving. What's going on?" With a Maddox, doing someone else a favor could mean any damned thing.

"Let's wait on them." Cord glanced at the door as he braced his arms on his legs and rolled the bottle of beer between his palms. "I don't feel like explaining it twice."

Hell. Jazz wondered if it was too late to just kick the bastard out and forget whatever the "favor" was. Thing was, Cord was well aware of Jazz's ire. Several years before, Jazz had tried to contact him to accompany him and Zack to DC to help Slade when he'd been in trouble there.

The message hadn't been answered for more than a year. By then it had been too late. Slade had been back in Loudon, the situation in DC resolved.

Slade's advice to both Jazz and Zack had been to let it go. Letting it go wasn't easy, though. If Slade hadn't returned, if the worst had happened, then they would have lost not just the man they called brother, but also the woman whose soul had nearly died when Slade had first left.

Jessie loved Slade with such strength that had something happened to him, Jazz didn't doubt she'd have drifted away until she was gone as well. A low knock at the door interrupted the memory, pulling his thoughts back to the present. Stepping to the door, Jazz unlocked it before turning the knob and pushing it open.

It didn't take long for Slade to enter the RV. Jazz tossed him a beer and leaned negligently against the counter, waiting until the door opened again and Zack stepped inside.

For three men who were essentially brothers as well as business partners, Jazz, Slade, and Zack couldn't have been more different, even in looks. Slade was dark blond, with refined features and an innate confidence often mistaken for arrogance.

Zack was the patient numbers person. He could tally up a construction job in his head so fast it amazed Jazz, and he was normally within a 98 percent margin of the actual cost or profit. Light-brown hair and patient gray eyes hid a man seething with the possible explosion to come, though. He was too damned patient and rarely shared his thoughts, let alone any feelings he might have.

Jazz was the people person. He was the one who took the calls from irate building owners or insurance agents. He didn't take much shit, but he knew the value of a calm word. At six six, with eyes too blue and strong mountain features, he was known to make even the stoutest man wary; he'd had to work on his people skills over the years. And he'd done a damned fine job of it, if he did say so himself.

She would have been proud of him . . .

His brothers were damned thankful.

They were friends, brothers, and partners in the building construction business, Rigor Construction, their foster father, Toby, had left them on his death. And now, fourteen years after his death, that business was thriving just as Toby had promised it would.

Only Slade had settled down, though. In Jessie, he'd found a woman who loved him and could put up with him at the same time. Zack was trying to deny who he wanted, but Jazz had seen that relationship building for several years. As for himself, hell, he couldn't get a ghost out of his heart enough to give it to another woman.

"We're all here now," he growled as Slade and Zack glanced over at him questioningly. "What the hell's this favor you're so intent on doing for us?"

Cord's expression hardened for a moment as his head

turned to stare back at Jazz. "How well you know that little kindergarten teacher you were swapping tongues with outside?"

Trust Cord to just throw a man's business in the street for everyone to haggle over. The fact that there was a fine thread of anger in his tone wasn't missed. Jazz was damned certain where it originated too.

"Swapping tongues?" Slade turned to Jazz instantly with a glare, well aware of who Cord was talking about. "Jazz, dammit, I told you to stay the hell away from Annie. When you break her heart, Jessie will kick both our asses."

Disgust edged at his friend's voice as Cord kept his gaze on Jazz for a second before turning to Slade.

"She's Jessie's friend, too, isn't she?" Cord pointed out. "You did a check on her?"

"Of course I did." Slade's dark-blond brows lowered as irritation tightened his lips. "What's this all about, Maddox?"

Reaching into the front pocket of his dark shirt, Cord pulled a slender flash drive from the interior before flipping it to the table where Slade sat.

"I checked her background myself," he said quietly. "Surface check was gold until I called a contact with ties to the university where she obtained her teaching certificate. There was definitely an Annie Mayes who received one, and she was definitely at the address given until just a few weeks before showing up here. What I found buried a bit, though, was the fact that she flew off to China with her lover—a carefully placed CIA asset—several years ago. Another check there found Miss Mayes happily teaching at a small private school for

American businessmen located in Hong Kong." Mockery filled his hard features. "We might think we're in BFE sometimes, but I've never mistaken Loudon for Hong Kong."

Jazz stared at the flash drive lying on the table for long moments before glancing back to Cord. "What was your interest? Why take the time to check anything out?"

Cord didn't always concern himself with what was going on in town; he left that up to his younger brothers. So why pick on a kindergarten teacher who kept to herself?

"I get real curious about folks teaching Kin's kids," Cord stated, the dark-emerald gaze glittering dangerously. "She has a new student coming into her class in the fall, one I look after personally. So I did the check personally. Then I started watching her. She spends a lot of time tracking Jazz and that just made me suspicious as hell anyway. And I owe you for being unable to help the three of you when you asked. That's why I followed up on the information and tried to learn who she was and where she came from. Something I haven't been able to do. The trail stops with the false identity. I want to know who she is and why she's here, and your interest in her hinders that . . ."

Meaning the strong-arm tactics Cord was known for wouldn't be missed and damned sure wouldn't go over well with Jazz or his brothers.

"She could be in danger," Slade pointed out in concern as he glanced at Jazz, then back to Cord. "A false identity doesn't always mean someone is hiding from the truth, or hiding any wrongdoing."

Like Jessie and Jazz, Slade had been concerned about some of Annie's odd habits. There were times she'd seemed to know things about them that she shouldn't. Once she'd referenced a business that hadn't been in business for years before she arrived in town. And her familiarity with Slade, Jessie, Jazz, and Zack from the beginning had made them all wary at first.

"If you say so." Cord wasn't listening if the shrug of his shoulder and chill in his tone were any indication. "I owe you though, so I'm giving the three of you the chance to figure it out."

Annie had been wary since coming to Loudoun. She avoided crowds unless school-related; even when attending the weekend lake parties, she rarely stayed long. Who was she hiding from?

"I don't know who she is," Cord continued, his expression tightening for a moment. "I don't care who she is. I want her out of Loudoun and out of that classroom before fall." The hard, intent look Cord shot him had Jazz's brows lifting mockingly. "Find out who she is and give me a logical reason for the false identity or get rid of her. You have ten days, then I take care of it."

He was fucking joking. Jazz almost laughed in his face at the ridiculous order.

"Like hell." All the lazy negligence Jazz was deliberately projecting disappeared at Cord's ultimatum. "You call that a favor, Maddox? I call it a personal fucking suicide wish. Stay away from her."

Jazz straightened from the counter, his arms falling from their position across his chest to drop to his sides as he faced the heir apparent of the Maddox clan. He didn't give a damn who Cord Maddox thought he was, or what he might have been in the military; he'd be damned if the other man would take care of anything where Annie was concerned.

"She's a liability." Icy determination filled the other man's voice as he simply stared up at Jazz. "The three of you know what that means. I can't track her, I can't identify her, that makes her a danger. I will not tolerate the threat to the family, Jazz and you should understand that better than anyone. We've lost enough already."

The reminder didn't sway him the way Cord had no doubt hoped.

"I said you'll stay the hell away from her," Jazz demanded, refusing to consider, or to allow, anything else. "If she's in danger then I'll be damned if I'll let you make it worse."

He and Cord were on a collision course if the other man thought differently.

"I gave you warning." Cord rose to his feet, watching Jazz carefully. "Ten days . . ."

"Three weeks, Cord." Slade didn't bother to demand, order, or ask. He made a statement as well as the concession of a deadline.

Three weeks, his ass, Jazz thought.

Jazz didn't bother to protest; nor did he demand anything even resembling a concession. He kept his gaze locked on Cord's, let the other man know where it counted that Annie, whoever the hell she was, was off limits.

He and Cord had known each other since they were

kids. They'd known each other far too long, Jazz thought, because he knew the core of the man Cord had become in the past ten years. And he knew the Maddox heir would have no problem at all ensuring Annie Mayes was out of Loudoun and no longer an unknown threat. But just because Jazz knew why, because he understood why, didn't mean it was acceptable.

"You finally let go, didn't you?" Cord asked then, his tone low, the somber resignation filled with regret.

Was that what Cord actually believed?

"What choice have I had?" Let go? Hell, even Jazz knew he didn't know the meaning of the term.

"Dangerous game you're playing, Jazz," Cord observed wearily as he pushed the fingers of one hand through his thick dark-blond hair. "She could be dangerous to all of us."

Dangerous? "A friggin' kindergarten teacher, Cord?" Disgust filled his voice. "How the hell do you figure?"

"Because she's lying about who she is and why she's here, which means she has an agenda here. One I can't figure out," Cord snapped. "That's not a risk I'm willing to take."

She was a threat.

Had it been anyone else, Jazz would have agreed. But it wasn't anyone else. It was Annie.

"Evidently she's a risk I'm willing to take." It was a risk he had no choice but to take. Annie wasn't a risk to the Maddox clan or the Kin and he'd be damned if he'd let either of them make her "disappear." He'd fight the whole mountain if he had to. "By the way, next time, don't do me any fucking favors, okay?"

Cord nodded, his expression tightening with merciless determination. "Good luck, then, I have a feeling you'll need it." Turning back to Slade, he nodded slowly. "You have your three weeks. I hope you don't regret it."

Cord moved past him and left the RV by the same door they'd entered. The shadowed, lake side of the parking spot edged into a narrow line of woods that separated the clearing from the parking area. It was a perfect spot to sit and watch those attending the weekend. It was also perfect cover for the Kin to move about and watch without being seen.

"Hell!" Leaning back in his seat, Slade ran one hand over his face before reaching back to rub at his neck. "I knew something was off. I just didn't expect this. Damn, why didn't I send someone out to check deeper?"

Jazz had considered it, but he'd backed off at the last minute. He hadn't suspected this, not consciously, but he knew he should have.

They'd all known something was off where she was concerned, but Jazz had to admit he wasn't exactly surprised by the fact that she wasn't who she said she was. There had been too many subtle clues that could have been passed off as eccentricities—but once the pieces of the puzzle fell into place, they explained that odd off feeling Jazz experienced around her sometimes.

"Are we telling Jessie about this?" Zack asked at that point, a single brow arching quizzically as he faced Slade.

Annie was Jessie's closest friend. The two women could get as giggly as teenagers whenever they were together. They borrowed each other's clothes, shoes, and purses and argued incessantly over their favorite shows.

"As if I have a choice." Slade grimaced, the look of

helpless resignation almost amusing. "I swore I'd never hide anything important from her again. I'm pretty sure she'd consider this important."

Yeah, Jazz thought, he'd agree with her, too.

"Ya think?" Zack grunted sarcastically.

"Where do we start?" Jazz pinned Slade with a hard look. He knew where he was going to start, but some information was better kept silent in deference to the ulcer Slade often swore Jazz and Zack were going to give him.

If Cord had already tracked Annie to the point that he knew she wasn't Annie Mayes but had been unable to dig up so much as a hint of her real identity, then their job would be next to impossible without going outside their normal routes for information. The Kin weren't just in Loudoun, nor were they all mountain-raised. It was a network that had begun in the mountains only to spread to encompass only God knew how much distance through the subtle web of family links, yet Cord didn't have the answers he wanted. Someone with a bit more finesse was probably needed at this point.

"We'll go over the report Cord put together first," Slade said, nodding to the flash drive. "I'm going to bet he's already checked with contacts in the FBI and marshal's office for witness protection or an agent op. That doesn't give us many tools to use ourselves."

He was going to paddle Annie's ass for this, Jazz swore. Damn her, if she was in trouble then she should have come to him, or Slade. She could have trusted them. She should have trusted Jazz at least.

"Why not just ask her," Jazz bit out, growing more pissed by the minute. "Confront her with the information Cord pulled up and see if she has the good sense to trust us."

Slade watched him doubtfully then. "She's Jessie's best friend, Jazz. Do you really think that would work?"

The two women were a lot alike in some ways, they'd observed over the past two years. So much so that Jazz suspected Annie would be just as stubborn as Jessie. But with Annie, he had a feeling they had more to fear than her anger. Annie would run.

"We do have options, though." Picking up the flash drive, Slade stared at it for long moments before closing his fingers on the small device. "I'll get a copy of this to you two in the next thirty minutes. Then I'll start making some calls, see what I have to work with." The look he gave Jazz was a warning. "Look, I know you're interested in her, but don't play with her, Jazz. Jessie will just get pissed off at both of us. If Annie gets hurt while she's in trouble, then we just may get hurt as well."

Sometimes Slade was far too intimidated by his delicate wife. And far too tightly wrapped around her little finger.

"Fuck you," Jazz growled. "Go take care of that little busybody you married and leave Annie—or whoever the hell she is—to me. That way, you and I don't end up pissed at each other again."

They'd spent the past year glaring at each other the way it was. Jazz would do something that would worry or upset Jessie, then Slade would rip into Jazz's ass. Hell, he was starting to feel like he'd acquired fucking parents. Something he sure as hell didn't need at this late date.

"Don't go off half-cocked, Jazz . . ."

He flashed his friend a confident, reckless smile.

"Hell, I'm always fully cocked when I go off, Slade, you know that," he drawled as he hid the tension building inside him from his friend. "Now get off my ass about it."

He had known too many things were off with Annie and he'd ignored the internal knowledge and warnings. Instead, he'd let her think she was fooling him, let her think she was watching him while he was slowly trying to draw her in, and she could have been in danger the whole time.

Bolting the door after Slade and Zack left, Jazz moved to the laptop he kept locked in a drawer and drew it free. Sliding into the leather recliner Cord had vacated earlier, he powered it up and signed into his email account.

Cord and Slade had their contacts; well, Jazz had his, too. Jazz knew a lot of women. Not all of them had been in his bed; a few of them he'd be wary of in a dark alley. There were a couple, though that he knew he could trust with his back at any time. Two of those ladies were damned dangerous in their own right. And if he was a betting man, they could acquire more information on Annie than Cord or Slade could dig up in twice the time.

Women, he'd learned over the years, were a hell of a lot smarter and most of the time more dangerous, than men ever gave them credit for.

It was because they were so damned pretty, and soft and sweet. Because they had such silken lips and delicate fingers that could bring such pleasure. They weren't hard and powerful like a man, so a man just didn't expect the wallop they could pack.

Jazz liked to think he was a bit smarter than most men. He never assumed a gently curved woman with a winsome face and painted nails couldn't throw a punch or pull a trigger. He damned well knew they could. And there were a few who killed the bad guys and felt good about it when they went to sleep at night.

Kate and Lara Blanchard were just such women. He'd covered their backs and saved their asses. More than once, actually. Now he was calling in the markers. He needed information. And he just might need them to cover Annie's ass for a bit while they were at it.

As he sent the emails Jazz could feel his gut roiling. Learning part of Annie's secrets had finally eased that nagging itch he hadn't been able to locate.

The itch was Annie.

It was hazel eyes that he knew weren't really hazel. Soft, light-brown hair that he knew was dyed. It was the way she stayed in the shadows when he could sense the hunger to come out and play. It was the way she moved, always ready to run. She was always ready to fight.

Whoever she was, she wasn't the quiet, soft-spoken teacher everyone had gotten to know in the past two years. She wasn't anything like the women who had shared his bed in the past, either. He'd known that Annie was different. And it was a difference he was going to figure out whether she wanted it figured out or not.

CHAPTER 3

In the two years since Kenni's return to Loudoun, she'd seen Jazz in a variety of moods. Being Jessie's best friend had allowed her to see him more often than she would have otherwise, though learning his connections to the Kin wasn't nearly as easy. Being part of Jessie's small, tight-knit circle of friends had ensured she and Jazz socialized fairly often. Kenni made certain they didn't share small talk as a consequence though. Sometimes, she simply forgot to keep her guard up where he was concerned, and that could be far too dangerous.

Not that it had been hard to avoid him for the first year or so. It hadn't. Jazz had been a lot busier while helping Zack run the small construction firm the three of them owned before Slade's return. After Slade and Jessie married, that had changed. Suddenly Jazz seemed to realize she was there and that she was female.

A female whose bed he hadn't been in yet.

Loudoun's playboy had pursued her off and on since, alternately teasing, arrogant, and just plain infuriating.

The one constant had been that curious, almost puzzled look at odd moments. As though he was trying to figure her out. As though he was trying to take what he knew and use it to explain what he didn't.

As he was doing two nights later at Slade and Jessie's.

His brilliant-blue eyes were trained on her, narrowed and intense behind that lush veil of black lashes.

His conversation with Slade was sporadic at best as they stood next to the gas grill on the back patio of Slade and Jessie's home. Jazz was leaning lazily against the deck railing, holding a bottle of beer in one hand. He sipped at it with absent movements, his expression brooding, the gleam of curiosity and suspicion in his eyes making her distinctly wary.

"Jessie, didn't you tell Jazz to stop trying to seduce me?" she asked her friend as Jessie moved around the kitchen behind her.

"That's rather like telling a leopard to change its spots," Jessie stated with a hint of laughter in her voice. "But I did try."

Jessie didn't seem too offended by the fact that her alley-cat friend wouldn't stop trying to seduce her other friend.

"Did you do it without laughing?" she sniffed at the carefully contained laughter in her friend's voice.

Jessie did laugh then. The sound was affectionate, cheerful, but not in the least concerned that Jazz was ignoring her request.

"Well, tell him to stop dissecting me with his eyes now," she muttered as she tore lettuce into a large bowl for salad. He was making her nervous. It was distinctly uncomfortable.

"Jazz," Jessie called out, much to Kenni's chagrin. "Stop dissecting Annie with your eyes, please."

The curiosity on his face turned to amused disappointment as he shook his head at her. Kenni could only roll her eyes at the complete uselessness of the attempt. Evidently Jessie had pretty much given up trying to convince Jazz to leave Kenni alone. That, or her friend was secretly cheering the lecherous man. She didn't doubt that one, either.

"He's not very well trained." Jessie's laughter spilled into her voice as she made the observation. "I'm sure he just needs a firm, feminine hand and he'll tame right down."

Kenni turned her head slowly to shoot the other woman a glare. "Stop trying to encourage him, then?"

Jessie only spread her hands and gave Kenni a helpless look. "I just did as you asked, right?"

"Yeah, right," she muttered, turning back to the salad ingredients she was prepping as Jessie finished making sweet tea and filling a pitcher with ice.

Setting the lettuce aside, she pulled the celery and carrots into its place and began dicing them. She had to force herself to focus on the job because her eyes kept straying to Jazz. The feel of him watching her, his gaze piercing, demanding the answers to whatever questions gleamed in his eyes, was distinctly unsettling. Hell, he was even making her hands tremble in nervous reaction. No one had ever . . .

A sudden sharp, slicing pain jerked her attention back to the knife and the blood spilling from her upper palm where the blade had somehow sliced her flesh.

Blinking, she stared at the scarlet fluid spilling from her hand in confusion. How had she done that?

"Oh my God, Annie . . . !" Jessie cried out behind her as both Slade and Jazz rushed into the kitchen.

Slade grabbed a dry dish towel from the top of the counter and wrapped it around her palm, applying pressure as Jazz took the knife from her other hand.

It all happened so fast. Blinking in disbelief, she watched as Slade eased the towel back from her hand several minutes later to reveal a shallow, bloody gash.

"This is all your fault," she said, glaring at Jazz as he pushed Slade's hand back, checked the wound, then folded it over again to apply firmer pressure.

"Sure it is," he agreed with completely false regret.

"If you hadn't been staring at me like a hungry mongrel," she all but hissed, trying to pull her hand from his grip.

"Stay still, darlin'," he demanded gently, ignoring the insult while retaining his grip. "Slade and Jessie went for bandages, we'll have you all fixed up in just a few minutes."

"It takes both of them to get a friggin' Band-Aid?" she snapped. It could take hours if they managed to become distracted with each other. Just what she needed.

"This will take a bit more than a Band-Aid," he promised, peeling the edge of the cloth back again to check for bleeding. "I think you need stitches."

Blood was still seeping from the cut, staining Jessie's dish towel as Kenni stared at it in disgust.

"It doesn't need stitches." She couldn't believe she'd

done something so damned stupid. "Just give me a stupid bandage." A big one maybe.

She knew better than to let herself become so distracted while wielding a blade of any kind. It was one the first things Gunny had taught her when he'd put one in her hand.

"Scared of needles?" he asked, surprise reflecting in his voice as he stared down at her.

"Yeah, terrified." She deliberately didn't look at him as she lied to him.

If she was scared of needles, she would have been in trouble that first night when a bullet had lodged in her shoulder as her uncle raced from a burning hotel with her. She'd learned the next day the hell of having the bullet cut from her flesh with no anesthesia, no hospital support staff or doctor's care. Just Gunny's knife, the whiskey he'd made her drink first and his hoarse voice apologizing as she screamed in agony.

The memory flashed through her head, causing her to inhale roughly before pushing the memory back just as quickly. She didn't need stitches and she didn't need Jazz babying her.

"I said I was fine." A quick jerk of her hand and she was free, putting several feet between them as she checked the wound herself.

"Damn, you are the meanest woman I know," he retorted as he moved behind her and picked up the cloth before looking over her shoulder at her palm. "What would it take to get you to chill out?"

"What would it take to make you stop staring at me like you're trying to dissect me?" she countered as she bit back a curse at the pain radiating from her palm. "I'm

going to have to stop accepting Jessie's invitations because you're making me uncomfortable."

Unfortunately, it wouldn't work, but the threat was
worth a try.

"Yeah, she'll let you get away with that this month
just as easily as you got away with it last month," he
snorted as she rolled her eyes in disgust. Jessie and her
big mouth. "Keep your hand under the water while I
rinse the dish towel in the laundry room. I don't need her
yelling at me because you're still bleeding or because I
threw the towel on the floor."

Turning sideways, she shot his back a glare as he
disappeared into the laundry room. Moments later the
sound of water running and the strong scent of bleach
assured her that at least she didn't have to worry about
DNA lying around.

Not that Slade seemed suspicious of anything. From
the day Jessie had introduced Kenni to Slade, he'd just
seemed to accept her. She was Jessie's friend and it was
that simple.

Not that she thought anything could be that simple
with Slade Colter. No doubt he'd checked the background she'd submitted when applying for the teaching
position. Kenni was confident it would hold up unless
Slade went personally to the California university where
Annie Mayes had attained her teaching degree. That
might present a problem.

And it might not.

"Let me see." Jazz pulled her hand from the water as
Jessie and Slade moved back into the kitchen carrying
a first-aid kit.

"It's fine." She tried to jerk her hand from his grip

again, only to find he was just as determined to hold on to it.

"Stay still for a change," he growled as Jessie moved to her side. "Let me bandage your hand and Jessie can finish the salad so we can eat sometime tonight."

Let him do it? The very thought was shocking. How long had it been since anyone, even Gunny, had helped bandage a wound for her? Gunny made her do it unless she simply couldn't reach it and the damage was too severe to go untreated.

"That means it's time to put on the steaks," Slade announced as he moved to the fridge for the platter of steaks Jessie had been marinating.

"This is ridiculous." Eyeing her friend as she handed over the first-aid box to Jazz, Kenni let herself be pushed into the kitchen chair as Jazz pulled another close enough to prop Kenni's hand against his knee.

"You can't ignore a cut. What if it gets infected? That's dangerous, Annie," he assured her, but there was a sparkle of amused fun in his blue eyes that had her frowning back at him.

"You're so enjoying this," Kenni accused him.

"Of course I am." The playful smile on his lips dared her to join in and tease him in return. "Knowing it irritates you just makes me enjoy it more, too."

She knew better but still it was so hard to hold herself back. She wanted nothing more than to see which of them could push the other the farthest.

Dangerous. So very dangerous.

Instead she ducked her head, watching as he carefully coated the wound with an antibiotic ointment before applying gauze and taping it in place. He bandaged the area efficiently, careful not to apply too much pressure to the reddened skin while ensuring it was properly taken care of.

Hell, all she needed was one of the big Band-Aids. It really wasn't that severe.

"There you go. See how well I can take care of these little things, Annie?" Lifting his head he stared into her eyes, lashes lowered, the drowsy arousal in his blue gaze causing her to swallow tightly.

"Stop trying to seduce me, Jazz," she ordered, her own voice low, hoping Jessie couldn't overhear the conversation. "I don't have time for you and I sure as hell don't want to be hurt by you."

Black brows lowered heavily as he frowned back at her, his expression was no longer teasing. Deep sapphire eyes were somber now and far too intent to ignore. "I'd never hurt you, Annie."

He would pleasure her until she was screaming from it. He would make her ache for more, beg for more, until she was screaming his name in desperation. Then the day would come, and it wouldn't take long, that it would be over. She would be without his touch, his smile, and his laughter, and everything bright in the world would dim.

"You would destroy me," she whispered, knowing it was true. "I'm not one of those women you can seduce and then remain friends with, so please don't try because we'd both regret it."

His lips parted, though whether it was to agree or object she didn't know.

"Steaks are almost ready," Slade called out. "You have the rest of it, Jessie?"

"Salad's finished and the rest is in the fridge," she called back to him. "I'm just waiting for Jazz to finish playing Doctor Feel Good so I can set the table."

Doctor Feel Good? Give her a break.

"All done." Jazz moved so quickly he actually surprised her. "And I'm starved. I'll help Slade get the steaks in."

Beautiful, beautiful little liar.

She was so fucking good. So good that Jazz didn't know whether to be pissed off or amused. What she didn't know was the fact that her secrets were going to be busted. He would make damned sure of it.

Once she'd helped Jessie straighten the kitchen she'd had the nerve to say good night and just leave. It wasn't even dark yet. He hadn't had a chance to cop a feel, steal a kiss, or piss her off before she left.

What he had managed to do was to make certain the bloody dish towel they'd pressed to her hand was bagged and prepped to send out for DNA results. When he'd seen her cut herself he'd nearly frozen in such a gut-level reaction, it had shocked him. The fact that she had been hurt had been so offensive to him that he wondered if he'd ever be able to see her with a knife in her hand again. It was obvious she needed a little practice before using one again.

"How long before the DNA results come back?" he asked Slade as they watched Annie's taillights fade into the night.

"A few days to a week," Slade answered absently as he propped his foot on the railing and leaned against the post of the porch. "Bridget will send me the results and

I'll match them first against the personal DNA database I've set up before running them on the federal program."

If Slade was ever caught, there would be hell to pay. His fingerprint and DNA database for damned near everyone he'd come in contact with since returning to Loudoun included men and women the federal government was probably salivating for at any given moment. Unfortunately, it was 100 percent illegal as well, especially for a former federal agent.

"You think she has relatives in Loudoun?" Sometimes Slade's suspicions went in strange directions.

Slade shrugged at the question. "She reminds me of someone. I just can't place who. I've spent the majority of my life here, so I thought it seemed logical to start here."

Slade was damned good with faces, but the suspicion only followed his own that the color of her eyes was due to contacts and that her hair had been colored. Like Slade, he must have seen her somewhere, possibly even here in Loudoun. It wouldn't have been recently, though. A relative of a friend perhaps, or someone they'd dealt with in a business capacity.

"Let me know when the results come in," Jazz asked, heading down the steps.

"Leaving?" Slade's quiet voice was amused.

And knowing.

"I told Jessie good-bye before coming out here," he promised his friend. "I have things to do tonight."

"Things like heading to town to surprise Annie with a little visit?" Slade was no one's dummy.

"Seems like the thing to do. Make sure her boo-boo is still covered and all that." He chuckled as he threw his hand up in a farewell gesture and stepped into his pickup.

Okay, so he was chasing after a woman when he hadn't done so in a lot of years. It wasn't as though he were becoming involved or anything.

He left emotional entanglements to men like Slade and Zack. They needed the women they were focused on at such a gut-deep, primal level that it would destroy them should anything happen to those women. Jazz had learned years ago what happened to him when he let himself get emotionally entangled with someone and she died. As though he hadn't learned his lesson the first time when his mother had died. Hell no, he'd had to go and let himself get entangled with a little vixen who had walked into his heart without his knowledge. He hadn't even been aware of how important she was to him until she was gone.

Pulling out of Slade and Jessie's driveway, Jazz turned onto the main road and accelerated away from the house. The drive into town didn't take long, despite the curvy mountain road. In less than twenty minutes he was pulling into her driveway and turning off the truck.

Night had eased fully across the mountains, bathing them in mystery and the shield of darkness. Annie's house sat on the outskirts of town, about halfway up the quiet street. The houses here weren't as pristine and well presented as those closer to the town's center, but the gentle wear Annie's home was showing gave it a sense of character and life that the others didn't have.

The rental was a spacious, single-story brick with a fenced front and backyard. The grass was trimmed; no weeds struggled to take over even at the edges of the yard. It was clean, if empty of most of the feminine touches he would have expected. There were no flowers ready to burst into rioting color. No newly planted shrubs or even a potted plant on the wide front porch.

The house was dark but for the faint hint of light at the rear of the house, but he knew she was there.

The main door eased open as he stepped to the porch. Coming to a stop he just stared at her as she stood on the other side of the storm door without opening it or asking him in.

"What are you doing here, Jazz?" The wariness in her tone gave him a vague sense of discomfort. It bothered him that she didn't trust him, that she stayed on guard with him.

"Fuck if I know," he admitted, watching her through the glass. "I should be home getting ready to go to work tomorrow, not standing here wondering how I'm going to try to talk you into letting me visit for a while."

There was no way he could explain to her why he needed to be around her. He couldn't even explain it to himself.

To protect her?

He could buy that, he was pretty "hands on" when it came to his damsels in distress.

She looked away, her gaze going to the darkened street before she shook her head slowly. Unlocking the door she stepped back, watching him as though she expected him to jump her at any moment.

It wasn't trust—maybe more weary resignation than anything else—but he was in the front door. That was definitely a step in the right direction.

She'd changed from the jeans and T-shirt she wore

at Slade and Jessie's into a pair of soft cotton shorts and a tank top. She still wore a bra, though, where most women would have already tossed it to the side for comfort's sake.

Ready to run at a moment's notice, wasn't she?

He bet she had a small pack that contained everything she needed if she had to escape quickly. Hell, he knew she did. He still kept one himself. Just in case.

Moving inside he closed the doors behind him, locking them automatically as she moved to an end table and turned on the lamp there.

The soft, low light bathed the room in a gentle glow.

It was as sparse as the front lawn. There was no more there than what had to be. Couch, two chairs, matching end tables, and a flat-screen television. A flannel throw was tossed over the back of one recliner but there were no pictures, no mementos, nothing that would illustrate parts of her life as most women had. No knickknacks, flowers, framed prints on the bare walls, or books to mark her tastes.

There was nothing to leave behind if she had to run. No pictures of friends who could be endangered, no indication of where she might go or where she might hide.

This room made his chest tighten, made him hurt for her. It was as empty as she seemed to have been forced to make her life.

Fuck, who was she? What the hell had her so spooked that she thought he'd ever allow her to just disappear?

"What do you want?" There was an edge of defensiveness in her voice, that tone that never failed to make him want to show her exactly what they both wanted.

Looking around the room it was all he could do to tamp his anger down, to pull back the urge to demand answers. He wanted to give her no chance of lying, no way to wiggle out of the facts. Anyone forced to live on the run long enough to learn how to stay unencumbered would know how to lie and make it believable. He didn't want that between them. Nor could he handle the hunger for her that seemed to grow daily.

Damn her. He thought of little else anymore but her. It was bad enough before he'd learned that she wasn't who she said she was—and that she could be in danger. Now it was like a constant storm surge, battering at his self-control until he began to wonder if he'd make it another day without confronting her. Without claiming her.

He hadn't wanted like this since he was a young man, since he'd learned the danger in it. And even knowing that danger now, he couldn't seem to step back.

"I'm sorry I made you feel as though I were dissecting you at Slade and Jessie's." He held back a smile as suspicion instantly lit her gaze.

"Really?" She crossed her slender arms beneath her breasts, cocked those shapely hips defiantly, and stared back at him, plainly disbelieving.

"Cross my heart." He laid his palm over the middle of his chest as he watched her somberly. "That wasn't what I was doing at all." His hand dropped from his chest as his grin slipped free. "I was actually undressing you with my eyes."

She wanted to laugh, he knew she did. The way her lips tightened, the narrowing of her eyes to hide that gleam of amusement.

"Jazz, one of these days you're going to make me kick you," she warned him with convincing disapproval.

He might have been convinced if he hadn't caught that little twitch at the corner of her eyes when he winked at her.

"Come on, laugh, you know you want to," he dared her.

"What I want is to know why you showed up on my doorstep tonight," she retorted, glancing away from him momentarily.

When her gaze returned it was once again calm, though the suspicion still lingered. Watching him, her hand lifted to brush back her hair as it fell from behind her ear to brush against her cheek. She tucked the strands back with two fingers, though, rather than the three most women used. The odd little habit seemed strangely familiar, he just couldn't place it.

The bandage he'd put on her hand earlier was gone, he noticed then, the wound now covered with a Band Aid, albeit a large square one. And she acted as though it hadn't even happened. Or as though being cut, being hurt, wasn't exactly foreign to her.

"You're driving me crazy," he finally told her. "And the thought that you believe I'd hurt you irritates me, sweetheart. It irritates me a lot."

It bothered him more than he wanted to admit to himself. But as he stood there, facing her, he had to acknowledge to himself that her lack of belief in him had him questioning himself and what he might have done to make her distrust him.

"I don't believe you'd physically hurt me," she said

carefully, swallowing as the pulse at her throat began to speed up. "I never thought that, Jazz."

It was the truth.

She stared back at him directly, remorse darkening the hazel eyes as regret filled her expression.

Some of the tension that held his body taut relaxed. He hadn't realized how much it did bother him that she might be scared of him. Wary of his intentions, he could understand. Frightened of his strength, well, he'd have to do something about that, if it had been the case.

"Then how do you think I'd hurt you?" Stepping closer he watched the indecision in her eyes, watched as she considered moving back, running from him. In the end she stood firm, even when he reached out and tucked that falling hair back into place for her.

"Like this," she snapped, a little glare on her face. Her hands lifted to press against his chest when he stepped closer. "You use your soft words and your appreciation for a woman to seduce her straight into your bed. And it's all a lie, isn't it?" A hint of anger flashed in her eyes, and she did step back then. "You lie with every kiss, every touch, then you lie further when you convince them that walking away and staying friends will be so much more emotionally fulfilling than kicking your ass to the curb to start with."

Kick his ass to the curb? Hell, what had he done?

Of course staying friends was better than breaking hearts and leaving hard feelings. Hell, there was enough of that going around. There was no need for him to add to it.

"Damn, you definitely have an opinion on me, don't

you?" He wasn't angry, but he damned sure wasn't happy at the moment. "Where the hell do you come up with this crap? Because I haven't broken as many hearts as possible? Because I'm not moaning and moping because mine might have been broken? Really, darlin'? Don't you think that's just a little judgmental?"

His heart had been broken, though. It had been decimated to the point that it had taken nearly a decade to heal.

"No, I really don't." Her chin lifted stubbornly. "I know what I've seen out of you in the past two years and I know what I've heard. Your ex-lovers talk about you as though you're some sort of trophy they were allowed to hold for a while. Now all they dream about is one more night. Well sorry, but that just isn't me. I'd just go ahead and shoot you."

Damn, she was a bloodthirsty little thing, wasn't she?

He almost chuckled at the fierceness of her expression as it mixed with feminine arousal. She hadn't learned yet how powerful anger could make the hunger.

"Shoot me for what?" He feigned disbelief. "For seducing you? Because I want you, because my dick is perpetually hard?"

A flush mounted her cheeks then, her gaze almost dropping to his thighs as though to verify his claim.

"Your dick stayed hard before I ever met you," she accused him a second later, disgust snapping in her tone as she flipped her hand toward him disdainfully. "If you weren't such a damned hound dog, Jazz, things might have been different, but as it is the thought of being part of the Jazz Lancing fan club just doesn't sit well with me."

It didn't sit well with her?

So that was why her nipples were so hard they looked like little pebbles beneath her bra and shirt?

That straight little nose lifted, nostrils flaring as though some scent offended her, and Jazz could feel the dark core of sexual dominance rising inside him with a strength he hadn't experienced before her.

At this rate they were both going to end up regretting what he was coming far too close to doing.

Or maybe not—

"Keep lying like that, baby girl, and I'm going to show you how full of shit you really are," he warned her as she glared up at him, defiance and stubbornness tightening her expression.

"And how do you think you're going to do that?" Little fists clenched at her sides as she angled herself as though attempting to go nose-to-nose with him. "You couldn't show me a damned thing, Jazz, you're too busy protecting that cold little heart of yours while you're notching your bedpost like some collector."

Damn her.

Staring into her eyes he saw the anger, that it was a very small part of the heat driving her. Her breasts were heaving, hard little nipples tempting him to touch, to taste. And he was betting they'd be candy-sweet. Her hazel eyes were greener, a hint of freckles over her nose more noticeable, and he knew what arousal looked like in a woman. He knew how hunger brightened her eyes, flushed her cheeks, and plumped the curve of pretty breasts. And he knew she was showing every sign of it.

"Let me just show you how I'm going to prove it." Before she dared try to avoid him, he gripped her hips, lifting her against him, he wrapped one arm around her waist, the other around her back. His hand buried in the back of her soft hair, his fingers clenching in the silken strands.

Pulling her head back his lips slanted over hers, tongue driving past them as control exploded into a white-hot, searing lust he swore he'd never known before. Her kiss was like pouring gasoline to a fire. They were both burning out of control now.

She could slam his ass for his hunger, for lovers he hadn't touched since meeting her, and all the while lie through her teeth about her own need for him?

The hell she would.

She was practically shaking as her arms slid around his neck, holding on to him as though terrified he'd let her go. Her lips parted, a whispery moan leaving them as he tasted her with his lips and tongue, claimed her kiss, devoured the hunger he could feel in her response.

Pleasure consumed his senses. Her sharp little nails rasping against the back of his neck like a cat kneading in pleasure. She arched against him, her lips moved beneath his, taking his kiss as he took hers. And those tempting, firm little breasts, confined as they were in that bra, pressed into his chest, rubbed against it, and drove spikes of sensation straight to his dick.

God help him, he'd never wanted anyone . . . anything . . . like he wanted this woman.

CHAPTER 4

It wasn't supposed to be like this.

Kenni's senses were overwhelmed. Pleasure rose and surged through her body, blood rushing through her veins, her flesh sensitized and tingling with exquisite sensation at each brush of his body against hers.

It was incredible. It was more intense than she'd ever imagined it could be. And she'd really imagined it many, many times in her fantasies. Those fantasies were nothing compared with the real thing. Not even close.

His lips moved over hers possessively, his tongue pushing past, taking languid tastes of hers as heat built and surged through her senses. She was lost in the pleasure, lost in each taste of the wild passion she was given.

One hand buried in her hair, his fingers clenching in the strands and tugging at them erotically, sending sharp little bursts of sensation racing through her scalp. It wasn't pain, but a biting sensation of heat she might become addicted to.

But then she could become addicted to everything

about Jazz. Every touch, every note of his voice, the warmth of his body.

"Damn you." Hoarse, roughened with male lust, Jazz's voice whispered over her ear as his lips slid from hers, along her jaw, to nip at the lobe of her ear.

Kenni shivered at the rush of sensation that tore through her. His lips moved down the column of her neck, his tongue taking flicking tastes of her skin. Turning her head to his neck she let herself taste him as well, need surging through her, raking over her senses as she gripped the tough skin at the base of his neck and nipped it.

God, she loved the taste of him. It was all male and wild, like a storm coming over the mountains.

When he nipped her shoulder in return a moan escaped her lips, electric sensation racing through her at the feel of his teeth rasping against her skin.

Dizzying pleasure filled her, weakened her.

"How sweet you are," he whispered at her ear, the rasp of his cheek against her neck dragging a low moan from her throat.

She had waited for this, dreamed of it. Being in Jazz's arms, the spearing heat and aching, building tension rising inside her had her arching, needing to feel more of him.

"Jazz." His name slipped past her lips again, a desperate plea for more as he ran one hand from her back to her rear and lifted her closer to him.

"Spread your legs, grip my hips, baby. Hold on to me."

Her knees tightened at his hips, her head resting against the wall as he pressed his erection into the vee of her thighs. Separated by the material of his jeans and the thin cotton of her shorts, it was still little protection against the devastating eroticism. His hips rotated, moving against her, rasping the tender bud of her swollen clit with the material of her shorts.

Damp heat spilled from the feminine folds, saturating her flesh, slickening her, preparing her for him.

How was she supposed to hold out against him now? Deny him? It was a taste of ecstasy, of a dream she knew she should have never tempted.

"That's it, darlin', burn for me," he encouraged her, his lips moving along her neck, his teeth nipping at her flesh, sending flares of heat to the aching depths of her vagina.

She had waited for this for so long. She'd dreamed of it, ached for it. Yet she had never imagined she would come apart in his arms as she was now; that the pleasure could tear at her senses and dissolve every barrier she came up with against it.

"Damn. Not like this . . ." The rough, furious growl had her dragging her eyes open, staring up at him in shock as he set her feet on the floor and stepped back.

The icy chill sweeping over her was agonizing. Deprived of his heat, of the pleasure burning through her, she suddenly realized just how cold she had been for so long.

"What . . . ? Jazz . . . ?" Kenni swallowed tightly, her palms flattening against the wall to keep from reaching for him, from silently begging for him.

Just a few more minutes, she thought desperately. Couldn't she have had just a few more minutes?

Pushing his fingers roughly through his hair Jazz

stalked across the room before turning and glaring back
at her, his blue eyes intense behind the narrowed shield
of those thick lashes.

"You make me fucking crazy," he muttered, a hint of
anger burning in his eyes now.

The statement had her staring back at him in disbelief.

"I make you crazy?" What the hell had she done to
him this time? "You're the one who barged in on me
tonight, not the other way around." Anger instantly over-
came the erotic weakness that had invaded her knees.
Her hands went to her hips, outrage filling her. "I did
not ask you to show up here and start kissing me, Jazz
Lancing. You did that all on your own, so don't blame
me if you regret it now."

Damn him. Double damn him. What made him think
he could jerk her to him and make her want him with a
desperation that bordered on insanity, only to blame her
for it?

"I didn't say I regretted a damned thing." The low,
deep tone of his voice had her tensing at the warning in
it. "I said you make me fucking crazy."

"You were crazy long before I showed up." She flipped
her hand toward him dismissively. "Why don't you just
go on home and leave me the hell alone now. And
next time, call before you show up so I can leave before
you get here. You just end up giving me a headache."

And making her do things she knew were foolhardy.
Things like wishing she was back in his arms, like wanting to beg for more when she knew more would only
end up destroying her further.

She couldn't afford Jazz, her soul couldn't afford

Jazz. It was bad enough he was her greatest sexual fantasy and her deepest desire all rolled up in one sexy, hard, mountain-bred warrior. If she could be certain he wouldn't go to Cord, certain his ties to the Kin weren't as strong as they once were, then she would have asked him for help. Maybe.

Three months of watching him, though, tracking him, and still she didn't know if his loyalties would lie with her or with Cord and the Kin.

If anyone could have helped her, though, it would have been Jazz.

"Well, ain't that just too bad, sweet pea," he snarled, glaring back at her. "So I guess you just better get used to that headache because I'll be damned if I'll give you a warning of any fucking thing."

And wasn't that just like him. Stubborn, mule-headed man that he was, had been for as long as she'd known him.

"You're being unreasonable . . ."

"Well, excuse me," he snarled back at her. "Evidently that's what happens when I get this hard for a woman who refuses to come to me on her own."

Well, now, shouldn't that have just clued him in at some point?

"Who refuses to beg, you mean?" Crossing her arms beneath her breasts Kenni flashed him a disgusted look. "I won't beg you, Jazz, nor will I fawn over your dubious charms. I'm not one of your little harem bunnies."

There were nights, though, when she would have begged to be at least that much. She needed, ached, prayed that one day she would feel secure enough to let him hold her for a little while. For a night.

"It would be a damned sight better for both of us if you were," he muttered before turning and stalking to the front door. "I'm leaving before I end up saying or doing something we'll both regret. But this isn't over, sweetheart. Not by a long shot." At the door he turned back to her, his expression tight with such male dominance and complete arrogance that she could only stare back at him in surprise and disbelief. "Don't even think I won't be back, because I promise you I will be. And when I do, you and I are going to have a few things to discuss."

With that, he jerked the front door open and stalked out. The door slammed behind him, the force rattling the panes of glass in the metal door.

Kenni could only stare at the entrance, blinking in shock. He had to be the most irritating human she had ever met in her life. He didn't make a damned bit of sense. Evidently, in ten years that hadn't changed a bit.

But his kisses were like potent wine. Her senses filled with the memory of them as her hand lifted, her fingers touching the still-swollen curves. And even as irritated as she was with him, she wished his lips were still on hers, his hands caressing her. Even knowing it could never go farther than a night or two in his arms, she ached for it.

She ached for him.

And she couldn't have him, at least not for long. Not long enough to endanger him, not long enough for him to figure out the lies she was living.

Moving slowly back to the bedroom, she resigned herself to the ache Jazz created in her body. Her nipples were so hard that the rasp of her bra was almost unbearable. The swollen bud of her clit was aching with such heated need, she knew there would be no easing it for a while.

She hadn't known how hot, how intense she could burn in his arms.

She hadn't known how deep regret could be, or how much it could hurt to know that her time with him would be short, whether she went to his bed or not.

Her time as well as her life were limited, she feared. Because as soon as the Kin realized where she was, she would die. If she didn't learn who was trying to kill her and who had murdered her mother, then there would be no chance of survival. Risking Jazz to that fate was something she couldn't bear to do—and something she feared he wouldn't allow her to walk away from if he even suspected her real identity. God, she prayed daily he didn't, because Jazz would be the hardest one to escape.

CHAPTER 5

She was being watched, not hunted as she had been in the past, but Kenni could feel that vulnerable sense of eyes on her, tracking her movements and following her as she left the house a few mornings later. Keeping her steps relaxed and unhurried, she walked the few blocks to the café where she and Jessie met for coffee a few mornings a week.

This was the first time she'd been followed while walking there. The sensation drove home the fact that she'd perhaps grown complacent because she hadn't been bothered or noticed by the Kin since arriving in Loudoun.

For a moment she considered returning to the house and getting the small car she drove. That would only tip them off, though, she feared, let them see that she suspected they were watching her. It would only give her away. Let them wait, wonder. Maybe, just maybe she'd have time to identify who it was before they were certain it was her rather than who she said she was.

Who was watching her or how they were managing to follow her, Kenni wasn't certain. There wasn't much traffic moving through the streets; no single vehicle stood out or passed more than once. No one else jogged or walked along the sidewalk that morning, and no one seemed overly interested in her movements.

But the feeling was there.

Her forehead was tight with instinctive awareness, the sensitive skin between her shoulder blades prickling with it.

This wasn't the driving awareness of a weapon trained on her, or that hollow ache of panic that came whenever she'd been found before. It was more a feeling of simply not being alone when she knew she should be.

Keeping her steps purposefully unhurried, Kenni pretended she was simply enjoying the warm summer morning. If she had to run, she would; if she had to fight, she could. For the moment, though, she pretended to be completely unaware that she was being watched.

The light tan capris and white tank top matched with leather sandals she wore weren't the ideal clothes to have to run in, but she'd learned to be prepared over the years. She could get to more durable clothes within minutes if she had to. Gunny had taught her to never allow herself to be caught unprepared or without the clothes and tools she needed to survive.

Charles "Gunny" Jones had been her mother's half brother, one Kenni had never known existed until the night of her mother's murder. He'd shown up the night of the fire to meet with her mother, his deep-brown eyes filled with concern when he'd met Kenni. Later that night Kenni had walked in on her mother's murderer and nearly become a casualty herself.

She forced the memory back. She couldn't let herself become mired in the past again. The terror and betrayal she had felt that night had scarred her in ways she knew she'd never recover from. Everything she had believed in had died and all the trust that had been built through her life disintegrated.

Had it not been for Gunny, she would have died. He'd surged through the smoke and flames just in time to rescue her.

She'd escaped, but as they ran from the hotel someone else had been waiting. Someone who had put a bullet in her shoulder, leaving a reminder that she would never truly be safe. Her assassin could be waiting anywhere, at any time, if she wasn't careful not to give herself away.

Reaching the café Kenni pushed inside, her gaze scanning the area until she spotted Jessie and Slade where they sat on the far side of the room. It wasn't often Slade came with his wife; he claimed "girl talk" made him itch. Evidently this morning he'd decided to suffer.

Smiling at the couple Kenni moved across the floor as she hoped—hell, she prayed—Jazz wasn't with them. She'd had all she could deal with this week when it came to the local Romeo.

Jazz had been far different at twenty-three, she reflected. He had smiled and had fun, but he'd seemed to take relationships more seriously. Not that she'd known him to really have a relationship, come to think of it, but neither had he been screwing his way through the county.

"Am I late or are you early?" Kenni asked as she took the seat across from the couple and smiled back at Jessie.

Three months' pregnant and glowing with health and Slade's love, Jessie was radiant. The light, soft white sundress she wore made her eyes appear deeper, darker. It complimented her smooth complexion and dark brown hair while making her look more innocent than she already did.

"I think we were just very early," Jessie assured her with a small grin as Slade poured an extra cup of coffee from the carafe at his elbow. "Slade had an errand to run and finished up sooner than he thought he would so we came on over."

Adding sugar and cream to the steaming coffee, Kenni glanced at Slade to see his gaze on the bandage on her hand.

"It wasn't really that bad," she assured him, lifting the cup for a much-needed sip. "It just looked like I was bleeding out."

"It did indeed," he agreed. "Jazz mentioned running by your place to check on you after you left. Did he make it?"

Kenni lifted her head and glared at him as Jessie's smothered laughter had his lips kicking up at one corner.

"I thought you two liked me." Sitting back in her chair, she stared at the two in disappointment.

"We do like you, sweetie," Jessie assured her, her

brown eyes sparkling with amused affection. "I've just never seen Jazz like this. He doesn't know if he should be sweet or irritated with you. It's kind of cute."

"It's kind of scary." Slade grimaced, though his gray eyes gleamed with his own amusement. "I used to be able to predict what he'll do. That's not working anymore."

Kenni's brow lifted before she gave a little roll of her eyes. "You're telling me this why? It's not my fault the man is completely psycho."

Slade snorted at the accusation. "He's more psycho than normal, then," he pointed out. "Actually, Jessie's right, Jazz isn't normally so focused on one woman. I consider that a good thing. On a good day."

Her mocking comment was forestalled by the waitress. As she took their orders the old-fashioned bell above the entrance door announced new arrivals.

The couple that walked into the room was so unexpected, the sight of them such a shock, that only years of training helped her maintain her composure.

It was all she could do to set her coffee cup on the table and force her fingers not to tremble. In the time she and Jessie had been coming to the café this was the first time she'd seen members of the Maddox family there.

The Maddox Clan headed the Kin, a mountain-based militia group with tentacles reaching from one coast to another. What had begun as a small anchor group decades before her birth had turned into much more before she'd been forced to disappear. So much more that no matter where she'd run, they'd managed to find her.

Moving slowly across the room, the current wife of the head of the Clan, Lucia Neely Maddox, moved gracefully across the floor. Her long dark hair was piled haphazardly on her head and held with a clip. White linen shorts and a matching sleeveless blouse were paired with a pale yellow belt and matching strappy leather sandals. She looked cool and relaxed, and distant. Despite the friendly smile curving her pale-pink lips, Kenni could still see the cool reservation in the other woman's expression.

Behind her the eldest son of the family moved like a predator, his intense emerald-green eyes narrowed and suspicious as he watched everything while appearing to watch nothing.

Cord Maddox was rumored to be even harder, colder, than his father. He oversaw the Kin in the area and kept up with those in other areas while running his teams with a fierce determination that made a drill sergeant look like a Sunday school teacher.

And he and Mrs. Maddox were headed toward the table where she sat with Jessie and Slade. Now, wasn't that just what she needed?

"Annie, I was hoping to go to the school and clean out the classroom sometime this week," Jessie stated, dragging Kenni's attention to her. "My resignation was official the last day of school." Her smile was excited but tinged with a hint of regret. "I thought I'd get everything ready for the new teacher they're bringing in."

Lucia Maddox and her stepson were right behind them.

"New teachers are always welcome, but we'll miss you, Jessie." Lucia Maddox moved to the side of the table, allowing her to face Jessie.

"Luce, how are you?" Pleased surprise filled Jessie's face.

Rising from her chair, Jessie moved around her husband to give the other woman a warm, welcoming hug. "How are you doing?"

"Fine," Lucia answered, the warm smile that curved her lips not reaching the somber blue eyes. "Things have just been incredibly busy. I saw Slade's car parked outside and hoped you were here. I hadn't seen you in forever."

"Sit with us." Jessie waved her hand to the extra chairs at a nearby empty table. "Have a cup of coffee. It's been ages since we've talked."

"Cord?" Luce turned back to her stepson. "Are we in a hurry?"

She could feel his eyes on her, probing, icy cold. She knew that brilliant-green gaze would be like shards of emerald ice. Suspicion was a part of him, so deeply ingrained that she doubted he'd ever trust anyone.

"I'm sorry, Luce." Cool and lacking any regret he answered her, his deep voice pitched low. "I have to get those papers back to the house for Dad to go over." He turned to Slade then. "I hear congratulations are in order, though." A quirk of his lips hinted at the sincerity of the expression as Cord extended his hand to Slade.

"Thank you." Slade's grin was proud as hell.

Yes, the ties that bound Slade, Jazz, and Zack to the Kin were still just as tight as ever, if not tighter. It was there in the undercurrents of familiarity and friendship, as well as a hint of wariness the two men shared with each other.

"Ready then?" Cord turned to Luce, his powerful shoulders shifting, tension rippling beneath them.

"Of course." A little moue of disappointment shaped her lips as she turned back to Jessie. "I'm sorry, hon, maybe you could come out to the house one morning for coffee? Your friend could come as well. Annie, isn't it? You're a teacher as well?"

"I'm so rude," Jessie exclaimed in horror. "Annie, this is Luce Maddox and her stepson Cord. They live in that big old creepy house everyone talks about farther up the mountain." The laughter in Jessie's voice had Luce's eyes crinkling for a second in amusement. "Luce, Cord, this is one of our kindergarten teachers, Annie Mayes."

"Mrs. Maddox." Kenni accepted her handshake, thankful her palms hadn't become damp with nerves. "Mr. Maddox."

His handshake was firm, his palms callused. She was careful not to look at him directly, certain if she did then he would see her for the liar she was. Her brothers had always known the second they looked in her eyes that she was lying, or so they had always claimed.

"My father is Mr. Maddox," he seemed to growl. "I'm just Cord."

"And 'just' Cord will drive like a lunatic if I don't let him leave," Luce laughed softly. "Annie, do join Jessie and come for coffee one day. I'd love to visit."

"Of course," Kenni murmured.

There wasn't a chance in hell. She wouldn't step into that house if her life depended on it right now.

Cord might think she hadn't seen the dark hint of

disapproval in his expression when Lucia made the suggestion, but she had. Not that it mattered; he had nothing to fear where a visit from her was concerned.

Luce said her good-byes and moved ahead of Cord to leave. The brevity of the visit was frightening. They couldn't stay for coffee but they could stop, come into the café, and make a point of mentioning that she was only there to say hello to Jessie and Slade? There was more to it.

"Well, that's Luce for you," Jessie said, shaking her head. "I'd have thought she'd have stayed a minute to chat."

The worry in Jessie's voice had Kenni watching her curiously.

"Poor Luce," Jessie said softly as Cord and his stepmother disappeared from view.

"Poor Luce?" Kenni turned to her, deliberately keeping the inquiry in her tone mild. "Is she okay?"

"I hear she and Vinny aren't getting along well," Jessie said. "She should have never accepted his proposal so soon after his wife's and daughter's deaths. Now she just seems so unhappy."

Luce had married Vincent "Vinny" Maddox less than a year after his wife of over twenty-five years and his sixteen-year-old daughter had died. What had the woman expected? Though there were those who swore Luce and Vinny had been having an affair long before her sister, Sierra Maddox, had been killed.

"And there's nothing you can do to help her either way," Slade reminded her. "Let the Maddoxes take care of themselves, sweetheart, it's better that way."

"Yeah, well, it's not like Luce listens to anyone anyway." Jessie shrugged, her gaze resigned.

Thankfully, Jessie dropped the subject of the Maddox clan. It was a subject better left lying at the moment.

Kenni finished her coffee and the sweet rolls she'd ordered as conversation turned to less controversial subjects. Namely, whether or not Jessie could convince Kenni to help her clear out her schoolroom. Before they left the café, Kenni couldn't help but laugh with Slade as he tried to convince them that cleaning out the classroom could wait a week or two, then groaned in male resignation when Jessie told him to just give it up.

She enjoyed visiting with both of them, though they didn't talk as freely, nor did Jessie give her quite as much gossip on the locals, with Slade there. It wasn't often he joined Jessie, though with the pregnancy he had become very protective.

As they left the café Kenni looked around as though simply enjoying the view and the weather. Eyes narrowed against the sunlight as she looked for any possible threats. That earlier sense of being watched returned the second she stepped outside, stronger now than it had been before.

"Let us give you a ride home, Annie." Slade stopped her as she moved to the edge of the curb and prepared to cross.

"I enjoy the walk," she assured him as she glanced along the street for oncoming cars. "Besides, I have to do something to rid myself of the calories from those sweet rolls you insisted on ordering more of."

Slade chuckled at that as his arm curled around his wife's shoulders.

"If you're sure." He watched the street as well, his gaze sweeping the area in a way Kenni recognized well. He could probably describe everything he saw in exact detail this time tomorrow, she knew.

"I'm sure." She stepped from the curb, throwing her hand up in a careless wave.

As she stepped from the curb a sedan pulled out from a side street. In the second it took her to reach the halfway point, it was nearly on her. The acceleration was fast and as quick as she could move, Kenni didn't know if she could make it.

As though in slow motion she glimpsed the driver, flat dark eyes, carelessly grown beard and long hair paired with sunglasses. She would know him if she ever saw him again.

If she survived.

If she could just get across . . .

Her foot slid on the blacktop as she tried to push herself out of the way. It was too far to jump. She couldn't get enough traction with her sandals to get out of the way. She was too short to clear the distance otherwise. She made a mental note, if she lived, never to wear the damned things again.

She could feel the summer heat like a brush of fire against her flesh, hear the car speeding closer, and knew she wasn't going to make it. She couldn't make it . . .

A manacle latched around her waist, the hard jerk of her body taking her breath as she felt herself flying through the air, held so close to a hard, powerful body that when they hit the pavement she barely felt it. He cushioned her against his chest before he rolled them both behind a truck parked at the side of the street.

The car hit the curb, drove over it, then sped away with a scream of tires as Kenni stared at the brick facade of the building no more than a few feet from her, and listened to Jazz curse like a sailor only wished he could, behind her.

The hiatus was over, she thought fatalistically. They knew she was here now. They knew, and they wouldn't stop until they killed her, just as they had killed her mother and her uncle.

And she still hadn't figured out who it was or why they wanted her dead.

Fuck him. He was shaking.

Jazz could feel the pure terror that sent him tearing across the street to lift Annie from her feet and all but throw both of them across the distance to the front of the truck parked several feet from the end of the curb. He'd felt the vehicle as it brushed past them, missing them by scant inches as it swerved to catch them.

He'd find that bastard and when he did he'd make damned certain he was the one who skinned the man alive.

Fuck.

With his arms wrapped tight around the little imposter he held to his chest, cushioning her against him, the thought of the damage that could have been done to her delicate body caused his guts to cramp. He didn't think he'd ever been so damned scared in his life.

The second he'd seen the car accelerate toward her he'd known what was happening. There was no hesitating, no pause; he'd just run for her. If he had to take the hit to throw her across the road then by God that was what he'd do. The thought of seeing her broken . . .

He was sweating.

Adrenaline was pounding through his veins, rushing through his senses, and the horror of what could have happened flashed through his mind.

He could have lost her.

"Jazz! Fuck!" Slade knelt in front of them as Jessie rushed in behind him. "Goddammit, are you okay?"

"Did you recognize the son of a bitch?" Jazz hadn't had time to look. He'd been moving too fast, a haze of red in front of his eyes as the certainty of the fact that if he didn't move faster, then Annie would die, descended upon him.

"No tags on the car." Slade's gray eyes were dark, filled with anger and concern as he stared at Annie. "Annie, sweetie, are you okay?"

He reached out as though to touch her.

"No!" She flinched before trying to pull herself from Jazz's arms. Twisting toward him, she stared up at him, enraged. "Let me go now!" she hissed.

"Settle down, dammit," he growled. "Let me get you the hell out of here, then we'll fight it out . . ."

"Someone call an ambulance," one of the onlookers called out.

"No ambulance . . ." Panic was edging into her voice as she began struggling harder. "Let me go."

"Settle down, Annie, or you're going to draw more attention than you have to. Is that what you want?" Jazz snarled as he moved quickly to his feet, pulling her up with him.

"I'll get the truck," Slade muttered as more onlookers began crowding around them.

Jazz didn't bother waiting. He wanted her away from the gathering crowd now. He could feel the tension in her body, her muscles tightening to the point that he knew she'd begin fighting to be free if he wasn't very careful.

Instinct was a bitch. Especially a well-honed instinct for survival. She was primed to run, to hide and watch, to reassess the danger and relocate. That relocating part was what he intended to put a stop to.

"I'm right behind you," he bit out. Anger was building inside him, surging through him with the force of a tidal wave. His protective instincts were going crazy, rioting through his senses and sending pure, raw fury tearing through him.

Lifting Annie into his arms he held on firmly despite her attempts to get free and moved quickly across the street. He was aware of Slade standing in the middle of the road watching to ensure there were no other speeding vehicles turning onto the street.

Once Jazz had Annie safely across and was striding toward the maroon king cab pickup parked in the café's lot, Slade hurriedly escorted Jessie across the street—all but dragging her to the truck parked beside Jazz's.

"Let me go before I brain your damned ass." Annie's fist struck at his shoulder as he shoved her into the front seat of the truck. "I don't need you to carry me."

He caught her fist on the second swing; her aim would have plowed dead-on into his face. The little witch. Did she actually think he was going to let her just merrily continue on her way and walk home? It wasn't happening. He'd tie her to the damned truck seat if he had to.

She wasn't in shock. A quick look at her furious expression and he knew that wasn't a problem. Hazel eyes burned with green sparks of anger.

"Would you settle the fuck down?" he growled, glowering at her as her eyes narrowed up at him, instincts battling to run even as other, primal senses demanded she submit.

Submission just wasn't a part of this woman's nature evidently.

"Take. Me. Home." She might be crazy mad at the moment, but he could glimpse the fear in her eyes.

"Take you home?" he asked her softly. "Someone just tried to run you down and you want me to just drop you off at your house, by yourself, and drive away like a good little boy?"

Oh hell no. She must really believe he was some dumb mountain hick if she thought he was actually going to do that.

She was the most aggravating woman he had ever met in his life.

"That would be my preference," she snapped, lips tightening at she glared at him.

"I'm really not concerned with your fucking preference," he bit out furiously. "I'm more concerned with keeping your pretty ass intact at the moment."

Her eyes narrowed, lips pursing just slightly as delicate little nostrils flared.

Fuck. God, for just a moment . . .

A hard shake of his head forced the thought back before he glared down at her again.

"Sugar, you're just mad as a hornet right now, aren't you?" he accused her, amazed at the fact that she was angry with him. "Some bastard just tried to run you down and damn if you don't act like you're pissed because I saved your ass."

Her gaze flickered then with a hint of uncertainty. How he'd managed to knock her off guard, he wasn't certain, but he'd love to keep her there for a while.

"I'm pissed because some drunk asshole tried to run me down in the middle of town and nearly killed both of us," she retorted. "I want to go home, take a hot bath and some aspirins, and try like hell to forget it happened."

He almost laughed at the absurdity that she'd just spilled from those pretty lips. Like hell. She wanted to figure out if it was time to run yet.

Jazz shook his head, buckled her seat belt, then stepped back and closed the door before loping to the driver's side.

"I'm heading to my place," he muttered as he passed Slade.

"I'll meet you there." Nodding, Slade moved around the back of the truck. Within seconds they were both pulling from the parking lot and heading out of town.

"Jazz, I really don't want to go to your house," she stated as she realized they were heading in the opposite direction of her house.

"Sweetheart, right now, I really don't give a damn," he warned her. "I nearly watched you die in front of my eyes and that's going to take me a minute to get over. You can just suffer and put up with my company until I can get a handle on it."

It was going to take far more than a minute to do that. He didn't think he'd ever felt fear like he'd felt it as he'd watched that car bearing down on her.

"You want to tell me why someone decided to run you down in the middle of town?" he asked, certain he knew what her response was going to be.

Turning his head, he caught the telltale stiffening of her body.

"I have no idea what you're talking about," she retorted a second later, her expression actually confused. "It must have been a drunk or something. I'm a kindergarten teacher, for God's sake. Who doesn't like kindergarten teachers?"

God bless her heart, he was going to spank her for that one. A lie, wrapped in deception and practicing deceit. And she did it with such incredible sincerity. He'd known she'd pull something like this.

"Whoever was in that car," he countered instantly. "That was no drunk, so don't take me for a damned fool. He knew what he was doing and he knew who he was trying to do it to. So why don't you tell me what the hell is going on?"

He tried to keep from raising his voice. He wasn't a man who yelled often, especially at women. A loud man was too intimidating, his foster father Toby Benning had told him more than once. A nice even tone would get more results.

Well, he wasn't getting any results.

"And you think I know what's going on." She was

trying to deceive him with her voice, her eyes, her very expression.

Damn her, she was lying to him with such convincing sincerity that he found himself wanting to believe her. Unfortunately, he hadn't believed in fairy tales for a lot of years. He wasn't going to start now.

"Sweetheart, you and I are going to start butting heads here soon if you can't be honest with me." It was the most sincere warning he could give her, because at the rate she was lying to him, he was going to be spanking her before nightfall.

"Jazz, what reason do I have not to be honest with you? How would I know who was driving that car or what they were trying to do?" she exclaimed as she pushed her fingers through her hair and avoided looking him in the eye as she tried to avoid a bald-faced lie.

His hands tightened around the steering wheel. It would probably be a really bad idea to pull over to the side of the room and spank that pretty butt.

Still, lying to Jazz was a very bad idea.

CHAPTER 6

"When we enter the house be prepared." The heavy note of warning in Jazz's voice had Kenni turning to him, wariness stiffening her body even more than the near miss in town already had.

"For what?"

He gripped the steering wheel with both hands as a grimace contorted his face for just a moment.

"I mentioned the puppies a few weeks ago, remember?" The rueful amusement she saw in his face now had her curiosity aroused despite her best intentions.

"I remember," she answered, wondering what puppies could have to do with any of this.

"They're Rottweiler puppies." He almost grinned.

She could only roll her eyes. "Well, Jazz, I didn't peg you for the Pomeranian type," she assured him mockingly. "But I'm still not certain why Rottweiler puppies come with a warning."

"They're six-week-old rotties with more energy than a dozen Tasmanian devils," he said then. "The second you step into the house they're going to break away from their sire and dam and come after you like a herd of mini elephants. They love attention. Three of them especially love female attention. And they don't take orders real well just yet."

She remembered when the puppies were born, Jessie had been nuts wanting to claim one and Jazz had kept putting her off.

"Jessie hasn't gotten one yet?" she asked as he made the turn onto the gravel road leading to his house about half a mile into a valley.

"They're not weaned yet." The hasty, obviously practiced excuse would have been amusing if not for the fact that someone had just tried to kill her.

"Has Jessie picked out which one she wants yet?" she asked then, pushing the subject. Anything to take her mind off the memory of that car bearing down on her.

Blowing out a hard breath, Jazz reached back and rubbed at the back of his neck for a second before returning his hand to the steering wheel and muttering, "Not yet."

"Has she seen them yet?"

"Not in a few weeks." He frowned. "I've been busy."

He was lying. From Jessie's bitching she already knew Jazz had no intention of giving up one of those babies.

"You've been possessive," she corrected him absently as she watched the forested land outside the pickup. "What are you going to do to put her off now?"

Slade and Jessie were right behind them and if Kenni knew her friend then she knew Jessie would be on those puppies so fast it would make Jazz's head spin.

"I'm going to have to talk to Slade," he breathed out, the sound filled with resignation. "He'll tell her."

Kenni shook her head. "We're talking about Jessie's husband, Slade. Right?" she retorted. "Slade ain't going to tell her crap if it's going to upset her right now, Jazz. Stop fooling yourself."

His lips pursed in a display of male uncertainty. Seeing Jazz in the least bit uncertain was surprising.

"When I'm ready to let one go, then she can have first pick." He shrugged. "I'm not ready yet."

"You'll never be ready." She was certain of that.

"So?" That one word said it all. He simply wasn't going to worry about it. They were his puppies and he wasn't giving one away.

"Tell her Essie would be upset if you let one go right now," she suggested as she turned back from her perusal of the woods surrounding the truck. "That should help."

As she spoke the surrounding forests and mountain parted to reveal the valley and Jazz's two-story brick-and-wood home. The sprawling farmhouse was gorgeous. Red brick and red wood siding, green tin roof and a wide wraparound front porch.

The valley spread out below the house, a pond so large it was almost a small lake. A dock extended out into it with a canoe tied up to it. On the bank a covered, enclosed gazebo sat.

Green, green grass grew like a lush summer carpet, inviting bare feet and giggling children, summer cookouts and family reunions.

It took a minute to see what she was looking at, though, and when she did, it was all she could do to breathe. She hadn't been to Jazz's place since returning to Loudoun. But she'd been here when she was younger with one of her brothers when he'd stopped to talk to Jazz. The house hadn't been here then, just a single-story home that looked more like a shack. The valley had been here, though, and the pond.

She'd been sixteen. While Sawyer had looked over a car he was interested in, she had informed Jazz of exactly what the valley should look like. The house, the boat dock and canoe, and the gazebo.

She wondered if there was a bed in the gazebo as she'd told Jazz she wanted. A big soft one with lace sheets and pillowcases, surrounded by a mosquito net.

The big red barns were in their places. One for equipment, the other for hay and stock should he decide to have any. The stock consisted of what appeared to be two horses. They were older, moving lazily in the huge pasture that surrounded the stock barn.

He'd laid everything out as she'd suggested. That summer she'd been convinced she belonged right there. In the summer she'd have barbecues off the back porch, family reunions and family cookouts.

She couldn't see the back but had no doubt there was a two-level porch there, one holding the barbecue grill with its iron enclosure, the second level a covered porch with a wide swing and several outdoor tables.

He'd laughed at her, she remembered. His blue eyes had been full of amusement, but when her brother had glanced back at them his expression had been filled with brooding suspicion.

She'd flirted outrageously with Jazz that day and he'd been good-natured about it, she thought. He'd teased her gently, though not sexually. Winked at her a time or two.

He'd laughed when she warned him that if he wasn't careful she'd steal his heart and told her that "maybe" she already had. His maybes were always a little deceptive, though, she remembered. Jazz had loved playing with that word. And he still did.

Sawyer had decided it was time to leave then.

Strangely, he hadn't warned her against Jazz. He hadn't mentioned that afternoon, but she knew he'd gone to see Jazz again that evening.

"You have a beautiful place, Jazz," she said softly when he pulled into the wide parking area on the rise overlooking the sprawling backyard and pond.

She wanted to sob, but tears had been locked inside her soul years before and she didn't even know where the key was anymore.

"Thank you," he said simply. When she glanced over at him he was staring out at it as well, his expression somber.

Oh God, what had she truly lost that night? Someone had stolen more than just her family and her life from her. They'd stolen this man from a future she hadn't even had a chance of fantasizing about. Ten years and countless other women had passed between them now. Any tenderness he might have felt for a sixteen-year-old charmer was no doubt just a vague memory to him. But to her, it was a dagger straight to her soul.

"Come on, let's get in the house," he breathed out heavily. "I think I need a beer."

She needed something a hell of a lot stronger than a beer, she decided. A few good shots of whiskey maybe.

Something to deaden the overwhelming feeling that in bringing her here Jazz was getting ready to completely up-end her life.

She really didn't need her life up-ended the Jazz Lancing way. Hell, she'd almost prefer being chased by a car again. At least then, she would know what was coming.

Damn, it had been years since he'd remembered the stubborn determination he'd displayed when beginning to construct the property the fall Kenni had died with her mother in a hotel fire. They'd buried her and her mother, and according to the rest of the family, life went on.

It had gone on, but it had taken years to forget the pretty teenager. The only female whose father Jazz had ever gone to and asked permission to call on.

She would have turned seventeen that fall, and he knew he was too damned old for her. Twenty-three was a far cry from seventeen, but he wasn't about to stand and wait for one of those horny little teenage pricks to walk in and steal her heart.

He hadn't wanted her to know he was asking her father's permission to see her though. He'd been that certain Vinny Maddox would kick him in the teeth and tell him to go to hell. He'd waited until the afternoon she'd left with her mother to take their yearly shopping trip, then he'd gone to see her father and brothers.

Her brothers had yelled, threatened, and ordered him out of the house. It was the father Jazz had watched, though. Somber, intent, his gaze had seemed to look deeper than Jazz was comfortable with as he listened to all the arguments his sons could come up with. When they'd wound down, he'd asked Jazz if he loved Kenni, and he'd had to be honest.

Hell if he knew what love was, he'd told the other man, but when he looked at Kenni, all he wanted to do was make *her* dreams come true. He wanted to see her smile and hear her laughter every day, and he wanted to be there to share in all her triumphs. If there were failures then he wanted to be there so she would cry on his shoulder, not another man's.

The smile that had curled Kenni's father's face had confused him. For years Jazz hadn't understood it, until the day the other man had arrived to see the completion of the buildings that had gone up in the valley.

Kenni's father had nodded slowly, that sad smile quirking his lips again.

The older man looked out at the house, the valley, and blinked back the moisture in his eyes as he turned back to Jazz. "Sawyer told me last night you'd built what Kenni described to you before she and her mother . . ." He shook his head, then caught Jazz's eye again. "Do you know, Jazz, why I gave you permission to court my daughter?"

"No sir." There were few men Jazz gave such respect to.

"You honored me when you came and asked my permission rather than seducing my baby as many men would have done, but when you vowed that day not to take her to your bed until she was of age, you honored her," he said softly. "And had I said no, what would you have done?"

Jazz knew he hadn't expected the answer he got.

"I would have waited until she was of age and asked again." He'd shrugged.

"Why? I'm nothing to you." Her father had been confused then. "Why would my permission matter to you?"

"You're her father," Jazz had told him softly. "Without your respect, without your acceptance, she would never have been happy."

The older man had been startled. "You were going to marry her." He seemed to struggle for a moment with the thought, and with the tears that filled his eyes.

Surprised, Jazz had stared back at him. "Of course I was. Later. Not too soon. We both had some growing up to do . . ."

And Jazz had left it at that. But her father had looked out over the valley for long moments once again.

"She would have loved this," he said then. "She would have loved this . . ."

Why the hell had that memory returned, he wondered as he led his little imposter up the front walk to the porch. It had been years since he'd thought about it. Kenni had been a beginning that had never had a chance to begin, in some ways. She had been gone before he'd had a chance to call on her the first time.

And when it came to the house and grounds, she'd been right about the layout. Everything seemed to fit perfectly where she'd suggested. He hadn't done it just for her, he told himself. He'd told himself that for years.

He'd done it because she'd been right.

* * *

It didn't end outside.

The descriptions she'd given him that day of what she would do if the valley was hers, if the house she loved was built, had been carried out as though she'd drawn him a picture.

Following him into the house Kenni couldn't help but stare in wonder at the large open rooms, the hardwood floors, and the way light spilled through the large windows. The floors reflected the sunlight in muted gold tones while the open, airy floor plan of the first floor invited visitors to soak up the warmth and charm of the rooms.

A short staircase led to the master bedroom and a single guest room. Rather than the bedroom level sitting directly atop the first, though, it was slightly offset and rested against the hill rising next to the house. A balcony overlooked the pool area just as she'd told him she wanted.

God, she'd been sixteen, well, almost seventeen. She'd been so young and he'd been older, establishing Rigor Construction with his friends and planning his future. And that future had included things she'd dreamed of as a young woman when she dreamed of Jazz Lancing.

"The house is beautiful," she whispered as he led her through the large television room with its overstuffed couch, love seat, and recliners.

Next to the sliding glass doors and large pet door two Rottweilers watched suspiciously as four offspring hovered in excitement behind them. The black-and-tan canine family looked regal and far too playful all at once.

"Let's get some coffee. Slade and Jessie are coming in behind us." Jazz led her through the room. "You can meet the heathens later."

The doorway into the kitchen was gated, the four-foot-tall metal gate latching securely to hold back rambunctious pups.

Stepping into the kitchen, she nearly gave herself away. Her insides were trembling, her throat tight with emotion at the sight of the beautiful chef's kitchen. The gas stove and grill were set in the center of the room to allow the cook to socialize in the kitchen as well. Beside it was a prep sink while several feet from it sat the large country sink with its troughlike dark-bronze faucet.

Honey-oak cabinets filled the wall against the family room while large windows filled the other three walls. Marble countertops had ceramic tile on the walls above them in a soft cream with splashes of honey gold, soft bronze, and a hint of blue. The counters followed around the room beneath the windows behind the work island, stopping at the door that led to the porch outside. The rest of the kitchen was for dining, socializing, and relaxing.

Across from the work island was an exact replica of the huge dining set she'd grown up with in her parents' home. The rich dark wood of the table, slightly rough, with only a thin protective layer of polyurethane. Eight chairs sat around it; a wooden bowl in the center of the table held a few apples, some pears, and they were real. The china cabinet, buffet cabinet, and padded bench were so familiar that it was hard to believe it wasn't the same set.

Her chest was so tight she was surprised she could breathe. Emotion threatened to swamp her, to burn through her fragile control and leave her sobbing.

Why had he done this? It wasn't out of some overwhelming love, she knew that. He'd been a friend, one who flirted back with her gently but never made a single pass at her. Not the first touch, not even a kiss.

"You okay?" Glancing over at her as he stepped behind the work island to the coffeepot, Jazz watched her in concern.

"This is the most beautiful kitchen I've ever seen, Jazz," she whispered as she heard Slade and Jessie enter the kitchen behind her.

"And how he developed the taste to create such a gorgeous house and kitchen I haven't figured out," Jessie declared as she moved to the bar on the other side of the stove and grinned at Jazz teasingly. "His RV looks like it was thrown together. Nothing matches."

"Troublemaker," Jazz muttered in accusation as he pulled coffee cups from a nearby cabinet and set them next to the coffeemaker.

"I'm no troublemaker," she argued, leaning against her husband as he moved behind the stool she sat on. "By the way, I picked out my pup. Can I take him home today?"

"They're not weaned yet," he answered instantly.

"I can have him when he's weaned then?" Her eyes narrowed on him.

"I didn't say that," he growled as he measured coffee into the basket. "Stop harassing me, Jessie."

"And stop trying to save Annie from the inquisition," Slade told her firmly. "It's not going to work. I'm sure

Jazz is just as curious as I am about that little attempted hit-and-run in town."

"I've already endured Jazz's inquisition," Kenni responded firmly before turning a demanding look on Jessie. "I don't know how you expect me to know who it was? Like I told Jazz, everyone likes kindergarten teachers. It had to be an accident or drunk driver or something."

Jessie's expression slowly morphed to disbelief as Slade just stared back at her impassively. That wasn't a comfortable look, either. Slade wasn't buying her explanation, which meant Jazz wasn't, either.

"Coffee." The cup smacked against the counter in front of Slade as he moved to stand next to his wife.

Thankfully, her cup and Jessie's were placed more gently in front of them, but his expression had once again become brooding. The look he gave her assured her he didn't believe her explanation now any more than he had before.

"Jazz, you buying that?" Slade asked impassively.

"Oh yeah, Slade, I do." He nodded. "I believe in the tooth fairy, Santa Claus, and the Easter Bunny this year, too. Cinderella and Sleeping Beauty are good candidates as well, I think."

Kenni rolled her eyes as she leaned against the counter next to Jessie. Even her friend didn't believe her if that slow shake of her head and disappointed look were anything to go by.

"Annie, come on," Jessie said softly, disbelief lingering in her expression. "I saw that car when it pulled out. Whoever was driving knew what they were doing. And I think you know they did."

What now?

This wasn't the Kin; no one was trying to force anything from her, or take anything from her. The obvious concern in Jessie, Slade, and even Jazz's eyes as they watched her almost made her feel guilty for lying.

Almost.

She'd lost friends over the years. She'd found her uncle lying in his own blood, his face so beaten he was barely recognizable. Because he was trying to help her.

What would they do to Jessie? To her unborn baby?

She could never forgive herself if anything happened to Jessie or her baby because of her.

"Come on, I've been here two years. If someone wanted to hurt me then they had plenty of opportunity. Why wait?" It was a perfectly logical explanation.

Jazz and Slade's expression hadn't changed; if anything Jazz's had darkened.

"Drink your coffee," he said succinctly as he gestured to her cup then turned to Slade. "Let it go for now."

Slade's brows lifted in surprise before he gave a brief nod, a quirk of a smile at his lips. "I'll do that, Jazz," he agreed. "Just for now. But I think until we figure it out, I'll keep Jessie at home for a while."

"Slade . . ." Jessie's angry objection was met with Slade's heavy frown.

"Think about the baby, Jessie," Slade said, his expression torn as he glanced back to Kenni. "Until we figure out the threat against Annie, then you're in danger as well. And Jessie, losing you would kill me."

The truth of that statement was clear in his voice, his expression. His love for Jessie was unwavering, soul-deep. And Kenni could feel the guilt searing her, tearing at her with serrated teeth.

"Jessie, listen to Slade," Kenni told her friend before drawing in a deep breath. "Just until we see if there's anything to their suspicions. That's all."

It was all she could do to force those words past her lips before turning to Jazz. "Would you take me home now? Please?"

His arms went across his broad chest, a cool smile curling at the corners of his lips.

"No, baby, you're not going home right now," he stated, pure, hard-core determination deepening his tone. "You're staying right here until you and I get a chance to talk."

Kenni stared into his eyes, the brilliant blue watching her intently, boring into hers as she fought to remain still beneath his look.

He wasn't a man who dealt well with threats to his friends. She knew he saw her as more than a friend, but this was still uncalled for.

"Keeping me here won't change the fact that I don't know anything, Jazz." She rubbed at her arms for a moment, wishing she were standing in the sunshine, someplace warm, warm enough that the ever-present chill of fate wasn't breathing over her flesh.

"Well then, I guess keeping you here will ensure they don't try it again, won't it, sugar?" he said smoothly. "Because until I find out who and why, I'm going to make damned sure they can't get to you."

Kenni didn't break his stare; she didn't dare. Any sign of weakness and he would take full advantage of it.

Just when she was certain she couldn't hold his stare much longer, the excited yips of four immature Rottweilers sounded at the gate.

Jazz's gaze slid to the gate then back to her. The obvious, deliberate release didn't sit well with her. Damn him, he'd known she was wavering, so why had he just let it go?

"Well, I'm playing with the babies before I leave," Jessie declared, her tone less than pleased at her husband's intention of keeping her away from Kenni.

It was better that way, though, Kenni knew that. Now that she'd been found, now that the first strike had been attempted, it wouldn't stop. And until she could run, hide, then everyone she cared for or might care for would be in danger. She'd learned that lesson in the early years of this cat-and-mouse game her life had turned into.

"Come on, Annie, let these two bitch about us." Jessie grabbed her cup and headed for the television room. "We'll go bitch about them."

Slowly, Kenni took the coffee cup, glancing only briefly at Jazz's set face before leaving the room.

He might not be willing to let her go, but she'd leave, one way or the other. She'd learned how to escape and run a long time ago. The only difference now? She didn't want to escape, she didn't want to run yet. She wanted to enjoy the beauty of the home she would never have and the man she couldn't have, for just a while longer. Then she would run, but this time she had no idea where she could hide.

CHAPTER 7

Jazz watched from the kitchen, taking his time getting the steaks and the grill ready for dinner after Slade and Jessie's departure. Salt-rubbed baked potatoes were in the oven, a pitcher of sweet tea in the fridge. And there, in the living room, surrounded by puppies with more energy than some two-year-olds, sat the prettiest thing he was sure he'd ever seen.

Wary, damned defensive on a good day, but giggling like a schoolgirl now, she sat as four canine demons romped around her and decided she was their personal chew toy. Even their sire, Marcus, and normally distrustful dam, Esmerelda, put aside their wariness enough to let Annie pet them and assure them what a beautiful family they had.

He couldn't help but be surprised by the fact that she felt right there. In the middle of the living room in a house he hadn't been able to imagine another woman living in, this woman who called herself Annie just belonged.

Figuring out why would take a while, he thought.

God knew he wanted her in his bed, and he was as possessive as hell over her, but was it love? It didn't feel like the only love he'd ever really known, but then he'd been a hell of a lot younger then.

"Hey, ready to take a break?" he asked from the doorway as he unlatched the gate. "You could keep me company while I grill some steaks."

Her shoulders stiffened, wariness instantly marring the peace he'd glimpsed in her expression as she played with the puppies.

"Sounds good," she responded, giving the puppies a final pet before rising to her feet and turning to face him. "Those puppies are heathens, Jazz," she said, glancing down as the rambunctious babies jumped against her legs, not quite ready to stop having fun.

"They can be," he agreed, grinning as he opened the gate for her.

She slid past him quickly, giving him just enough time to close the gate before the heathens could follow her into the kitchen.

Latching the metal barrier he turned and watched her step to the sink, where she washed and dried her hands carefully.

The distrust in her gaze when she faced him moments later had his chest tightening in regret. Damn her. She had to find a way to trust him. Whatever she was attempting to do she hadn't managed in the two years she had been in Loudoun. Securing her safety was his highest priority; she may as well begin accepting that.

For now, he'd rein in the need for answers. Soon enough he would have to demand them.

"Grill's out back." He nodded to the porch as he picked up the steaks he'd prepared and laid on the bar.

Stepping outside he was aware of her following him until the door closed behind them and Annie stopped, taking in the view.

The porch wrapped around the house. At the end of the back of the house was the grill, located a step below the porch. The rock patio led to the pool with its waterfall and rock features.

Glancing back at her, he glimpsed the wistfulness in her expression. There was a hunger there, barely glimpsed, that had him wondering at the life she must have lived before coming to Loudoun. Each time he showed her one of the house's features that she hadn't seen yet, that almost hidden hunger would flash in her expression before it was gone again.

Grilling the steaks Jazz watched as she moved through the backyard, investigating the pool and natural landscaping. He'd tried to keep the look as natural as possible with miniature trees, flowers natural to the mountains around them, and a path made from stones he'd unearthed on the property itself.

It was a feature he'd created to go with the pool in those first months after the completion of the house. A place where he could think, where he could make sense of changes in his life that had altered too much of what he thought and felt.

As the steaks finished Annie returned to the house for the potatoes and assortment of sauces and butters he'd set out with the freshly baked garlic bread. Dinner was eaten in a comfortable silence as early evening began to ease over the mountains.

Refilling their tea glasses, Jazz drew her to the steps leading to the yard before drawing her down to sit on the step in front of him. They were just in time to watch the ducks, along with their ducklings, as they ventured from cover to frolic in the large pond.

"It's so beautiful here," she whispered as they watched the playful waterfowl. "I can't imagine anyplace more beautiful."

The wistful regret in her voice had his senses raging on alert as he sat behind her on the steps. He braced his knees protectively around her and propped his back against the wide post supporting the roof.

Lifting his tea, Jazz sipped at it rather than speaking.

"Do you own a lot of land?" she asked then.

"A bit," he agreed. "About a hundred acres."

"You could get lost in it." There was that vein of aching hunger inside her.

She wanted to get lost, he realized. She wanted to hide, and at the same time she was dying to live.

"You could," he agreed. "It's the mountains you could get lost in, though. They're so deep, so mysterious that whole clans live within them without ever being seen."

Her head settled on his knee as he let his fingers rub against her hair, the shell of her ear.

"What if someone comes looking for them?" she asked, the tension in her voice making him wonder if she thought she could find a haven other than Loudoun.

"Depends on if they want to be found. If they don't want to be found, then they won't be. And enemies disappear when they come searching for them," he assured her.

Her breathing hitched.

God, he wanted to demand those answers again.

He wanted to make her tell him what she was running from, what she was so scared of. But he'd already pushed her to the point that Jazz had sensed her shutting down, pulling away. Whatever she was running from, whoever she was hiding from, Annie feared it more than she feared anything else.

"When I was thirteen, I slipped into those mountains to disappear," he told her, giving her a grim smile, wondering if she would do the same. "Damned foster system sucked here then. I'd been in so many foster homes they didn't know where else to send me. And, well, being a burden wasn't my idea of fun." He gave a short, almost amused laugh. "I wandered around I don't know how long, several days. There was water, but I had no idea how to find food. I was about starved out when this old man, Castor Maddox, just steps out from behind a tree, shakes his head at me, then proceeds to set up a fire and roast this fresh rabbit he'd caught." He chuckled at the memory. "After I ate, he pulls me up and we walk down the mountain to this farm a few miles from here. Toby Benning's place. He and his wife had lost their only son about ten years before. So this old geezer takes me to the door, and when Toby opens it, old man Maddox pushes me toward it, swats me on the back of my head, and tells me to mind my manners and not shame him." He glimpsed her smile. "Well, being the badass I thought I was, I turn on him and just ask him what damned business of his it was?" He shook his head, a part of him hating the memory, another part amused by it. "'Cause I found you, boy, makes you part mine, he said. Mind yourself now, don't make me come back."

"You weren't alone anymore," she whispered softly. "He wanted you to know you did have someone."

The aching loss in her voice had him wishing there was something he could do to ease it.

She felt alone. He could hear it in her voice, sense it with an instinct he didn't quite understand yet.

"We all have someone, baby," he promised her, wishing he could find a way to convince her that if no one else was, he was there for her. "Sometimes, we just don't know it."

She had him, all she had to do was meet him halfway. He knew she was in danger, and she was smart enough to know she wasn't fooling him. She had to tell him what the hell was haunting her, soon. There wasn't a lot of time left. One of the three weeks Cord had given them was gone, and he knew the other man would be making a visit soon. Cord wasn't one to sit and wait on a deadline, even if it was his own. He'd be touching base soon, and the confrontation might not be pretty.

No, sometimes, Kenni thought, you find out you have no one at all. But she kept the thought to herself as she drew away from him and rose to her feet.

"I should leave, Jazz. I can't stay here." But she hated to go. It was so peaceful there, so warm and so much a part of Jazz. But it was also a part of the young woman she had once been, the one who had believed with all her heart that Jazz belonged to her.

How naive she'd been that summer. So innocent and

certain of herself, of her heart. She would stare at Jazz, and he always seemed to know it. He would smile at her, wink, or lower the ever-present sunglasses he used to wear before arching a brow as though asking what she wanted or if she had any idea what he could give her.

What she had wanted had shocked her at the time. No doubt what he could have given her would have shocked her as well. Would he have been surprised? she wondered.

She doubted he would have been, not then or now.

He rose as well, took her hand, and led her back into the house.

"We'll talk about it after I clean up out here. Go on in and visit with the pups for a bit more, I'll be finished before you know it," he promised as he opened the door for her and shooed her inside.

Kenni moved into the television room where the pups were racing one another across the floor, barking for the sheer hell of it while their parents napped, confident the babies were safe. She was envious of that sense of security, of protection. It was something she hadn't felt in so long that she'd almost forgotten the sweetness of it.

Wrapping her arms across her breasts Kenni moved to the wide sliding doors that Marcus and Essie lay in front of. The view of the side of the pool also afforded her a view of the grill deck, where Jazz was closing the steel appliance.

The shaggy fall of his thick black hair at the back of his neck made her fingers itch to burrow through the heavy strands. Broad shoulders stretched beneath the cotton T-shirt, strong shoulders.

And he would gladly stand in front of her and protect her from any danger she faced. It was a terrifying thought.

The memory of Gunny's blood, so much blood, pooled on that warehouse floor was a nightmare. She'd waited, but he hadn't come back. His belongings had been thrown around the warehouse, some of them broken. His knife—he would have never left without it—lay in the blood, a testament that something terrible had happened to him.

Because he'd tried to protect her.

Covering her lips, her fingers trembling at the memory, Kenni had to fight back the tears that would have filled her eyes.

Gunny had gone AWOL from the marines the night her mother had been killed. He'd dedicated his entire life to keeping Kenni safe and trying to find out who had given the order to kill his half sister and her daughter. He had given his life to protect her.

Jazz would do the same, she knew that now. He would stand in front of her and every Kin and Maddox who tried to harm her. And he would die. Jazz, Slade, Zack—they would all give their lives if they had to, too strong to realize they couldn't win against the force that would descend on them. And even if they did suspect they were going to die, still, they'd give their last breath reaching for a miracle.

She couldn't let that happen. Slade had his own family, a son, a wife, a baby on the way. The Kin would destroy all of them.

God, what was she going to do?

Pressing the fingers of one hand against the glass, Kenni tried to convince herself he would let her go home. If she could get away from him for just a few hours, then she could run. The Kin would follow her and no one else would be hurt.

Until they found her.

And they would find her, they always did.

Turning away from the view outside she moved to the couch, staring at the puppies as they settled down against their parents, obviously ready for a nap.

She continued watching the pups play as Jazz made his way into the television room, sitting next to her and watching her for long, silent moments.

"You have to take me home," she told him, still watching the pups. "Everything's fine, I promise, Jazz."

It was so hard to walk away from him knowing she wouldn't see him again.

"Don't lie to me. And we both know you're lying," he stated warningly. "I won't let you leave while someone's out there trying to hurt you," he continued softly. "Not yet. Give me a day or two to find that driver first. I promise, Slade and Zack are searching for him. It won't take long to find him."

"Jazz—"

"Don't fight me on this." Brushing her hair back from her shoulder, he let his fingers brush against the bare skin, the slight rasp of callused flesh sending a shudder of pleasure racing down her spine.

Her heart was speeding out of control, her flesh so sensitive, so starved for touch, that the stroke of his fingers had her inhaling sharply in reaction

"You'll break me," she whispered, desperate for him to touch her, terrified of what tomorrow would bring if she let it go any farther.

"Not in a million years," he promised as his head lowered to her shoulder, his lips brushing over the curve, weakening her.

Oh God, how he weakened her.

A gasp left her lips when he lifted her, pulling her across his lap as his head lowered, their gazes locking as his lips whispered over hers. The softest brush of a kiss and she ached for so much more.

"Jazz." What he made her feel was dangerous, for both of them.

"Come on, baby." He breathed into that stroke of exquisite pleasure as a grin tugged at his lips. "Be bad with me. Just for a minute. We'll deal with the rest of it later."

"Your minutes last for a long time, Jazz," she reminded him, achingly aware of his fingers lifting the hem of her top.

"As long as I can make them last, darlin'. As long as I can make them last."

He wasn't playing anymore.

If she'd thought his kisses were dominant, experienced before, then they were catastrophically so now. Slanting over hers as he laid her back along the couch, his hard body coming over her, he taught her the meaning of pure, aching hunger. With each deep, penetrating kiss, each lick of his tongue. With each touch of his fingers he drew her farther into a whirlwind of pleasure she didn't have a hope of resisting.

She didn't want to resist.

She needed him. Needed to taste him as he tasted her, touch him, hold this memory to wrap around her during the long, lonely nights to come.

Tugging at the material of his T-shirt, she pulled at it until her hands were stroking his sides, over his back. She gloried in the feel of his muscles tightening at her touch. When her nails raked against his flesh, a muttered groan rumbled from his chest, rough and hewn with male lust.

He pulled back, his shirt gone in less time than it took her to realize he'd actually jerked it off. Then his lips were at the side of her neck, his teeth scraping, his tongue flickering over sensitive flesh until she arched to him with a desperate cry of pleasure. Sharp, hot kisses ran down her neck, the buttons of her blouse released, the sides falling away from the lacy material of her bra.

The front catch was no obstacle. Flicked open, the cups pushed aside, and Jazz's marauding lips were given free rein.

His teeth gripped one nipple, tugged at it until she opened her eyes to stare back at him in dazed fascination. His eyes were so blue, such a startling dark hue, she felt mesmerized for a moment. Then her gaze was caught by his teeth surrounding the cherry-red nipple. He released it, extended his tongue, and licked over it like a treat he'd long awaited.

"Sensitive?" he asked softly as the lick had her flexing involuntarily.

"Yes." And she couldn't help but arch closer for more.

"Get ready then," he warned her. "Because I think I could spend hours just pleasuring your pretty nipples."

His lips parted, covered a peak, then sucked it into his mouth with greedy lust.

Sensation spiked in the tip, slammed through her, struck at her womb, and dragged a desperate cry from her lips as it started all over again. Like electricity, zapping crazily from her nipple to her lower stomach then to her clit. She could feel the slick heat of her response spilling from her vagina to dampen her thighs. Her clit swelled, throbbed, and tormented her with its need to be touched as well.

As her hips arched Jazz pushed his knee between her thighs, wedging it against the aching center of her body as he gripped her hip with one hand. Her thighs tightened on the pressure, hips lifting, stroking against the denim-covered muscle of his thigh as his lips moved to her other nipple.

Sparks flew across her vision when his mouth consumed the tight point. Tightening on it, suckling it as his tongue raked across it. Sensation upon sensation. His teeth gripped it, then he sucked it in his mouth again as his fingers captured the damp tip of the nipple he'd pleasured first.

Gripping it between his thumb and forefinger he applied just enough pressure . . .

"Oh God, Jazz . . ." She couldn't bear it. It was too much sensation, a mix of such pleasure and pain, and yet her body couldn't get enough of either sensation.

Her hips worked against his thigh, rolled and pressed, thrust and arched as her clit scraped against the material of her panties. Each arch against the hard muscle of his thigh applied a pressure that stroked the hard little kernel to such a blaze of need, she felt tortured by it.

"Ah, darlin', how sweet you are," he groaned, his lips lifting from her nipple, moving back to her neck, then to her lips once again.

And she couldn't get enough of his kisses. Especially when his fingers continued to caress her nipples with sharp, hot flares of sensation. His thigh pressed and rubbed against her, tormenting the bud of her clit as her vagina wept with need.

She was ready to weep with need.

Her hands were in his hair, her head tilted back on the couch as his lips and tongue moved down her neck once more, spreading those stinging little kisses back to her breasts.

"I told you we should have knocked."

"Yeah, so we should have."

At the sound of the two amused, feminine voices, Jazz was moving. Before the third word was out of the first woman's lips he had her behind him and a lethal black handgun trained on the speakers.

Not that it seemed to faze them.

Hurriedly fixing her clothes behind the shield of Jazz's broad back, she heard his muttered curse and looked up to see the two women watching them curiously. She expected raving beauties. What she saw instead were two women who were quite pretty, but weren't the model beauties she would have expected.

The identical twins stood just inside the entryway to

the family room. Dressed in denim, hiking boots, matching tank tops, and matching holstered handguns clipped to the low-slung band of their jeans, they looked like teenagers playing cops and robbers.

Long black hair was pulled into ponytails that trailed down their backs while dark sunglasses were pushed to the tops of their heads. The only difference between the two women was the thin white scar that marred one suntanned face.

Both watched her and Jazz with violet eyes surrounded by thick inky-black lashes and reflecting both amusement and steely determination.

And Kenni had no idea who they were, or what they were doing there. If they were Jazz's ex-lovers there would be problems.

She wasn't the only one unsettled by their appearance, either.

The two adult Rottweilers stood in front of their puppies, low growls rumbling in their throats while glancing at Jazz every few seconds for direction.

"Why aren't Marcus and Essie biting them?" Kenni muttered.

The two women might not be raving beauties, but they obviously knew Jazz really well.

Flicking her a look from the corner of his eyes, Jazz shook his head before jerking his T-shirt from the floor and pulling it back on with quick, obviously frustrated movements.

As the material covered his hard abs Marcus gave a low, warning growl.

"He wants to bite them," she said behind him, keeping her voice low.

"Sugar, I can hear you," the one with the scar informed her with mocking sweetness.

"Sugar, do I seem like I care?" Before she could stop herself she jabbed her fist against Jazz's ribs. "Sugar? Is she for real?"

His head jerked around, surprise in his blue eyes as they met hers.

Essie growled, the low rumble of a concerned momma, a dangerous sound.

"Ease up," Jazz ordered the animals firmly, resignation filling his voice as he replaced the handgun beneath the couch and sat up slowly, glancing back at her for just a second.

Frustration filled his brilliant-blue eyes, but if she wasn't mistaken there was also a hint of anger there. He wasn't happy with the interruption.

"Annie, meet Kate and Lara Blanchard," he breathed out heavily. "They're friends as well as business associates."

"Hmm." Propping her elbow on the cushion behind her, Kenni's eyes narrowed on the back of his head before turning to the two women once again.

"Hey Annie," Kate, the one without the scar, greeted her with uplifted brows. "Could we borrow Jazz just for a minute? There's a problem with a job we're working on and we need to talk to him about it."

They were kidding, right?

Lara gave a soft, knowing laugh. "Now, don't be so suspicious, sugar," she advised. "We really are friends. I swear, neither of us introduced ourselves in the Biblical sense to Casanova here. And we just need to chit-chat, I swear."

She turned to Jazz, seeing the hardening of his jaw, the dangerous set of his expression. Whatever the hell was going on, it was more than she was being told and she didn't care much for that at all.

"When you're finished, Casanova, I'm going home," she told him softly. "So try not to take all night because I may leave without you."

The look he shot her was brooding and filled with latent male dominance and warning.

Yeah, she was really going to let that one intimidate her.

"I won't wait all night," she promised. "When I'm tired of waiting, I'll walk home."

"And when I catch up with you there'll be hell to pay," he growled back at her.

Rising to his feet, he strode to the dogs then bent and spoke close to the male's ear. Marcus lifted his ears, his proud, intelligent gaze watching everyone behind his master. As Jazz straightened and motioned the other two women to the kitchen, the male Rottweiler focused on her.

Kenni had a feeling Marcus had been given his orders to keep her there. And that dog was big enough to make damned sure she stayed.

Narrowing her eyes on their retreating backs, she decided they had half an hour and that was it. At that point their little meeting would be finished. Then she was going to kick Jazz Lancing's ass.

CHAPTER 8

Kate and Lara Blanchard looked like the girls next door until you paid close attention to their eyes. A hint of the bitterness and disillusionment lingered in their violet gazes. It wasn't their eyes Jazz was concerned with tonight, though, it was the information he knew they must have, otherwise they wouldn't have shown up like this.

Arriving without notice indicated they'd learned something they wanted no one else to hear, and these girls didn't trust phones. Not cell phones, landlines, or any other traceable form of communication.

They were paranoid, suspicious, and distrustful. A hell of a combination in two women who were a little on the short side, curvy, and decidedly feminine. They were also damned loyal when it came to those they chose as friends, and willing to fight to the death to protect someone they believed in.

Those traits added to their surprise arrival sent tension racing through his body. Muscles tightened, all his senses went on alert as that gut-deep awareness warned

him that their information could be far more important
than he could guess.

Closing the door as he stepped to the porch, he let his
gaze move between them. They wouldn't have shown up
if it wasn't important, but there was a hesitancy about
them that warned him of their uncertainty in telling him
whatever they'd learned.

He'd never seen these two uncertain.

Twilight filled the valley now, not quite dark yet daylight had given its final farewell just before their arrival. Shadows stretched out along the porch, helped
along by the heavy vines of honeysuckle that grew thick
and heavy along the front of the porch.

Kate and Lara slid along those shadows to the porch
swing hanging in front of the windows next to the door
while Jazz moved to the chair, his back to the honeysuckle, across from them. He watched the two women
silently, sensing the tension emanating from them as
they stared at him consideringly. It had been a lot of
years since they'd been this uncertain around him.

They were two of the most efficient investigators he'd
ever known. They could uncover information others
were certain couldn't be found. Give them a puzzle and
it wouldn't take them long to fit all the pieces in their
place, and that was what the job was to them. Each case
was a puzzle, Kate had once explained to him. A puzzle that had to be solved.

They weren't speaking yet. He knew them well
enough to know their silence was an indication that
whatever they'd learned was either excessively dangerous, guaranteed to piss him off, or both. When it came

to the woman calling herself Annie Mayes, he had no doubt it was probably both.

"Is it that bad?" he asked quietly, his gaze flicking between the two of them.

The sisters glanced at each other, sharing some silent communication that only twins have before turning back to him.

"It's difficult," Kate answered him as she sat back fully in the heavily cushioned swing and rested her elbow on the arm of the seat while gripping the chain with her hand. "I'll tell you, Jazz, I don't think I've ever been so torn between information and a friend in my life."

His jaw clenched with enough force that he wouldn't have been surprised had he heard his back teeth crack. It was several seconds before he could release the tension enough to speak.

"What's making it so difficult?" This was one of only a few instances that either woman had hesitated to tell him what he needed to know.

"I'm very uncomfortable with this." Kate sighed. "I feel like I'm betraying her, even though it's fairly obvious she distrusted us on sight. What she's been through, how she's survived so far, amazes me."

For all her strength and tough attitude Kate had an incredible soft spot for survivors. Unfortunately he couldn't afford to allow that soft spot to influence their decision to turn over the information.

"She's facing a nightmare, Jazz, and it's about to become your nightmare if you decide to stand behind her. If you'd prefer not, then let us know before we leave.

We'll find her someplace safe to hide. We'll do our best to protect her."

The resources the two women had were extensive, he knew, but there wasn't a chance in hell he was letting Annie go.

Leaning forward, he gave each woman a long, direct look before speaking. "This morning someone tried to run her down in the middle of the street as she left a café." He deliberately hardened his tone, his expression. "She's in danger and I *will* protect her, with or without your help. But, if you hold back what you have and something happens to her—"

"You would never forgive us," Kate finished for him, her voice heavy as she rubbed at the back of her neck. "God, it's been years since they attacked . . ."

Kate broke off and turned to her sister once again. This time it was more than just concern that reflected in her expression. This time, Jazz saw a hint of fear.

"Tell me." Lara turned back to him, one hand clenched on the arm of the swing, the other in the cushion beneath her. "How well do you know the Maddox clan, Jazz?"

That was the last question he expected to come from either of them. What the hell could his connection to the Maddox clan have to do with any of this?

The question gave birth to a suspicion, though—one he refused to contemplate.

"Why?" He could feel the hairs rising at the back of his neck now, a primitive response to whatever was coming, a warning that whatever it was could change his life forever.

"From what we've learned in the past week—" Kate

breathed out heavily. "—Cord Maddox, and possibly his two younger brothers as well, head a mountain militia group stretching God only knows how far. They call themselves Kin. The same Kin that murdered her mother and have chased her across just about every state in the nation as well as parts of Canada and Mexico. They're tenacious."

Yes, the Kin were tenacious, merciless, and thorough. Most were former military, all were from the mountains that bred and nurtured them, and every damned one of them inducted into the Kin was bound by loyalty, and in many cases by blood, to the Maddox clan.

How Kate and Lara had gotten so much as a whisper of information concerning them was surprising. The information they had was damned unbelievable.

Every muscle in his body tightened to a breaking point. Jazz could feel the punch line coming and the implications of it had his senses stilling while a cold, murderous rage began to simmer inside his soul.

"The night her mother died she was rescued by her uncle, but not before she was shot. She was only sixteen. Since that night, from what we've uncovered, she was nearly killed in three other attacks over the past ten years. Rumor is, two years ago they found her uncle in a Chicago warehouse where he was brutally tortured for information on her whereabouts. They say he died without ever admitting who she was, or where she was. His body was never found, and she was never seen nor heard from again. Now we know why. He sent her to hide right beneath their noses."

Kate and Lara watched him, their gazes expectant, wary. Did they think he'd have already spat a name out?

No, because the only name he could come up with he dared not allow himself to voice. Rousing hope even enough to voice her name and learn he was wrong was more than he wanted to face. It was far more than he could bear to risk.

He shook his head, swallowing tightly.

No. He wouldn't let himself consider it . . .

But still, his breath felt suspended in his chest, fury, pride, and disbelief ripping through him.

"Who is she?" He knew, God, in his gut he knew. Just as he'd known the first night he met her as Annie Mayes. When he'd stared into hazel eyes and knew the color was wrong. The hairs on the back of his neck had lifted then as well.

Once again the two women glanced at each other, obviously uncertain how to proceed.

"Jazz . . ." Lara spoke up, obviously hesitating.

"I asked you a fucking question." He came out of his chair, his hands plowing through his hair as he stalked to the end of the porch, his fingers gripping the railing in a desperate grip.

He turned back to them slowly. "The two of you owe me, Kate," he reminded her. "Don't think you can hold back on this."

"Dammit, Jazz . . ."

"Answer the fucking question. Who is she?" he snarled, suspicion and blind fury surging through him.

Kenni stood perfectly still, silent at the side of the door that hadn't quite closed securely.

There was no way to save the situation, she thought.

Kate and Lara Blanchard had brought the truth and there was no way to keep that truth from Jazz now.

Her fists clenched at her side.

Every fear she'd lived with every day of her life for the past two years rose inside her, tormenting her with the knowledge of what could happen now. He could betray her to the Kin, or he would die for her at their hand. Once he learned the truth, he'd realize that, too, and she wasn't certain she could bear it if his choice was betraying her. But neither could she bear it if he died for her.

She should have never returned to Loudoun. Surely there was some other part of the world where she could have hidden. With the identity in place and already established by the real Annie Mayes, there must have been a safe place to exist other than here.

She hadn't wanted to exist, though, she realized. She hadn't wanted to keep running, being found, watching friends die. She hadn't wanted to continue living a lie and she hadn't wanted to die never knowing if the family she had loved had ordered their mother's and sister's deaths.

But neither had she wanted Jazz to know the truth. Not yet. Not now.

How had he known she wasn't really Annie Mayes? What had she done to make him suspicious? And what was she going to do now? Because she knew there was no way to keep the truth from him.

A sudden awareness of her had Jazz turning his gaze from Kate and Lara as the kitchen door pushed open and she stepped to the porch.

Darkness shrouded her, wrapped around her. What little light was available allowed him to glimpse the pain and fear in her expression, though, and the sight of it had every protective instinct he possessed rising hard and fast inside him.

The twins rose slowly to their feet, surprised, more than a little nervous as they stared between Jazz and the woman he'd known as Annie.

"How did I give myself away?" she asked the twins. The fear he heard in her voice stripped him to his soul.

From the moment he'd met her something had stilled inside him, going alert, waiting, watching. Aching for her.

Somehow, he'd known, Jazz realized. He had known who she was, he just hadn't wanted to see it. Admitting it seared him with guilt and the knowledge he'd failed her.

"You didn't give yourself away," Lara told her softly before Jazz could answer her. "It was the Kin that gave you away. Cord Maddox's curiosity tipped someone off, I assume. His search into Annie Mayes has caused several other searches from what we've learned. Each of those searches turned up the same information we found."

"That Annie Mayes is actually in China," she answered. "Wonderful." She turned to Jazz. "Why would Cord give a damn about some schoolteacher?"

Cord's suspicious nature was well known. He would have wanted to know who was teaching any child he'd taken under his protection.

They were all watching him now, waiting for an answer.

He was going to kill Cord, it was that simple. And if he learned the other man knew or even suspected who she was, then he would make what the Kin could do look like a picnic.

"Kenni," he whispered, knowing—God, could it be true? "Kenni . . ."

A bitter smile tipped her lips. "You should have just let me leave earlier, Jazz," she replied. "It would have been so much easier for both of us."

Oh, he really didn't think so.

"Kenni." Lara shifted restlessly at the comment, forestalling Jazz's instinctive rejection. "They know you're still alive and they know where you are, but running isn't going to save you. You already know that."

Jazz kept himself still, silent. The rage coursing through him was like a fever, a furious, burning surge of such force it was all he could do to remain standing in place.

"No, but it would save those I care about, Lara," Kenni stated as she acknowledged Lara's argument, bitterness filling her voice. Shoving her hands into the pockets of the capris she wore, she stared back at Jazz. "They killed Gunny." Her voice almost broke. "I came back to the warehouse and there was so much blood—" Turning her head she stopped, one hand lifting to cover her lips before she drew in a hard breath. "They will kill anyone who tries to help me."

Her shoulders straightened then, her slight body giving a small, almost imperceptible shudder before she stilled it. God he wanted to see her face, her eyes. He wanted those contacts out, he wanted the color out of her hair. He wanted to see the woman she had become, the woman who had been stolen from him.

There was no getting those years back, no way to take

the horror of what she had lived from her memories. That innocence was gone forever, but the woman was still here. She was here and she was alive, and by God he intended to make certain she stayed alive.

"Kate, Lara, you can bunk in the guest room," he growled at the other two women as he stomped across the porch, gripped Kenni's arm, and despite her instinctive attempt to break free pulled her into the house.

"What are you doing?" There were no tears, no anger, just hard determination in her voice now. "Let me go, Jazz."

Let her go? Yeah, he was going to get right on that.

"Shut the fuck up. And stop fighting me or I swear to God, Kenni, I will paddle your ass."

This was the second time he'd made that threat. She was getting rather tired of it, Kenni thought dismally as Jazz all but dragged her through the kitchen, television room, then up the short flight of stairs to the master suite at the top.

The bedroom door slammed behind him, the crack of wood against wood sending an involuntary flinch through her body. The moment he released her she swung around to face him, a blistering tirade on her lips until she glimpsed his expression. It was so tight, so hard, it could have been hewn from marble. The fury raging through him burned in his eyes, though. They were brilliant, like a faceted gem slicing into her before he walked away.

Eyes wide, staring at the apparition stalking across the hardwood floor of the bedroom to the French doors, Kenni couldn't help but draw in a hard, fortifying breath.

Throwing the doors open he stalked out to the deck, his arms extended, fingers gripping the railing before him as he stared into the darkness beyond.

The deck stretched out from the bedroom, the railing surrounding it securely. The only way to reach it was from the bedroom. There were no steps, no access period to the patio below. Now, this was a feature she hadn't thought of. The deck also shaded the patio outside the living room where Marcus and Essie and their pups often played.

Laying her hands on the railing as she stood several feet from him, Kenni stared down at the water, sadness washing over her. Large flat stones filled the perimeter of the pool, just like a pond. Just as she had dreamed when she was younger.

He'd built the house she'd dreamed of, the pool she'd longed for. The gazebo by the water, the small dock, just as she'd described to him so long ago.

"Why did you do this, Jazz?" she whispered. "Build everything as I dreamed?"

Tension poured from him. It vibrated from him and thickened the air until it felt smothering.

"Why didn't you contact me?" His voice grated with fury. A fury that lashed at her, tightened her chest, and reminded her of all the nights she had dreamed of contacting him, dreamed he came for her, rescued her. The fact that he hadn't answered her question became buried by so many emotions, so many memories.

How many nights had she cried for him, cried for her mother, her family? How often had she cried for the brothers she had trusted before the bodyguards sent with her and her mother destroyed her life?

She'd learned fast that the black knights far outweighed the white ones, and damsels in distress were just screwed. She'd learned that the night she found Gunny lying in a pool of his own blood.

"You once told me there are no knights in shining armor," she whispered. "And I've realized, I'm no Cinderella . . . I couldn't contact you, I couldn't let you know, because I refused to be the cause of your death as well."

She smoothed her hand over the railing, noticing the wood was free of roughness. It had been sanded, stained, and treated until no chance of harm existed from stray splinters. If only there were a way to smooth life so easily.

Jazz turned to her slowly, towering over her, his expression still livid. If he'd come out here to cool down or to get a handle on the fury, he'd obviously failed.

Kenni jumped to move back, but she was too slow and a heartbeat later his fingers were locked around her upper arms as he glared down at her, the blue of his eyes so bright he was frightening.

"Jazz . . ."

"Why the fuck didn't you contact me?" he repeated. "Why, Kenni? Why didn't you let me know you were alive?"

His voice didn't rise, it roughened, grated, the sound of it more intimidating than she wanted to admit.

"You don't understand, Jazz," she whispered. "I couldn't . . ."

"You wouldn't," he snapped. "Ten years, Kenni. You could have called me, or Cord . . ."

"No . . ." She would have never called Cord, Deacon,

or Sawyer. And she sure as hell wouldn't have called her father.

"Why, damn you?" The guttural tone of his voice had her breath. "Tell me why!"

"Jazz, please don't," she whispered, shaking her head, trying to pull free of him.

"Tell me why, damn you. Why?" His voice rose just enough to assure her his anger was slipping its leash. Not that she feared he would hurt her, but she did fear what he might do if all that excellent control he possessed slipped free.

"Because you're Kin. You're Kin and I couldn't be sure you wouldn't go to Cord." The cry tore free of her, ten years of hopeless, aching regret and loss, ten years of having everything and everyone she trusted taken away from her. Her throat was so tight she could barely speak, her heart racing with fear and pain and the overwhelming sense that she was no longer in control.

Releasing her, his fingers lifting one by one until he was no longer touching her, until he could step away from her as though he didn't trust himself to be close, Jazz stared at her in disbelief for a moment before his expression hardened.

"Because you didn't trust me." His voice was harder, no longer filled with heat or even anger.

"I trusted *you*." Damn, her hands were shaking. Pushing them into the pockets of her capris, she stared back at him, wary of the steely gleam in his gaze now. "But I trusted Kent, Jimmy, and Greg as well. They were family, cousins I'd known all my life, men my brothers sent to watch over Mom and me."

The horror of that night was like a scar inside her

soul. She could still feel the punch of that bullet as it tore into her shoulder, shredding her flesh and sending her to her knees as she tried to run. The smell of the smoke, the heat of the flames . . . the sight of her fragile, beautiful mother hanging limply, held upright only by Greg's hands around her throat.

"Gunny saved me that night. He was Momma's half brother, she said no one knew about him. He gave up his whole life trying to find out who kept sending my family to kill me." She couldn't help the bitter, agonized laugh that left her lips. "My family, Jazz. It was always family, always Kin sent to kill me. Men at my brothers' command." The sneer that echoed in her voice wasn't intentional, but fitting. "And you think I should have called you? How was I to know you wouldn't call Cord, no matter what I told you? Because I knew, just as I know now, how you trust him."

"Cord isn't behind this, Kenni," he bit out, his arms going across his chest as she stared back at him in disbelief.

"And you would be willing to bet my life on that?" Stepping back from him, Kenni watched him carefully now, remembering where his loyalties lay.

He was Kin.

From an early age he'd been marked as part of the militia network. His mother had been Kin, as well as his uncle before they were killed just after Jazz's fifth birthday. The foster system might have raised him, but the Kin had ensured he'd eventually ended up with a family willing to nurture him.

A family sworn to the Kin as well.

His ties to the group were too strong, his loyalties to them too deep.

"I wouldn't bet your life on anything or anyone. Not then or now," he snapped, disgust coloring his voice as well as his expression. "But I know the man Cord's become just as I remember the man who grieved for his mother and his sister until we didn't think he'd recover himself again. The twins were little better."

Frustration tightened his face, gleamed in his eyes. He was torn, loyalty to the Kin and to friendship suddenly in conflict. And Kenni wasn't certain which would win.

"The man Cord has become doesn't matter," she retorted, the ache of being unable to trust the men she had loved from the day of her birth like a dagger in her heart. "Even if he isn't involved, the fact is that until he learned I wasn't really Annie Mayes, there had been no threats against me. Now, within an hour of having been face-to-face with him, I was attacked again." Turning away she stalked into the bedroom once again, rubbing at her arms to dispel the chill racing over them, the sense of rising danger heading her way. "I saw the driver. I can't place his face." Turning back to Jazz, she found it difficult to meet the intensity of those blue eyes. "But I've seen him before, a long time ago, and he's Kin. And all Kin get their orders from Cord, Deacon, or Sawyer Maddox. My brothers."

Even now, ten years later, that knowledge was like acid eating through her soul.

Her brothers. Only four men could give the order to harm her or her mother. Those four men were her father and three brothers. Only they had the power to give a kill order.

"I don't care where the orders are supposed to come from, Kenni," he ground out, the fury in his voice deepening it, giving it a primitive, harsh rasp. "But I'll tell you right now neither your brothers nor your father was involved. I'd bet my life on it."

Kenni swallowed tightly and clasped her hands together in front of her. Fear was curdling in her stomach, threatening to bring her dinner back up.

"Will you bet my life on it? Are you going to tell them?" Her voice was faint. It was all she could do to force the words past her lips.

God, he couldn't do that. She hadn't been able to prove the identity of the person giving the orders yet. But then it didn't appear she was going to. Gunny had taught her how to survive, but the investigation process hadn't been in the lesson plans.

"Your brothers were a mess for months," he bit out, pushing his fingers through his hair furiously before glaring back at her. "Cord still gets drunk every year on the anniversary of his mother's death and what he believed was yours. They suffered, Kenni. Guilty men don't suffer like that."

He was asking too much of her. Ten years of running, uncertain who to trust or where to run, and he wanted her to just let go of all that?

They wouldn't care to kill Jazz as well, or Slade, Zack, or Jessie and her unborn baby.

"I can't take the chance." She refused to. "They've killed anyone willing to help me, Jazz. Friends Gunny trusted, then Gunny as well. All I had left was the identity he put in place for me in case of emergency. I can't bear to lose anyone else I care about because of this." Her voice hitched painfully, one hand reaching out to him beseechingly. "You have to let me go . . ."

"The hell I will." He was on her before she realized what was happening, his hands gripping her arms again, jerking her to him. "You're going nowhere, Kenni."

"Don't force me to go unprepared, Jazz, please." The plea was rough, forcing itself past a throat tight with tears. "Don't make me run like that."

"Run!" Nose-to-nose, he drew his lips back into a snarl, his gaze burning into hers like laser fire. "I fucking dare you to run. The minute you do, I'll call those brothers of yours. I'll tell them everything I know, Kenni, and when they catch up with you there will be hell to pay for thinking, even for a second, they'd ever harm you."

"And if they get themselves killed instead?" The cry was torn from her, the thought of her brothers hurt, or killed, more than she could bear. "Even if they're not involved, Jazz, they're in danger. Just as you, Jessie, Slade, and Zack are in danger if you try to help me." She gripped his arms desperately. "Let me go!"

"When hell freezes over . . ."

CHAPTER 9

Kenni wasn't prepared for the depth of heat and hunger Jazz unleashed on her. She wasn't even certain what caused it.

When his lips moved over hers, though, they were wild. This wasn't just erotic hunger. The feel of his need, the heavy groan torn from the very depths of his soul as he picked her up in his arms and moved for the bed, tore away the last fragile shield she'd kept around her heart.

She was defenseless now. All the aching hunger and need she'd trapped within her for the past years poured free. And every desperate emotion that had silently gathered inside her for this man was revealed.

She should have left Loudoun months ago. But she'd held on instead and eagerly awaited each glimpse she'd had of him. She may have pretended to herself that she avoided him, but Kenni knew now, very little had mattered other than keeping her identity hidden, and seeing Jazz.

And she had waited for this. For the stomach-clenching pleasure that swept over her as Jazz laid her back on his bed, his lips moving to her jaw, running down the sensitive line of her neck, and igniting the most exquisite sensations in their wake.

How was she supposed to live without this now? she cried out silently as Jazz leveled up, then quickly turned her to her stomach.

The gasp that parted her lips was one of excitement and surprise.

"Stay there," he growled as she moved to turn back. "Right there, or I won't have enough control to get my damned boots off, let alone my jeans."

Kenni buried her face in the comforter, her fingers clenching in the blankets beside her head at the guttural sound of his voice.

"Damn, you have the prettiest fucking ass, Kenni," he groaned as one boot could be heard thudding to the floor. "It has the sweetest little curve. Makes a man want to do nasty things to it."

She trembled, a shudder of anticipation racing through her. She'd heard just how erotically intense Jazz could get. How his bedroom games could go for hours. How he could go for hours.

"Spread your legs for me," he ordered, the graveled sound of his voice sweeping through her senses and laying any objections she might have to waste. "Slow and easy, baby."

A whimper escaped her lips before she even realized she'd voiced it. She spread her legs for him, uncertain in this position, unable to see him or to gauge his intentions.

"Takes trust to just lie there, doesn't it, Kenni?" he

said before she felt his lips at her ankle like a sensual brand. "To just let me look. Or touch."

A fingertip caressed the material running between her thighs, the sensation causing her to jerk at the exquisite pleasure as it lanced straight to her swollen clit.

"Your pussy's so wet your panties are damp, isn't it?" he groaned.

Kenni whimpered, forcing her hips to remain still rather than lifting to him and begging for more.

Callused, warm hands cupped her rear, squeezing gently as she felt his weight move to the mattress between her thighs. Then his hands smoothed over her hips, up her side as he came over her. She shivered as he brushed his lips against her ear and felt his larger body covering her, sheltering her.

Hungry male lips moved to her neck, her shoulder. The heat of his erection, iron-hard and throbbing, pressed against her rear.

Rolling to his side Jazz eased her to her back, his blue eyes mesmerizing as she gazed up at him.

"Ah, Kenni," he crooned, his voice rough, possessive. "I waited far too long for this."

His lips covered hers again, sipping, licking at her tongue, drawing her into chaos, causing her to forget to question what he had waited for.

Lifting her hands to his biceps, her nails bit into the hard, powerful muscles as he pushed her cami up her stomach to her breasts. His lips eased from hers as he pulled back, his eyes heavy-lidded, watching as she lifted her arms and allowed him to pull it free of her.

His hand lowered, cupped the weight of one breast

and as she watched, his head dipped down, lips parting to cover one hard, aching tip.

Kenni cried out, arching closer to the feel of his lips suckling at first one hard tip then the other. Deep, heated pulls sent shards of sensation forking from the sensitive nub to the weeping center of her body before striking at the swollen kernel of her clit.

And his hands were never still.

Strong, callused fingers and palms stroked and caressed her body, fueling the flames burning through her senses.

"That's it, baby," he crooned as her fingers buried in the heavy length of his hair to hold him to her. "Show me what you like."

Show him?

She could barely breathe, let alone guess at what she liked. Every touch he gave her, she liked.

She wanted more.

When he captured her nipple between his teeth and tormented it with his tongue, she lost her breath. Tremors of sensation rocked her body, tightening her muscles as she whimpered against the storm building inside her.

Above her, Jazz groaned as though in pain before releasing the swollen tip. His lips moved from her breasts, hot, hungry kisses spreading lower as he hooked his fingers in the band of the boy shorts she wore and pushed them over her hips.

Desperation had her arching, aiding the removal of the last barrier between his flesh and hers. She needed to get closer to him. She had to still the pulsing, aching sensations tearing through her as they tightened in her vagina and around the sensitive flesh of her clitoris.

"Jazz." Heat rushed over her as she felt his nails rasp along her side to her hip. His lips brushed against her abdomen, little flicks of his tongue driving her crazy with pinpoints of prickling pleasure as his other palm caressed her inner thigh, slowly parting her legs farther.

"Kenni, so sweet." He nipped at the side of her hip then licked across the little burn.

"You're killing me." Whimpering, desperate to ease the aching need tormenting her, Kenni tried to arch closer to him again.

"I'll make it all better, baby," he promised as he eased between her thighs. "You just lie right there and I'll make it all better."

Kenni's eyes jerked open as his shoulders settled between her thighs and his hands slid beneath her to cup the curves of her rear.

"Jazz!"

Heated, hungry lips settled on the sensitive folds between her thighs, his tongue laving the tortured bud he found there with exquisite, fiery licks.

Wicked blue eyes locked with hers, his gaze daring her, tempting her as his lips tightened on the little nubbin to suckle at it with gentle, tormenting draws.

Her hands clenched in the sheets beneath her, her breath locked in her throat. Small, desperate mewls escaped her lips, and pleasure rocked her senses.

She was certain the tightening spirals of pleasure were going to tear her apart. Every muscle strained toward the rapture growing closer, and just when she was certain she would explode with it he eased the pressure of his lips, pulling her back from the ecstatic edge.

"No. Don't stop." Her hands flew from the sheets to bury in his hair instead.

"But it gets better, sweetheart," he assured her, his voice deeper, darker. "Let me show you how good it can be."

Wicked. Those eyes were so wicked as he lifted her closer and then *licked* her.

Parting the swollen folds, he tongued the sensitive inner flesh lazily. Flicking against the clenched entrance to her vagina, he rimmed the opening before testing it with the tip of his tongue. Pleasure seared her, burned against already sensitized nerve endings, and sent sensation clashing through her senses.

Too much. Not enough. Too easy. Not easy enough. She didn't know if she needed more or if she needed less sensation. All she knew for certain was that his tongue was lethal. It teased and tempted, licked and tasted until Kenni was desperate for release.

She'd never felt pleasure like this. She'd never known it could be this intense, this exquisite. Lightning-swift, forked trails of lashing sensation tore through her senses, setting off explosions of such heat throughout her body that she felt tortured with pleasure.

His tongue teased and tasted her intimate flesh, his lips captured sensitive skin, suckled at it and heated it. He tortured her with such pleasure she was begging, nearly crying for ease before he captured her clit between his lips, suckled it into the heat of his mouth, and flicked his tongue over it, around it—rubbed against it.

The implosion ruptured her senses with ecstasy.

Bright, livid color exploded behind her closed eyes as her body tightened, shuddering uncontrollably beneath the violent lashes of ecstasy.

Spasms tore through her, stole her breath, and left her gasping for air.

Sensation was still rocketing through her when he moved. He rose between her thighs, coming over her as a blunt, heated pressure tucked at the entrance of her vagina and began pressing against it with steady force.

Kenni struggled to open her eyes, to catch her breath. Forcing her lashes open she looked down in time to see the heavy, blunt tip of Jazz's erection as it disappeared inside her.

Her senses screamed out in pleasure and in pain. Eyes wide, she let fascination and shock hold her in their grip as she felt her inner flesh rippling around the intruder, tightening and pulling though mere inches penetrated.

And there was a lot left to go.

"Damn, Kenni, you're so tight," he groaned as his lips pressed against her shoulder. "So hot . . ."

Kenni bit her lip, her senses so immersed in the sensations tightening inside her that she hadn't considered he would be unable to fit.

"I'm sorry." She wanted to please him, wanted her body to please him. "I'm so sorry, Jazz."

He eased back as a dark chuckle parted his lips. "Sorry? Oh God, Kenni, you're fucking exquisite."

Pausing at the entrance his hips bunched, power gathered in his thighs, and a second later the broad, heavy flesh forged harder, deeper inside her as the fiery pleasure became a deep, burning discomfort that shocked her body and tore her free of the building waves of ecstasy pulling her into another release.

Kenni forced back a cry of pain. She didn't want him to stop. She didn't want to disappoint him. She'd waited so long for this, for his touch, his possession. The pain would be okay soon. Surely it would.

She stilled beneath him, forced her fingers to uncurl where they gripped his back, her nails to ease from his hard flesh.

He still wasn't fitting.

Kenni nearly whimpered at the knowledge that it would hurt again.

"Ah baby." The deep rasping croon eased some of the fear.

She would endure much worse for this man.

"It's okay," she whispered. "I'm okay, Jazz."

His lips eased over her shoulder, her neck. Slow, whispering caresses that had her senses pausing, waiting to see what he would do.

His hips didn't move. Despite the contractions of her vagina around his thick length, he remained still but for the throb of the thick crest buried within her grip.

"You're perfect." His voice was strained, his muscles tight as his kisses drifted to the tops of her breasts. "My perfect sweet Kenni. No one's ever given me such a precious gift."

She'd never imagined giving herself to anyone else. Every fantasy, every desire since she was sixteen had been centered on him. His lips were easing over her upper breast to the still-hard tip of a nipple. She loved his lips on her nipples. She would endure a little pain for that pleasure.

Only it was better than before.

She was shocked at the cry of renewed need as it escaped, surprised she had the breath to make the sound.

As his lips surrounded the hard tip and he sucked it firmly inside the heat of his mouth, those hard lightning forks of sensation ripped from her nipple to the painfully stretched flesh he was invading.

A spasm rippled through the muscles clenched around his erection as Kenni felt the slick, heated slide of her response ease around the intrusion.

With every pulse and clench of the flesh surrounding his cock, Jazz's lips became hungrier. He suckled at first one nipple then the other until the striking bolts of pleasure had her hips lifting to him, the pain of the penetration merging with the pleasure whipping around her again.

Jazz didn't ease back at her response. Instead, one hand clamped to her hip as his lips and tongue pleasured the hard peak and he thrust against her again. The hard flesh buried to the hilt inside her, filling her, stretching her so tight around him that his throbbing length caressed all of her vagina.

"Jazz." Her hands gripped his biceps now as new sensations began tearing at her, tearing through her.

His breath rasped as her ear. A groan tore from his lips while powerful, corded muscles flexed against her.

"Lift your knees," he rasped at her ear. "Grip my hips, baby."

His hand slid from the curve of her hip to her bent knee to guide it into place. Once she was positioned as he wanted his hips shifted, the full length of his erection settling deeper inside her.

Kenni whimpered at the increased sensation, her knees automatically tightening on him as a rough groan vibrated against her ear.

"That's it, Kenni," he whispered. "Hold on to me, because heaven help us I don't know how long my control is going to last."

Her lips parted to question the comment when he moved. Pulling his hips back, he shifted his erection inside her, moving against delicate responsive flesh. Pleasure clashed with pain. Her vagina rippled and clenched around him to hold him inside before the heavy flesh settled in place once again.

That slight movement ignited a trembling response.

"More," she whispered brokenly as she shifted against him. "Do it again."

Jazz gripped her hip with one hand, his hold tight as his breath rasped at her ear. "Ah hell, Kenni, your pussy's so tight, so sweet around my cock."

The erotically explicit words combined with the tingles and static pleasure had her muscles tightening around the intrusion with swift clenching spasms.

It was devastating. Fiery pulses of electric sensation began racing through her, building, throwing her ever closer to a pleasure she knew would destroy her.

"That's it, Kenni," he groaned, his voice tight. "Move against me like that."

Her hips were shifting, moving against him, forcing his erection deeper.

Each hard thrust of his cock had her flying higher. The rasp of his erect flesh impaling her, retreating, only to surge inside her once again, deeper, harder, renewing the sense of pleasure-pain as he stretched her inner flesh. "That's it, baby," he groaned again, lifting himself to his knees in front of her.

Hard hands gripped her beneath her knees, pressing her legs back and spreading her farther. "There now, keep milking my cock, baby. Let me watch. Let me see you take me."

Kenni cried out, the carnal intensity of his expression as arousing as the feel of his hard flesh penetrating her and his explicit demands spurring her.

Each thrust inside her tightened the bands of sensation burning and swirling through her senses. Each heavy penetration stretched delicate flesh, rasped against painfully sensitive nerve endings.

She was only barely aware of her cries as he moved harder against her, his thrusts increasing as he came over her again. Catching his weight on one elbow, he used the other hand to grip her hip again as his thrusts grew harder, faster.

Perspiration beaded on his shoulder, sliding along burnished gold flesh and catching in the short hairs growing across his chest.

Kenni stared up at him, caught, held by the intensity of the electric blue burning between lowered lashes. Pleasure began racing faster, harder. Slick flesh slid against slick flesh; breaths rasped from their chests as pleasured moans sounded through the room.

Her inner muscles clenched with hard, rapid ripples of response that tightened around her clit. Her nails bit into his biceps, her breathing became harder.

Kenni could feel herself unraveling.

Jazz's gaze held hers as his erection pounded inside her, pushing her harder, faster.

"Jazz . . ." His name was a breathless cry; was rapture.

She couldn't stop the explosion that tore through her and hurled her into a vortex of such ecstasy that for a heartbeat she wondered if she'd died. Wildfire consumed her, rapture hurled her from peak to peak as she heard Jazz's heavy groan and felt pulsing heat spreading through her inner flesh.

Another blazing rush of pleasure overtook her.

Perspiration soaked her body and the flaming pleasure hurled her deeper, harder into a vortex she never wanted to escape.

She wanted to stay forever in the crashing waves of ecstasy, locked against his hard body, feeling his pleasure merging with hers. This was where she was born to be, in his arms, his pleasure . . .

Oh God, just let her stay here forever because reality was going to shred her soul when the danger returned.

Kenni slept.

A deep hard sleep indicative of an exhaustion as much emotional as physical.

Sitting on the side of the bed after running a cool cloth over her thighs and the swollen folds of her pussy, Jazz found himself staring into the darkness of the bedroom, more confused than he could ever remember being in his life.

He'd broken so many personal rules with this woman that he'd stopped keeping count. But tonight he'd broke one he'd set in stone.

He'd forgotten to wear a condom.

The memory of being surrounded by slick, tight

muscles, the feel of her pussy milking his erection was so fucking good. So God-help-him sweet all he wanted to do was experience it again. To work his cock into the fist-tight grip of her pussy and fill her with his release over and over again.

He wanted to risk his soul with a woman who hadn't even trusted him with the truth of her identity.

Biting back a curse, Jazz rose to his feet and made his way through the house. Checking the locks on doors and windows, giving Marcus and Essie a pet before gazing at the pups, sleeping with such innocence.

Years of moving from one lover to another, never allowing one of them to become emotionally attached to him, never letting his emotions become invested in any of them. Because they were already invested in a woman he believed was dead.

"This isn't right," Cord whispered as Jazz stood at Kenni's grave site, hours after the funeral.

He hadn't heard her brother approach, hadn't known anyone was there. Staring at the mound of bare dirt, so focused on whatever gut-wrenching agony gripped him that nothing else had mattered.

"No, it's not right," Jazz agreed.

"Listen to me, Jazz, that's not my sister in there." Cord swung him around so fast that Jazz could only stare back at him in surprise, then in shock.

"What are you saying, Cord?" His heart was suddenly racing, an edge of hope rising inside him.

"You heard what that witness said," Cord snapped, rage burning in his green eyes. *"She was running from the hotel when she was shot. We have to find whoever grabbed her and ran with her."*

The hope died just as quickly.

"A druggie, Cord?" he whispered. "Your dad sent a dozen men to check that out, you were with them . . ."

Cord looked away, shaking his head slowly. When he turned back, Jazz saw the hopelessness that filled his brother's gaze.

"What's going on?" Cord whispered then. "There were three bodyguards with them, Jazz. How did this happen? How did it happen?"

Because the bodyguards had turned against her and her mother and attempted to kill both of them.

The hotel fire had been deliberately set—Vinny Maddox, Kenni's father, had learned that much. An explosive device set on the floor Kenni and her mother's suite was located on. The detective investigating the case reported that smoke inhalation had killed the mother and daughter, and the flames had destroyed their delicate bodies.

Moving from where the pups slept, Jazz made his way to the kitchen where the two silent Blanchard sisters sat with coffee and electronic tablets.

Pausing behind them he stared at the file pulled up on Kate's screen. The investigator's report from the fire in question.

"What are you thinking, Kate?" He turned to her, seeing the purpose in her eyes.

"I'm thinking she'll never be safe until we figure out who wanted her dead to begin with," Kate stated softly. "And from what she said, there's a high chance that could be family. Perhaps one of her brothers."

Jazz shook his head. "Not her brothers. Go ahead and eliminate them; I'd bet money neither Cord, Deacon, nor

Sawyer was behind this or knew about it. They learn she's alive then hell will hit the Kin until they find out who was behind it."

"Let's see if you're right," Lara suggested as she lifted a grainy, color photo from the small mobile printer they were using.

Taking it, Jazz stared at the vehicle that had nearly run Kenni down that afternoon.

"Where did you get this?" he asked her.

"Bank cameras." A grin tugged at her lips. "I couldn't get his face, but I got the side of his head. If nothing else, maybe, one of her brothers will recognize that, or the car. Everyone knows about the attempted hit-and-run," she pointed out. "He shouldn't think it strange if you're trying to find out who attempted it."

She was right.

He stared at the picture himself. There was something about the profile of the driver that nagged at him. A familiarity he couldn't place.

"No doubt Cord will be here as soon as he hears about it," he told them. "Hide your car in the barn before daylight. It should fit nicely in one of the empty stalls and there'll be no chance of it being seen, even if the barn's checked."

"I'll do it." Kate rose from her seat and left the house silently through the back door.

Not even her footsteps were audible as she went across the porch. If he hadn't known what to look for, he wouldn't have seen her grip the railing to vault soundlessly to the ground below, either.

As he watched Kate move across the yard he was aware of Lara watching him closely, too thoughtfully.

She was a dangerous woman when she let herself think too deeply.

"She's the one, isn't she?" Lara asked softly as her sister disappeared. "The reason why Jazz Lancing never gave his heart to a woman. Someone else already owned it."

There was a thread of sadness in her voice, one Jazz couldn't quite place.

"Yeah," he admitted remembering the woman-child Kenni had been, and how easily she had snagged his heart. "She's always owned it, Lara."

She nodded before turning back to the tablet and sifting through files for long moments.

"Jazz?" she asked softly when he said nothing more. "Do you think you might have a brother somewhere? One who hasn't already given his heart away, that is? Maybe one who doesn't see the imperfections?"

The scar. She pretended she'd forgotten it was there, that it didn't matter, but Kate had told him years before just how very aware Lara was of it.

"I think, Lara, you don't have a single imperfection. And anyone who sees one needs his ass kicked," he told her gently.

Lara rarely showed her vulnerabilities to anyone, especially if her sister was around. Kate was incredibly protective of her younger twin. She would kill the man who broke Lara's heart.

"Yeah, there's that," she agreed, her voice brighter now.

A false brightness and one he had no idea how to fix.

"We'll find out what's going on here." Lara glanced back at him, her gaze set and filled with determination.

"Then you can find that brother of yours for me. How's that?"

"I don't know, Lara." Moving around the bar, he met her gaze again. "I think you and Kate need to head home. I don't want you two involved in this."

Her brow lifted slowly, a move he knew wasn't a good sign.

"Really?" she drawled.

"This isn't your fight," he pointed out. If anything happened to her, or to Kate, then he doubted the other twin would survive.

"Just as we weren't your fight when you barged head-long into that gang of bikers to save us," she reminded him, her tone cool. "Forget it, Lancing, we're not going anywhere, so you're wasting your breath. And not because we owe you anything. Everyone who died trying to help her and her uncle was working alone, on their own. Gunny and Kenni stuck together, making it harder for the two- or three-man teams that went out after them. That's why they survived, until they caught her uncle alone."

"It's not coordinated." Jazz straightened then, staring at her in surprise as the truth hit him. "It hasn't been a Maddox objective, or she would have been dead that first night. The Kin are never sent out in such small teams. It's always a unit, always precisely planned." And if a hit was ordered, a Maddox was always there to ensure the plan was followed.

"If that's true, then it looks more like a few with a single objective in mind. But who would benefit from Sierra's and Kenni's deaths?" Lara asked.

"Answer that question," Jazz growled, "and we've solved the problem."

"If it's just a few, then facing a group surrounding Kenni and asking questions, someone's going to get scared and fuck up," she guessed. "We need Slade and Zack on this."

He nodded thoughtfully. Slade and Zack weren't the only ones they needed on this. Cord, Deacon, and Sawyer needed to know their sister was alive and threatened by Kin. That would tip the scales.

The trick would be in convincing Kenni to tell them. Or risk her hatred by telling them himself.

"Let's wait twenty-four hours," Jazz suggested. "The two of you head into town, see if you can hear or see anything. Come back here tomorrow night and I'll arrange for a meeting with Slade and Zack."

"That'll work." Kate nodded, though her expression was still concerned. "Finding out who it is won't be easy unless she cooperates, though. She hasn't moved to find out who's trying to kill her in two years. She might be too scared to know, Jazz." Sympathy softened her face. "How terrible to believe the very people you trust the most are the ones trying to kill you. Her own cousins striking out at her must have been horrifying."

She might be too scared to know, but he wasn't.

"That's why we're going to take care of that little thing for her. It's not a fight she should have to face herself. The fallout will be bad enough."

CHAPTER 10

How to find a killer when you have no idea of their identity or motives? It was a question Kenni had asked herself for two years now.

Gunny had been investigating her mother's murder and the Kin as they ran. He'd kept her out of the investigation, though, kept her as closely guarded and hidden as possible. She'd run errands, kept watch when he met with contacts he wasn't certain of, and drove when he was tired.

When she'd argued he'd just turned the "look" on her: his expression like stone, his brown eyes devoid of emotion. And he'd keep looking at her like that no matter how hard or how long she argued. When she was finished, he would pick up where he left off and she would end up doing exactly what he wanted her to do in the first place.

His stepfather had raised him in the marines and then he'd joined himself even before he'd graduated high school. It was all he'd known until his half sister had found him just a few years before her death.

One look, he told her once, at the delicate woman whose eyes were identical to his and he'd melted. He'd loved the sister he'd never had a chance to know so much that he'd gone AWOL from everything he'd known to save her daughter.

How had he known the danger she was facing, though? What had her mother told him that had him running with her and refusing to contact her family until she was well enough to make the decision herself?

What had he known that kept him running with her, chasing information to identify the person behind her mother's death?

"It was the bodyguards, Kenni," he would murmur as he tracked each second of her and her mother's time in New York. "Cousins. If only your father or brothers can command these men, then who gave the order?"

She hadn't had an answer for him. And now she didn't have an answer for herself.

Puppy growls drew her back from the past to the four Rottweiler pups playing at her side where she sat on the smooth stones of the patio the next afternoon.

The runt, fierce and always eager to rumble, was trying to pounce on his sister and steal the squeaky little squirrel he'd decided he was in love with yesterday.

He'd become so possessive over that damned furry toy, she'd started calling him Squirrel. The name had stuck. It was ridiculous, but even more ridiculous was the fact that he'd responded to the name from the beginning.

"No, Squirrel, leave Aggie alone. She was playing with it first," Kenni chided the rambunctious male pup as he used his teeth to tug at the only female's ear with fierce little growls.

A puppy woof, demanding and irritated, was Squirrel's response as Aggie gripped the toy in her teeth and turned her back on him. "You're being bad, Squirrel," Kenni said, wagging a finger at him in disapproval. "Aggie will snap at you again."

Squirrel gave a puppy growl before batting at her hand then going after the toy again.

Squirrel was only about half the size of the other pups but with enough attitude for three Rottweilers. With one black ear and one brown, the quick little pup tried for the toy again only to have Kenni block him once more.

She couldn't help but be amused by his determination. If he would just settle down for a minute Aggie would drop the toy and amble away to find something else to play with instead. If he would settle down—it took sheer exhaustion to get him to do such a thing, though.

Sitting curled on the stones next to the four pups as she gave the parents a break in watching them so they could nap, she tried to make sense of the past ten years. But then, she'd been doing that since she hit Loudoun.

She should have fought Gunny harder. She should have made him tell her what he was learning as he learned it. That was, if she'd known when he was learning something. She normally didn't find out until he was heading toward the next clue. And all those clues seemed to come with another near escape from Kin sent after her.

"We're changing that pup's name, right?" Jazz asked

from the sliding glass doors where he propped himself against the frame and watched her.

Her stomach got that jittery feeling again, while her thighs tightened against the moisture that began to gather immediately. Damn him. All she could think about whenever she looked at him was what it had been like as he'd taken her.

"He likes his name." She shrugged. "It suits him."

Scratching at his jaw, Jazz frowned at the pup in confusion. "He doesn't look like a squirrel, Kenni."

Turning to Jazz, the pup woofed, bounding over to him, only to trip over his own feet before reaching his goal. Sprawled out in front of Jazz, canine bemusement evident on his face, Squirrel struggled back to his feet where he then stared up at Jazz in pride, as though he'd done something completely awesome.

"Why hadn't you named them yet?" she asked as Jazz straightened from the door frame and moved to sit on the stone bench a few feet from her.

Reaching down to pet Aggie when she moved to him quickly, he grinned at Squirrel's hurried possession of the furry stuffed toy the female abandoned.

"Maybe I was going to let Jessie name them?" he answered, his gaze locking with hers as the use of the word *maybe* had her eyes rolling in exasperation.

"Maybe? Really, Jazz?" She was probably one of the few people who knew when that *maybe* began.

"Maybe." His lips quirked as she saw the memory in his gaze as well.

Maybe was Jazz's greatest lie.

Maybe I don't give a damn . . . That had been his

response to Cord when her brother had informed him that Kenni was far too young for him.

He had given a damn. He wouldn't have touched her and she had known it. At least not then he wouldn't have.

"I went to talk to Vinny the day you and your mom left for New York." His eyes turned somber as they darkened for a moment with whatever emotion he was feeling.

"What about?" What could he have possibly had to discuss with her father?

"You." His eyes locked with hers then. "I asked for his permission to call on you when you returned home."

She blinked back at him in surprise. How old-fashioned. She would have never guessed he would do such a thing.

Squirrel moved to her side, butting against her in a bid for attention as she felt her heart beginning to race, her hands to shake.

She hated it when her hands shook. It gave her away every time. It revealed how much something meant to her, how important it was to her.

"You were going to call on me?" she asked carefully.

"I wanted to court you, Kenni," he told her softly. "Your brothers yelled and cursed and threw their fits and the whole time Vinny just stared back at me." A low, self-deprecating chuckle left his lips. "When Cord, Deacon, and Sawyer finally shut up, he gave me his permission. I was going to be there when you returned. Maybe take you for a drive." A frown pulled at his brow as gave his head a little shake. "Then you were gone. Just that fast."

Turning her head away, Kenni had to fight her tears.

He surprised her. He'd always surprised her, she realized. She never would have imagined Jazz would do something so traditional.

"I had no idea you were even interested." She'd daydreamed, fantasized, but never thought for a second that any of those fantasies had a chance.

"I had no idea what your father would say," he returned, his voice soft, his gaze still far too dark. "You were only sixteen. I was twenty-three, but the thought of waiting while some teenage bastard stole your heart seemed a little idiotic to me. But then, I wasn't aware of how little you trusted me at the time, either. I might have changed my mind if I had known."

Trust.

"It wasn't a lack of trust." Rising to her feet, she brushed the back of her borrowed shorts off before turning and staring out at the pool. "It was the thought of what would happen to you." Wrapping her arms across her breasts as she fought back the chill invading her, Kenni stared at the water as it trickled along a streambed before falling into the pool. "The first month or so, I didn't call because I was terrified, and I could tell Gunny simply had no idea why Momma was dead and suddenly I was being hunted. But we knew it was the Kin. You were part of the Kin, and I knew if I called you then you'd call my brothers, my father . . ." She shivered at the memory of her terror during those days.

"You knew I'd protect you," he snapped.

Kenni whirled around. "With your life," she retorted fiercely. "You would have protected me with your life if that was what it took, Jazz. And I couldn't bear the thought of it."

"Damned right I would. Then and now!"

"There you go then." A mocking flip of her hand emphasized her point. "That's why. And I'll be damned if I'm going to keep arguing with you about it."

"No, you're just going to keep running, aren't you, Kenni? You've run for so long you don't know anything else," he accused her, the censure in his voice lashing at her guilt and her temper.

His expression was so arrogant, so knowing, it made her crazy.

"I've been in Loudoun for two years, Jazz. How does that constitute running?" The accusation stung, though, whipping at some hidden guilt she couldn't put her finger on.

A mocking smile twisted his lips. "No, Kenni, Annie Mayes came to Loudoun. Kenni Maddox is still running because she can face dying easier than she can face learning who's trying to kill her."

The retort enraged her.

Fingers curling into fists she faced him, knowing it wasn't true. It couldn't be true.

"You are wrong." Shaking, trembling, she stood in front of him, her finger pointing in his face furiously. "I lived . . ."

"Well by God I didn't." Jazz came off the bench so fast she could only blink up at him, surprised, a part of her suddenly wary at the icy fury revealed in his gaze.

"What . . . ?"

"Look at this place," he demanded as he grabbed her shoulders, quickly turning her to stare out at the valley she'd envisioned as a teenager. "This house, the property. Every fucking detail I could remember. Everything a sixteen-year-old flirt wanted, I built after they told me you were dead. After you began fucking running without a single thought to the people who loved you, Kenni. Who grieved for you."

She could hear the emotion in his voice, the grief that roughened it, that tore past the control he exerted on every emotion he kept locked inside his soul.

He had grieved for her.

He had loved her.

Every dream she'd ever had was locked in this man, and that, too, had been taken from her.

Agony exploded in her chest. Her heart felt as though it were shattering all over again at the tortured despair in his voice. At the knowledge that he had cared so much, and she hadn't even known.

"It wasn't like that, Jazz . . ." She felt as though she were dying inside. As though her soul were being ripped from her chest all over again.

"Then what was it like?" Voice rising, he pulled her around to face him again, his hold on her shoulders almost desperate as he glared down at her. "Tell me, Kenni. Tell me what it was like."

He hadn't realized how furious he was, how enraged it made him to know the hell she'd suffered without him to protect her.

"You turned your back on me and on your brothers." Lowering his head he snarled down at her, seeing the pain as it transformed her face but unable to lie to her, or himself, that it was acceptable. "I grieved, Kenni. I built your home believing you would never see it, that you'd never know just how fucking serious I was about you. And all that time you didn't even fucking care enough to let me know you were alive."

"I didn't know because you didn't tell me, Jazz," she whispered, her voice hoarse, filled with pain. "You treated me like a child barely out of diapers that summer. How was I supposed to know?"

"The same way I knew you belonged to me. Then." Releasing her, he stepped back. Pushing his fingers through his hair, he had to forcibly rein in the need to demand she acknowledge emotions even he couldn't make sense of. "That was then." His jaw clenched furiously. "A long fucking time ago, Kenni. It was a damned fantasy, because the young woman I was falling in love with that summer didn't exist anywhere but in my imagination evidently."

When she didn't say anything he turned back to her, his chest tightening at her pale features and the pain reflected in her face.

She didn't cry. Tears didn't fill her eyes. She just stared up at him with such misery, such agonized, dawning knowledge in those hazel eyes, that for a second guilt flayed his conscience. Then his anger returned.

Hazel eyes. God, he hated that color. That wasn't her eye color any more than Annie Mayes was her name. And he hated it. He hated the color and he hated the lie it represented.

"What do you want?" she whispered then. "What do you want me to say, Jazz? I can't take it back, and I don't know that I would even if it were possible. I couldn't risk you . . ."

She couldn't risk him? By God, he was going to show her risk.

"Take those contacts out today." First things first. "Before you do anything else get those damned things out of your eyes. They offend me."

Confusion flashed across her expression. "They offend you?"

"They offend me, Kenni," he growled. "I don't want to see Annie Mayes when I stare back at you or while I'm fucking you. Get rid of them or you'll wish you had."

It was all he could do to keep his hands off her, to keep from taking her right there where they stood. God he wanted her—needed her. He was on fire for the touch of her.

"You know I can't . . ."

"Annie Mayes doesn't exist here," he snapped before she could finish. "No more lying, Kenni. I won't let you keep pretending you didn't make the choice to hide from everyone who loved you. Everyone who would have helped you long before now. Keep lying to your brothers if you have to, but you will not lie to me any longer."

Kenni had only a heartbeat's warning before his lips came over hers with a hunger and dominant determination she wouldn't have expected. Powerful, experienced, they moved against hers, parting them and tasting her with his tongue. Like a fire pouring through her senses, he burned away any thought of protest before it had a chance to be born.

Pleasure raced past the agony torturing her, gathering force and swirling through her senses until nothing else mattered. Until only his touch filled her reality, only his hunger sustained her.

Gripping his shoulders, Kenni lifted closer to him.

Had it only been the night before that he had first taken her? How had she survived without his touch since? How had she survived without him, period?

Her nails bit into his hard flesh, tested its strength as his callused palm gripped her hip, his fingers flexing against her touch-starved flesh. How had she lived without this? Without the hunger that poured over her whenever he touched her?

"Damn, you're like a drug I can't get enough of." His voice rasped with anger and lust as his lips moved to her neck, his fingers caressing from her hip to the side of her breast, trailing waves of fiery pleasure in their path. "I don't want to get enough of."

His lips settled at her shoulder, his breathing nearly as hard as hers. She felt his withdrawal, though. Before he ever lifted his head and stared down at her with aching regret.

Brushing his thumb beneath her eye, he trailed it to her lips then slowly eased away from her.

"I have some calls to make," he breathed out heavily, tension pouring from him in invisible waves. "The next time I see you, Kenni, it better be you I see. Neither of us wants to deal with the fallout if it's not."

Did he really think the fallout scared her? Seriously, what was the worst he could do? What was the worst he would do? Tell her brothers on her?

He wouldn't, not because of the contacts.

So why was she standing in the bathroom after her shower that evening and staring into the dark-emerald color of her own eyes.

She hadn't paid attention to her eye color in years.

She always wore colored contacts; the natural color was far too incriminating. Maddox green it was called, because the color ran so strong in the Maddox male line that the children were invariably born with it.

Her brothers' children would no doubt be born with that gemlike eye color, whereas hers, if she lived long enough to have any, likely wouldn't.

The thought of a child instantly brought to mind the image of an infant, innocent wonder filling brilliant-blue eyes. A thick cap of pitch-black hair, strong features, and the promise of a charming rascal to come. Or feminine features, with a hint of mischief gleaming in the sapphire depths.

Jazz's child would be marked with the gift of mesmerizing charm and amused wonder, no matter the mother who gave it birth. But should she give him a child, Maddox blood mixed with Lancing Irish traits?

Her heart melted at the very thought of the strong, stubborn, laughing children they could have had. If she and her mother had returned that summer.

He would have been waiting for her. To court her, he'd said. The quaint, old-fashioned term would have been amusing in other circumstances. But it hadn't been amusing when Jazz had told her he'd wanted to court her.

He hadn't said he wanted to fuck her or tie her to him, or any of the other phrases that would have denoted simple lust as she would have expected.

He'd wanted to court her. Take her for a drive. Call on her.

The ache that wounded her heart at the thought of what she'd lost went far deeper than she'd imagined it could. Past her soul, past the very depths of her woman's spirit and beyond. She felt forever injured at the knowledge of what her life could have been.

Because he'd loved her.

He hadn't seen it in those terms.

He said he hadn't wanted to chance some dumb ass stealing her from him if he waited.

He would have courted her until she was eighteen, then they would have married. And she would have been a virgin on her wedding night.

The look on his face when he told her about the visit to her father had assured her of that. Pop would have made that clear. He'd have insisted on it. Jazz had been twenty-three—too old, Pop would have thought, for his innocent daughter. But something Jazz had said or done that day had convinced him to give his permission for the courtship. To take the chance that a young man as wild as Jazz would have kept his word.

Only one thing could have tipped the scales in Jazz's favor. Pop would have had to be convinced Jazz loved her. Otherwise, he would have barred Jazz from her until she was twenty-one at the youngest, and her brothers would have made the rule stick.

A shudder tore through her. Even after all these years she couldn't imagine her father or brothers attempting to hurt her, either.

They ruled the Kin. They gave the orders and they were highly possessive of that ability. They would never countenance even the suggestion that another do so.

Pop had loved her. He had to have.

He had slipped her candy when she was little and Grandmother Maddox had forbidden it. Momma had laughed at the rule, but she didn't slip Kenni the good stuff. That had been Pop. Chocolate bars, chocolate milk, and decadent candies whenever he went into Nashville.

He'd been firm, but he'd loved her. That had to have been love in his eyes when he watched her momma, too. And when Kenni would run to him and throw her arms around him for a hug, he'd always wrapped his around her and hugged her like he was terrified he would break her.

And her brothers?

Jazz . . .

She'd lost them all.

The sob that tore from her shocked her. The ragged, lost sound was one she hadn't heard in so long she barely recognized it.

A cry.

She hadn't cried in seven years, and God help her if the tears she'd held inside broke free now they would never stop.

"Poppy, hold me now!" Pushing past her father's office door by the simple means of rushing around the two men posted to keep others out, she'd invaded the meeting he was in and rushed to his desk. "Please, Poppy, I hurt me. I hurt me."

Stopping, she pointed to the skinned knee, lips trembling, tears spilling from her eyes as she stared up at her surprised poppy.

"I hurt me, Poppy," she told him again, breath hitching. "And Cord won't let me play on the swing no more, 'cause I hurt me."

He'd swept her into his arms, but not to rush her from

the meeting. No, he'd sent the men to wait for him in another room while he cleaned her knee, put the pretty princess Band-Aids on it, then smacked a kiss to it to make it get better faster. And when Cord had entered the office Poppy had told him firmly to take his Kenni outside and let her swing. *"Sometimes a princess has to skin her knee, son,"* he'd told her concerned brother. *"It's the only way she'll learn how not to break it later."*

She couldn't keep doing this to herself.

She couldn't let herself remember how her life had been before her mother's death. She had to remember what it had been like after. Cousins hunting her, mercilessly tracking her down only to shoot at her—and more than once the bullets had actually struck her.

They were men she'd been raised knowing. Friends of her brothers, close confidants to them. Men she would have trusted with her life before the night three of them had killed her mother and tried to kill her.

They weren't playing.

They weren't pretending.

They would have killed her. And she still didn't know why.

She didn't know why . . .

What had she done? What had her mother done?

What crime could they have committed to cause an order to go out to hurt them?

Another of those dry, horrible-sounding cries tore from her chest again as she gripped the towel wrapped around her and sank to the floor. Wrapping her arms around her knees Kenni buried her head against them as she fought back the tears, fought back the agonizing howls of loss that wanted to escape. The screams of injustice, of ten years running away only to find herself back where she began and being forced to see everything she'd lost.

Everything she'd ever loved.

She'd lost everything.

Even the man she hadn't known loved her.

CHAPTER 11

How long she sat in the bathroom floor, drawn into herself, Kenni wasn't certain. The waves of pain sweeping through her seemed never ending, ripping through her soul with a power she'd never before experienced.

There was no relief from the emotions breaking free inside her. Her eyes burned, her throat ached, and a band of agony tightened further around her chest.

It hurt to just breathe.

"Kenni . . . ?"

The sound of Jazz's voice, soft, so very gentle, had her freezing. Tightening her fingers in her hair, she tried to tell herself it was okay. It really was. She wasn't crying. He wouldn't walk away from her and leave her to hurt alone.

"Look at me, darlin'," he ordered, his large hands framing the sides of her head to lift it, to reveal her face as he stared down at her, his expression gentling. "What's wrong, Kenni?"

How could she tell him? How could she describe the agony racking her? The knowledge she'd lost his heart before she even knew she had it? The realization that even after all these years, she still had no idea how to save herself?

And the pain was destroying her.

She knew men didn't handle tears well, and God help her, she couldn't bear it if he walked away from her because of them.

"I'm not crying," she whispered, hoping the lack of moisture would convince him.

She refused to let herself cry.

His expression immediately turned brooding and dark. He frowned down at her, those sapphire eyes darkening as heavy, inky lashes surrounded the most outrageous blue she'd ever seen for eyes.

"Maybe you should cry, Kenni." The heavy sigh came as his arms went around her back and beneath her knees. A heartbeat later he straightened, holding her close to his chest and moving into the bedroom.

"Big girls don't cry," she whispered, repeating Gunny's words as Jazz sat down in the large chair a few feet from the bed. "When it can't be fixed, tears won't help. If it can be fixed, tears aren't needed. Right?"

He stilled against her so completely for a second that he didn't even breathe.

"God, Kenni." Pressing her head to his chest a second later, his arms tightened around her, holding her to him as a feeling of complete security washed over her.

She could feel his heart beneath her ear, the bare flesh of his chest warming the side of her face.

"All I wanted to do was come home." She remembered that, remembered all the silent tears she'd cried those first two years. "But every time we stopped long enough to try to figure out how I could do that, they found us." Her fingers tightened on his lower arm. "And I always knew who they were." Faces flashed across her memory. "Men I was raised with, Jazz. Men who were trying to kill me."

"Your uncle killed them all?" he asked, his fingers stroking over the side of her head. "He wasn't able to question them?"

Gunny didn't question, he interrogated with merciless determination.

"Sure he did." She shuddered, remembering the one time she'd watched one of those interrogations. "They said they were following Maddox orders."

She'd never been able to completely believe it. The fear that drove her, the will to survive and make someone pay for her mother's death had kept her from contacting her family. It had kept her from contacting anyone tied to the Maddox clan.

Especially Jazz. If she'd been wrong, if her brothers were involved and he'd died, the added grief would have done what the Kin had been trying to do. It would have killed her.

"I'm giving it the benefit of the doubt, Kenni," he whispered. "Because if anything happened to you, I wouldn't be able to live with myself. But for the record, there's no way in fucking way in hell your brothers are involved in this."

This time, he didn't mention her father. The exclusion would have been deliberate. For some reason, between his last defense of them and now, he wasn't so certain of her father.

Poppy . . . A dry sob hitched her breath at the thought.

The weary resignation in his voice was another burden on her shoulders. He believed in her brothers, trusted them, and that was something Jazz didn't do easily.

"Tell me, Kenni," he asked as the throttled sound of the sob escaped. "How long has it been since you cried?"

What did it matter? How long since she'd lived, or how long since she'd had a single second of peace? Those questions made far more sense.

"Why?" Why would he care? Hell, what did it matter?

"Curiosity," he answered smoothly. "Not many women I know that don't cry."

How long had it been?

Frowning, she watched, kneading the hard biceps in front of her face with subtle strokes of her fingertips while the muscle flexed beneath her touch.

"My eighteenth birthday," she finally answered. "Tom and Jason Keye caught me just outside Dallas, heading to meet with Gunny. They were going to rape me before carrying out their orders. They laughed and called me a crybaby. I realized Gunny had been right, tears didn't help."

Seconds later they were dead before Kenni realized the sounds she'd heard were Gunny's rifle.

"Tom and Jason," he murmured softly, but the tension in his voice was an indication of the fury he was burying for the moment. "We heard they'd moved to California."

"Yeah," she agreed, though the acknowledgment was a bit absent.

It had taken a minute for her to realize she was naked, and all that separated her from the heavy erection beneath her rear was the towel she'd had wrapped around her earlier. Because Jazz was naked as well.

He'd showered. Damp hair and shower-fresh flesh caressed her senses as his fingers trailed from the side of her head to her neck. Tilting her head up, Kenni stared into the somber, darkening depths of his sapphire eyes.

How would she be able to bear it when her time with him was over? When he was no longer touching her, when the chance to be touched by him was over?

She hadn't known how much she needed him until he'd pushed his way into her life and gave a damn that it appeared she might be in trouble because the identity she was using was false.

"I told myself for years I couldn't have felt for you what I knew I felt that summer," she whispered painfully. "That sixteen was too young to know what love was, and it wasn't as if you'd even brushed my lips with yours let alone actually kissed me. But every time I considered a lover, or the possibility of leaving America entirely to escape, you stood in my way, Jazz. The thought of never seeing you again was so abhorrent I couldn't consider it."

Those long, inky-black lashes lowered over the brilliant blue of his eyes as his expression softened into lines of pure male sexual hunger.

Beneath her hand his chest rose and fell harder, his breathing speeding up, just as his heartbeat did. Cupping her cheek with his hand, he slid his thumb sensually over her lower lip.

"Hell, I built your fucking house, Kenni," he growled, not so much angry as perhaps exasperated. "Not to mention that friggin' gazebo with a bed in it like you wanted. And not a single damned woman has shared either with me. I think that pretty much proves I was damned serious."

As he'd said earlier, he was serious *then*. That didn't mean he was nearly as serious now. But Kenni had realized she didn't really care which club she had to join, she wanted more of Jazz. Desperately. Now.

She closed her eyes, barely holding back a moan when the fingers buried in her hair tugged her head to the side. His lips settled just beneath her ear, against the line of her jaw. The flesh there sizzled with pleasure as sensitive nerve endings caught the sensation and sent it racing across her body.

Involuntary shivers ran up her spine while a breathless moan escaped her lips. God, she ached for him, needed him. It wasn't just the pleasure, it was the sense of finally being where she was supposed to be, if only for a little while.

She should be resisting this need, pulling back, reminding herself of the danger, something other than closing her eyes and reveling in the sensations. Because God knew, she would pay for this later. For every second of pleasure he gave her, Kenni had no doubt the pain would be worse in the not-too-distant future.

His teeth scraped against her neck, his tongue following as it flickered over her already sensitized flesh. It was like wildfire exploded through her senses, drenching her in the most incredible warmth.

"Like that, do you?" he muttered, his voice thicker, grating with hunger. "I love that little sound you make as your breath catches, but let's see if I can do something to warrant a moan. Just a little one, if you can. If I deserve it."

As he spoke, his head moved lower to the bend of her neck. There his teeth gripped the flesh for just a second, raked over it, then burned a path to the rise of her breasts as the arm behind her levered her back. As he licked over the hard tip of her nipple with slow, hungry strokes, each rasping caress sent forked trails of blistering sensation straight to her womb.

Moaning, arching into his hold, she tried to press closer, to feel more.

She needed to feel more.

Then his lips were on hers. Slanting over them, his tongue pressing between them as he began to sip from her kiss, to feed her the heady pleasure of his hunger as spiraling need stripped her to nothing but sensation.

And Jazz made damned certain there was plenty of sensation.

His lips moved over hers, rubbing against them, slipping between them, branding her with the hunger she could feel in each hungry kiss.

His fingers found the hard point of her nipple, gripped it, rolling it between his fingers and exerting exquisite pressure against the nerve-ridden flesh.

Sensation erupted in the hard tip, flashed through her body, clashing in her lower stomach.

Kenni was only barely aware of her hips moving. Each jagged burst of sensation erupting through her, obliterating more of the common sense she knew she was supposed to have. It was there, somewhere, just waiting for Jazz to let it come out and let her see the folly of her actions. It had to be.

Until then, she wanted to sink into the white-hot pleasure. She wanted to live within the heat wrapped around her, she wanted to burn in his touch.

She wanted to touch. If he would just release her wrists.

A cry, muted and hoarse, tore from her throat to fill their kiss as his fingers gripped her nipple again, tugged, pressed, and had flames searing a path to her womb.

Oh God, she needed. She needed Jazz . . .

His need for her, the overriding hunger and overwhelming drive to possess every part of her, was only growing stronger. Not by the day, by the minute. By every shattered look of longing, every pain-ridden gleam of love he glimpsed in her eyes when she looked at him, and every soft, whispered sigh of desire whenever he touched her.

Everything about her—her scent, the sound of her voice, the touch of her hand, shy smiles and hungry looks—only made him want to tie her tighter to him.

She was destroying him and she didn't even know it.

Trailing his lips from hers to caress the line of her jaw again, Jazz had to force himself not to turn her to him, to slide beneath her slender thighs and have her ride him as he stared into those beautiful dark-emerald eyes.

"Jazz, wait . . . please." Breathless, rough with desire, her voice had a groan tearing from his chest.

Wait?

She had to be joking.

Lifting his head enough to stare into her flushed, sensual features, he knew the wait was going be very short indeed.

"I want to touch you now," she whispered, staring up at him with such somber need that she broke his heart. "I want to give you pleasure, too."

There wasn't a chance he could bear it. She would have him insane in minutes. But her hunger for it filled her face, her eyes. She needed, for whatever reason, to steal the last vestige of sanity he possessed.

"Good God," he whispered as she slid from his lap. "And here I thought I'd have some control this time."

"Control is highly overrated." Rolling to her side she stared down at him, her expression heavy with feminine need.

"I'm not entirely certain this is one of those situations," he told her, though he was definitely curious over what she had planned.

No doubt she had every intention of driving him crazy.

How much could a little innocent like her know, though? Surely he had the self-control to endure whatever she dished out.

Or so he thought.

What he forgot to take into account was his reaction to her and the effect she had on him whenever she was near, let alone touching him.

She kissed him like a woman desperate to build memories, to fill as much of her soul as possible with sensation and warmth.

At first slow, exploring his lips with hers, tasting them with her inquisitive little tongue. Jazz remained at her mercy, never taking his eyes from her as his heart ached for her.

* * *

She was convinced she would be running soon.

Like hell!

Jazz was more than willing to be the recipient of the pleasure; he could be a bit selfish like that, he decided. But his would-be-runaway was done running. She just didn't know it yet.

Encouraging her hunger with each kiss, with each lick of her soft teasing tongue, he learned just how completely arousing a woman's innocence could be.

Or maybe it was just Kenni's innocence that was so damned arousing.

With each kiss, with each hungry stroke, the sensuality that was so much a part of her built until her own needs began consuming her.

Hell yes.

This was what he wanted.

Her hungry lips and quick hot tongue taking what she wanted.

A groan broke from his chest as heated kisses moved down the side of his neck. And damn, it felt good. Turning his head, he let her have her way.

Let her play.

Let her think he was actually going to let her run whenever she decided it was time to go.

Hell, she'd be lucky if he let her out of his bed.

Kittenish little nails pricked at his chest as she tested his muscles. She must have liked what she found in the feel of his flesh because she kneaded it again.

"Damn, darlin', how I love your kisses," he groaned, his jaw tightening at the catch of her breath when he spoke.

His Kenni liked hearing his pleasure.

Her teeth raked at his collarbone, that rasp of sensual hunger causing his already engorged dick to swell further and his balls to clench with a surfeit of sensation.

"Ah, baby, that hot little mouth will make me crazy."

She tightened against him, a little whimper vibrating over his flesh as her lips and sweet tongue moved lower.

"Kenni, darlin'." He stretched against the rasp of her nails running down his chest, nearly to his navel. So fucking close to the heavy weight of his cock as it lay against his lower stomach.

Her kisses continued over his chest. The flick of her tongue over the hard disk of his nipple had his teeth clenching. When she delivered a lingering kiss to it he had to curl his fingers into the arms of the chair to keep from grabbing her and dragging her over his thighs where she could ride them both into exhaustion.

"Kenni, you're going to make me crazy," he groaned. "That hot mouth of yours destroys me."

And she had no mercy.

Lower she went until his fingers tangled in her hair, his muscles tightening to the breaking point.

Sweet, hot kisses—the head of his cock pulsed, throbbing with the need for attention.

"Come here, baby." He watched her as he glimpsed the uncertainty that flashed across her face.

And uncertainty was something she should never feel while in a bed with him.

As he tightened his fingers in her hair to pull her up his body, the hot swipe of her tongue over the head of his cock had him stilling in shock and exquisite pleasure.

"Kenni, you don't have to . . . Sweet mercy . . ."

Fuck!

It was good.

Her mouth encased the sensitive crest, damp heat milking it, pretty lips surrounding the thick flesh as she stared back at him in dazed fascination. And as she drew on the throbbing crest, that quicksilver tongue of hers tormented it.

Damp heat flicked against the sensitive head, rubbed at it, tormenting flesh already so sensitive it was all he could do to hold back, to keep from filling her sweet mouth with his release.

"Fuck, Kenni." His fingers tightened in her hair. "Baby, it's so good." She drew back, her tongue still lashing at the eager flesh before sucking him in again.

Slow, experimental. She was letting herself get used to the feel of his hard flesh as she demanded the intimacy with greedy licks and slow, suckling hunger.

"Ah hell. Damn." Weak with the surfeit of pleasure, Jazz let his head rest against the back of the chair, only barely aware of the fact that it was grinding into the cushion behind him.

She took him deeper, filling her mouth and rubbing her tongue against the ultrasensitive spot beneath the throbbing head. Each rubbing stroke against the nerve-ridden area sent pulsing fingers of pure ecstasy to race over his cock and arrow-straight to his already tormented testicles. Each slow rippling caress had his balls tightening, clenching with the need to spill his release to her hungry mouth.

"That's it, baby," he groaned. "Just like that. Sweet Kenni, your mouth is killing me."

Each suckling stroke of damp heat was pushing him past the point of no return.

"That's it, darling." Breathing was almost impossible. "Ah hell. Yeah. Suck it harder, baby. That's it." Her mouth tightened, drawing him deeper. "How fucking good your mouth is," he groaned. "So hot and sweet."

Holding the base of his eager flesh, she widened her eyes as he began moving. Drawing his hard flesh nearly free of her lips before pushing in again, slow and easy. He watched. Watched her take him. Watched her sweet lips stretch around the width of him as he felt her sucking him inside.

"I've dreamed of fucking your mouth," he bit out as his balls throbbed warningly. "Of sinking my cock past those pretty lips as you suck, hungry for the taste of me."

Moving his hands from her hair to the chair arms again, he clenched the material desperately. His muscles tightened, sweat breaking out on his skin as heat began to consume him.

"Fuck, Kenni, I'm going to come. Baby, sweet Kenni." He thrust inside her mouth again. Once. Twice.

His fingers returned to her hair, clenched, held her still and felt her mouth tighten further on him. He thrust past her lips again. Once. Twice.

God.

Pulling from her was agony.

Forcing his cock from the heat of her mouth, from her licking tongue nearly undid him.

And his control was shot.

"Ride me, Kenni." Lifting her along his body, Jazz guided her leg over his hips as he held his cock ready to sink inside the sweet heat awaiting him. "Let me feel you take me, baby."

Teeth clenched, Jazz watched as the engorged head of his cock parted the smooth, silken folds of her pussy.

Slick, wet heat began stretching around the engorged crest. Parting, taking him, her silken honey flowing around the penetration.

"Kenni, that's it, baby," he rasped, both hands gripping her hips as he pushed deeper, harder inside her.

Watching her face, his hands caressed from her hips to her swollen breasts. There he found the plump nipples atop her swollen mounds, ready for his fingers to rasp and excite.

The silky heat of her pussy enveloped him, wrapped around flesh throbbing with the exquisite sensation.

Ah fuck. It was so good his toes wanted to curl with the pleasure.

"Fuck me, baby," he groaned, his voice graveled as her sheath rippled around his cock, sucked at it.

Hips bunching, straining, the need to push inside her, to stroke in to the hilt, was nearly overpowering.

Kenni's hands braced on his chest, her nails pricked the flesh, and her hips moved with increasing speed. Taking his cock deep with each downward thrust, her head fell back in pleasure, perspiration gleaming on her creamy flesh, giving it a satiny sheen.

Soft, desperate mewls of pleasure slipped past her lips and just when Jazz was certain he couldn't bear the pressure another second, complete, searing pleasure engulfed his cock.

Tight. So fucking tight.

Like a silken vise tightening and rippling around his erection, her internal muscles milked the entire length of his shaft.

Jazz's hands tightened on her hips, the fragile hold he had on his control completely disintegrating.

"Jazz! Yes. Oh God, yes!"

All sense of reality disappeared as he felt her unravel, the pulsing ripples of her inner flesh milking his cock until he exploded with complete rapture.

Quick, heavy thrusts.

Rapture tightened in his testicles, taut bands of pleasure so extreme Jazz knew that holding back his release wasn't happening.

He was dying.

His cock was so engorged, pounding with a furious need to come, that perspiration poured from him with the battle to hold back.

To feel her—

Stroking inside her, thrusting hard, heavy—her pussy gripped, milked his shaft. Tightened further with each contraction of her orgasm.

Tighter than ever—so fucking hot—

His release took him by surprise.

As her pussy rippled around him, gripping him like a vise, it was like a direct switch to his balls.

The first hard pulse of release tore a shattered groan from his lips. Arching, pushing deeper inside her with each furious ejaculation spurred ecstatic waves of sensation to tear through him. In some distant part of his soul, Jazz knew his fate was sealed. This woman was his. And there was no debt too great if it meant ensuring her safety and their future together.

CHAPTER 12

What had she allowed to happen?

How had she come to a place where the very thought of being without Jazz was almost more than she could bear?

All because of some damned fluke that sent Cord checking to be certain of the background she was using. Since when did he begin running teachers' backgrounds? Things like that he left to men like Slade and several others in the county with federal ties.

Hell, how could she have stopped her brother from checking deeper into Annie Mayes's background? She couldn't have. No matter what she'd done or the contacts she might have formed, there was no stopping Cord's instincts. They were phenomenal.

And he was nosy.

He just couldn't keep his nose out of her business, could he? He'd always been such a damned busybody, making her crazy by snitching on her with Momma and Poppy when she least expected it. He'd even told Poppy how she was watching Jazz that summer, after telling her she had to stay away from him.

Stay away from Jazz?

The very thought had been inconceivable. It was all she could do not to beg Jazz to kiss her, to show her why she was so mesmerized by him. But she hadn't told Cord that. She'd known better, because he would have immediately had Momma and Poppy send her to a convent or something.

Momma wouldn't have allowed it, though. Her mother would have been concerned, perhaps, but she would have also been terribly amused by her sons. Their protectiveness was something she'd warned Kenni she may as well get used to, because they would always feel it was their privilege to watch after her.

But they hadn't watched after her.

That summer was the first in years that her brothers didn't accompany her and her mother to New York. There had been some job they'd had to complete. One that couldn't wait for any reason as far as Poppy had been concerned.

She pushed the memories back. She didn't want to remember the flames and the blood.

Leaning against the open balcony door the next morning as a cool breeze whispered past her, she remembered telling her mother how she felt about Jazz on the drive to New York that summer.

That was part of the shopping tradition. Every summer they went to New York for three or four days. On the drive there her mother would always ask her about whatever boys she was interested in. That summer, though, Kenni hadn't dated; nor had she spent much time on the phone with any of the young men who called her. For that reason her mother had asked her who'd managed to steal her heart.

Once a year, Kenni could tell her mother anything. The rule was, what happened in New York, what was said in New York, stayed in New York. Momma never told Poppy her secrets, and her brothers never learned of them. What Kenni confided stayed just between her and her mother.

God, she missed her momma.

Kenni had never had to worry about her place in her mother's life; she had known Sierra Maddox loved nothing in the world as much as she loved her husband and children. But her relationship with her daughter had been special. They were girls together. They shopped and laughed and Kenni knew she could tell her anything.

She'd had no one to talk to since her mother's death. There had been no one to dry her tears when she'd cried, no one to soothe her when the pain of being hunted had torn her soul to pieces.

Gunny had kept her alive, though a few times it had been close.

He hadn't been good with tears. If he saw even a hint of them he'd disappear until the danger of them was gone. He could handle her silence, he could handle her staring off into space, steeped in her agony, as long as she didn't cry.

So she'd learned not to cry. Having him disappear for hours on end had terrified her. She'd always been scared he wouldn't come back for her.

Then he hadn't come back for her.

She hadn't even cried then, she thought, frowning absently as she rubbed at the chill racing over her arms. He was supposed to be meeting with someone who had information on the Kin. No big deal. He'd sent her to pick up the car he'd arranged to buy from some dirty, shifty-eyed old guy on a back street.

When he hadn't arrived at their prearranged meeting place, she'd gone looking for him.

Swallowing tightly she pushed the memory of what she'd found away. She couldn't deal with it right now, either. Right now she had to gather her courage and her strength to slip away from Jazz.

She had no car, no decent shoes, and getting away from him was going to be next to impossible, but she had to go. She had to get out of Loudoun, preferably alive, and figure out what she was going to do.

And where she was going to hide.

Unfortunately, she couldn't think of anyplace else to hide. Without her contacts hiding would be much harder as well. She'd taken them out as Jazz had asked, then they had completely disappeared from the bedside table where she'd put the small case.

The rest of her contacts were at the rental house, hidden with her laptop. Contacts, alternative ID, and a little cash. She might need them. If Jazz caught her running they wouldn't do her a damned bit of good, though.

Drawing in a deep breath, she left the comforting silence of the bedroom and headed downstairs to the kitchen instead. Entering the brightly lit room, she wished she'd stayed in the bedroom.

Stepping past the doorway she was suddenly pinned by half a dozen gazes, and all staring at her eyes.

Kate and Lara, along with Jessie, Slade, Zack, and Jazz, watched her from where they sat around the large kitchen table. Steaming cups of coffee sat in front of them, plates of doughnuts and croissants beside their coffee cups, as tension thickened in the room.

"Geez, and I thought Jazz's eyes were bright," Lara muttered. "You're right, Jessie, there's no mistaking who she is."

Just fucking great.

Slicing Jazz a condemning look, she wondered if he even had the good grace to realize the risk he was making her take.

"Coffee?" Jazz asked, his expression completely innocent, as though he hadn't forced her to remove the color-dimming contacts. Rising from his chair he moved to the coffeepot, grabbed a cup from beside it, and filled it quickly.

That didn't keep the others from staring at her.

"Morning, Jessie, Slade, Zack," she greeted, ignoring the comment on her eyes. "Slade, I thought you were keeping Jessie away for a while?"

It would have been best if he'd done just that.

"Oh yeah, like I was going to miss this," Jessie snorted. "Finding out my best friend is none other than the missing Maddox Princess was more than I could pass up. Come on, Your Highness," she teased then, her brown eyes sparking with laughter. "You know me better than that."

Kenni almost grinned. Jessie could do that, take

something that should piss Kenni right off and make her laugh instead.

Rather than giving in to that urge, she turned to Jazz as he moved to her with a cup of coffee.

"Snitch," she accused derisively. "Really, Jazz? You couldn't even hold out and let them see me first? They may not have even guessed."

The look of disgust didn't even faze him. He just winked, those wicked blue eyes laughing at her.

"Sweetheart, trust me, they would have guessed. Besides, you were sleeping and wouldn't talk to me," he pointed out. "I had to tell someone and Kate and Lara were tired of talking about you."

She slid a look to the other two women. They really weren't pulling off the whole innocent-expression thing. Then she turned to Slade.

"I need to leave," she told Slade, the only person she believed would have Jazz's safety uppermost in mind. "Would you please take me back to the house?"

Slade just watched her for a long silent moment before his gaze turned to Jazz. A second later his lips quirked in amusement.

"I would, Kenni, but he'd kill me before I got you out of the house. I'd hate to make my children an orphan today."

"Versus tomorrow, or the day after that?" she asked him, amazed that she sounded so calm, so cool. "Really, Slade, I'm sure you've seen the report these two busybodies dug up." She flicked her fingers toward Kate and Lara. "No one survives attempting to help me. Is that what you want for Jazz? For yourself?"

Kate and Lara glanced at each other in mocking surprise.

"Busybodies?" Kate murmured to her sister. "That's one of the nicest insults we've ever received."

Kenni had hoped the two women weren't as insane as the rest of the group seemed to be. She'd hoped in vain.

"She's just as overdramatic now as she was as a teenager," Zack observed as he sat back in his chair and lifted his cup for a sip of the steaming liquid. "Hell, Kenni, you should know better than that. Whoever's betraying your father can't possibly pull together enough Kin to come against us. Why do you think your father and Cord do little things like come to one of us when someone we know has come to their notice? We could divide the Kin if we wanted to, and they know it."

Arrogance.

Every damned one of them was so arrogant and self-assured it was sickening.

The problem was, she had no idea if they were right or wrong. Ten years was a long time when it came to loyalties and how they might switch. Just because these three hadn't been in the military didn't mean they weren't strong enough to garner the respect and loyalty of those who were or had been. Charismatic and intelligent, they were natural leaders with little desire to actually lead unless they had no other choice.

"What if it's not a case of betraying him?" she asked, the pain of that thought as deep and jagged as it had been when Gunny had first suggested it. "He remarried well before that first year was out."

The rumors that Vincent Maddox and his current

wife, once his sister-in-law, had been having an affair weren't new to Kenni. Even Gunny had begun to suspect her father was behind the death of her mother and the attempts to kill Kenni.

"Vinny hasn't been exactly sane since the funerals," Slade remarked somberly, his gaze meeting hers. "And from what I understand he calls her by your mother's name more often than he calls her by her own. Besides, there's no way he could pull something like that off without Cord's knowledge. And there's not a chance in hell your brother would have gone along with it."

If only she had the luxury of believing in her brother with such strength. Even if he wasn't involved, if she went to him, she could be risking his safety—and she refused to do that.

"Then who? Who?" The cry tore from her, more jagged and loud than she intended. "Tell me how anyone could kill Vincent Maddox's wife and make numerous attempts against his daughter without either Vincent or his sons knowing? How?" Strangling back her fury was impossible.

It was that sense of betrayal, though, the overwhelming, agonizing knowledge that no one else wielded that much power within the Maddox clan or the Kin. Vincent, Cord, Deacon, or Sawyer had to know. The Kin was too tight-knit for anything else.

"Jessie." She turned to her friend, desperate for a voice of reason. "Talk some sense into them."

"I did." Jessie blinked back at her as though in surprise. "I convinced them to let me come with them this morning so I could talk some sense into you. Kenni, you can't do this alone anymore. It's going to take a team.

That's something you've never faced your enemies with. It's not just you and Gunny anymore, or a lone friend trying to help from another location. It's a concentrated effort by men who wield a tremendous amount of power. But it will only work if you reveal yourself."

So much for the voice of reason.

Kenni dropped her head as she lifted a hand to rub at her temple. She was getting a headache. She hadn't had a headache in years. Come to think of it, she might remember getting several headaches that last summer. Each one coming after dealing with Jazz and his youthful arrogance.

That arrogance was slightly more developed now.

"That's why you're all here? To convince me to reveal myself?" She had to laugh, but there was little amusement, only amazement and outrage "You're kidding, right?"

"Kenni, by revealing yourself you force your enemies' hand. You throw them off balance by upping the ante. For whatever reason, learning you're here made them panic enough to try to take you out in public. That was a mistake. Let's ride their panic and give them the one thing they obviously don't want."

"I can't deal with this," she snapped, furious that they would gang up on her and try to convince her to do the one thing she feared could have the Kin converging on her in greater numbers. None of them would survive that. "Take me back to the house, Jazz. Please."

They had no idea what they were dealing with, or the merciless brutality the Kin could display.

The look he gave her assured her that wasn't happening.

"Drink your coffee, sweetheart, you're going to need it," he advised her firmly. "And before you completely lose your mind, remember the price you'll pay if you slip out on me."

He would call her brothers.

Rolling her eyes in complete disgust, Kenni moved across the room to the back door, opened it, and stepped out to the deck. She definitely needed to finish her coffee before dealing with him.

She may need a whole pot of coffee first.

Jazz watched her leave, the feminine disgust and fury that filled her expression at odds with the uncertainty there.

She had no intentions of being part of the discussion regarding her safety or the Kin.

"She's going to run, Jazz," Kate warned him, drawing his attention from Kenni back to the table.

"She will." Jessie nodded, her brown eyes dark and filled with fear for her friend. "I can see it in her, too. She's completely distancing herself, pulling back from any emotional connections to allow herself to make the move."

Yeah, he'd seen that in her as well. Strangely enough, it made him hard.

His dick was like steel in his jeans, and the thought of melting that distance was a challenge he knew he wouldn't refuse for long. He might last five minutes after the others left.

"Are you sure about her brothers, Jazz?" Lara asked then. "There's no way they're involved in this?"

"They've grieved for ten years," Slade replied as he

sat back in his chair and regarded the rest of them. "Especially Cord. Kenni was his shadow while she was growing up and he was damned proud of her. Every year on the anniversary of what he believes is her death, he gets skunk-drunk and doesn't talk about anything but Kenni and his mother. He feels guilty for not being there for them. It was one of only a few times he hadn't accompanied them."

"Chances are pretty slim then." Lara nodded before looking down at her papers and making another note.

"Chances are zero," Jazz sighed. "But I swore not to contact him. She's adamant that her family not be told she's still alive."

"Fear they'll be hurt? Or is she really convinced one of them is involved?" Zack questioned.

"I'm not sure." Running his hands through his hair before rubbing the back of his neck in frustration, Jazz tried to make sense of the woman Kenni had become. "We have less than two weeks left before Cord comes looking for answers, though. I have that long to convince her to trust him."

"Well, good luck on that one," Kate sighed. "She really didn't seem inclined to trust anyone the other night or now, let alone family. Thankfully, we don't need her to initiate the investigation into who ordered her mother's death."

"Kin won't trust the two of you," Jazz warned them. "You're not from Loudoun, nor are you blood-related to anyone tied to the Maddox family."

Kate smiled. One of those soft, seductive little smiles that he'd seen entrance men when she turned it on them.

"Now, sugar," she drawled as sweet as any southern

belle. "Don't you know men talk, too? I just have to find the right one, at the right time, who's had just the right amount to drink. That's not as hard as you think it is." The deliberately suggestive wink had him almost feeling sorry for whomever she chose as prey.

The door to the porch was pushed open hurriedly and Kenni stalked inside. Anger and accusation filled her brilliant-green eyes. The look only made him harder.

"You called Cord," she hissed, that anger transforming into rage as she stood glaring at him. "Why would you do that, Jazz? You promised."

"I didn't call Cord," he denied, his arms crossing over his chest as he narrowed his gaze on her. "Trust me, if I had, the whole fucking clan would be here."

A little trust wouldn't hurt, he thought mockingly. She could give him her virginity, but she refused to trust him. Now, wasn't that some shit?

"Well, he just pulled in," she snapped, fear and a haunting ache shadowing her gaze. "I swear to God, Jazz, tell him who I am and I promise you, you'll never find me when I run."

Before he could counter the threat she turned and raced through the house, returning no doubt to the bedroom.

Son of a bitch, could this get any more fucking complicated?

Turning to Kate and Lara, he nodded toward the direction Kenni had taken in an indication that they retreat as well. If the twins were going to be investigating the Kin, he didn't want Cord knowing who they were before the investigation started. No doubt he'd run their backgrounds the second he caught sight of them, but those two were damned good at covering themselves. Better to let them establish whatever cover story they came up with before Cord knew they were there.

No sooner had the twins disappeared from sight than Marcus let out a warning woof to alert Jazz that someone was crossing the yard and heading for the house. The yard and pool was his territory as far as he was concerned, and he didn't care much for trespassers.

"Easy, Marcus," he called to the Rottweiler before turning to face the windows looking out on the back porch. Hell, it wasn't even noon yet. No one should have to deal with Cord Maddox before evening at the earliest.

Seconds later Cord stepped onto the porch. Six two, lean, powerful and glaring at the world, ready to take it on. He'd been trying to take it on for ten years, too. The loss of his mother and baby sister had been too much for the other man's overdeveloped sense of responsibility and love.

He'd never stopped blaming himself, and Jazz knew he never would.

Cord didn't bother to knock. The stares leveled on him as he stepped into the house couldn't have been comfortable. Like a bug under a microscope he was pinned by all of them, assessing, suspicious, and wary.

"Maddox, what the hell do you want?" Jazz bit out, irritation threatening to spill over in the other man's direction. He hadn't tamped down the anger from their last little meeting, and adding to it might not be a good idea. For either of them.

A dark-blond brow lifted with lazy arrogance while cynical humor curled at the corner of his lips.

"Not in the best of moods this morning, are you, Jazz?" he observed as he moved to the coffeepot, found himself a cup, and poured the last of the steaming liquid into it. "Get up on the wrong side of your little schoolteacher?"

Cord knew she was here. They'd expected that. Still, the comment didn't sit well.

"Wrong direction to go in, Cord." He'd end up teaching the other man his manners with a fist at this rate.

"Interesting." There was no amusement in Cord's expression, despite the smile that quirked his lips as he opened a cabinet door and pulled out the creamer Jazz kept hidden.

"Just make yourself at home," Jazz invited, the heavy mockery in his tone fully intended as Cord stirred a heaping spoon of the creamy powder into his coffee.

"I thought I was." Turning, Cord faced the room, sipped at the coffee, and waited.

What the hell he was waiting for, Jazz didn't even want to guess.

"Miss Mayes doing okay?" Cord asked when no one volunteered to guess at what he wanted. "I heard there was an accident in town the other day?"

Jazz knew why he was there but wasn't going to make it easy for Cord. A surefire way to make a Maddox suspicious? Make something easy for them.

"She's doing fine," he growled. "She thinks it was some drunk driver."

That drew Cord's attention long enough for the others

to unobtrusively slide their papers and files beneath laptops or tablets.

"Hmm," Cord murmured before sipping at the coffee once again. "A drunk driver, you say?"

"Are you saying anything different, Cord?" Slade asked before Jazz could voice the question.

Cord leaned back against the counter, stared at the slate floor for long moments before lifting his gaze once again and meeting Jazz's.

"The driver of that car doesn't drink," he stated, his eyes narrowed as they met Jazz's, suspicion now filling the emerald orbs and making them brighter.

Jazz tensed.

"You know who it was then?" he questioned the other man. "You here to tell me who he is, or just trying to piss me off?"

"Probably both," Cord drawled lazily, his lips thinning in obvious irritation. "Which do you want first?"

"The name."

All he needed was the name.

"The driver was Joe Fallon," Cord stated. "But you're not going to get to question him. See, this is where I get to piss you off. Or you get to piss me off."

Adrenaline was building, pulsing in his blood with a demand for action.

"What makes you think I'm not going to question him?" He'd tear that fucking mountain apart if he had to.

For the briefest moment rage flickered in Cord's emerald gaze before disappearing as though it had never been there.

"Because he's dead." Lifting the cup to sip again,

Cord watched him too intently. "Deacon, Sawyer, and I went up the mountain to his cabin this morning to ask him about it. It appeared he'd been shot just as he came through the door into the kitchen of his cabin." He set his coffee cup on the counter before turning back. "Now, I just gotta ask, Jazz, you kill him?"

Jazz, Slade, and Zack had an agreement with the Maddoxes. Anything that demanded action against Kin, they'd notify a Maddox. Any action against anyone Slade, Zack, or Jazz was known to affiliate with, and the brothers came to him. Just as they had with Kenni.

"I didn't get the chance." He would have, if he'd known who to kill, if he'd had a chance to question him first—but not without first observing the pact they had. "I hadn't learned who took a swipe at her yet."

For a moment Cord's jaw bunched, the carefully banked anger finding no release, no relief.

"It wouldn't have taken you long." Cord breathed out, the sound rife with frustration as a grimace contorted his expression. "Dammit, Jazz, what the fuck is going on? What's that woman involved in that had Fallon trying to race right over her ass?"

Demanding, arrogantly presuming he deserved an answer, Cord faced them, his gaze meeting Slade's and Zack's first before turning back to Jazz.

"She's not involved in anything, Cord." There were days that dealing with more than one Maddox was more than a man could handle. "What the hell was Fallon involved in that had him racing down the street like a fucking maniac?"

Slade and Zack watched the exchange silently, but Jazz could see the look on Slade's face. The other man was ready to jump between Cord and Jazz at the slightest provocation. Slade was still trying to play the big brother, though Jazz hadn't needed a big brother in a lot of years.

Cord shifted his shoulders before placing his hands on the counter behind him and staring back at all of them fiercely. He wasn't happy and wasn't bothering to hide it.

"That the story you're sticking with then?" Cord questioned with obvious doubt. "Come on, Jazz, this is me and we both know better than that. Fallon hasn't been off that mountain in months, then one day he just decides to run some little schoolteacher over? Does that make sense to you?"

None of this had made sense since the night Cord had revealed that Annie Mayes wasn't Annie Mayes.

"That makes more sense to me than your suggestion that she somehow deserved it," Jazz bit out.

A grimace tightened Cord's face. Evidently, he was enjoying dealing with him about as much he was enjoying dealing with Cord.

"That wasn't what I said, dammit. I said she's involved in something and you damned well know she is." Maddox straightened then, the glare on his face increasing as his gaze swept the room. "And every damned one of you is going to play innocent?"

Deep-green eyes finally settled on Jessie. "You playing this little game with them?"

"It's not a game." Jessie smiled sweetly as she propped her chin on her hand and regarded him with a far-too-pleasant smile. "They're very innocent."

Cord could only shake his head to that one. "Jessie, you used to be such a good little girl," he sighed heavily. "Slade's corrupting you."

"That's beside the point," she assured him with a smile. "In this case, they really are innocent. If Annie was up to something, I would know it. And I know she's not, so mind your manners, please."

For a moment Cord's face softened and Jazz remembered hearing Kenni tell her brothers that a few times. *Mind your manners, please, or I'll tell Momma* was the full threat.

"Mind my manners." Shaking his head once, he turned back to Jazz. "You know nothing, right?"

"That about covers it," Jazz agreed.

And Cord wasn't buying it.

"I'll remember that when I prove differently. When I do, Jazz, we're going to have problems," he warned, heading toward the door he'd used to enter the kitchen. "I'll go before you end up pissing me right off. That wouldn't be good for either of us."

Wasn't that the truth, Jazz agreed silently.

"And Jessie." Cord turned to her slowly, his gaze implacable as it met hers. "Only one person ever said that to me—to mind my manners, please. She was the best of all of us, but she's been gone a long time now. I'd appreciate if I didn't have to hear it again."

With that, he stalked from the kitchen, the door closing silently behind him before he strode from the back porch and into the yard.

The grief and agony he'd glimpsed on Cord's face when Jessie spoke only strengthened his belief that Cord would never be a part of a plot to kill Kenni. Discounting her fears and telling Cord the truth wasn't going to help her trust him, though.

"Poor Cord," Jessie whispered then, her brown eyes filled with remorse. "I guess I should watch repeating those little asides Kenni's bad for, huh?"

Yeah, that might be a good idea, Jazz thought ruefully. *A damned good idea.*

CHAPTER 13

She was the best of all of us, but she's been gone a long time now . . .

Kenni tried to tell herself her brother could have faked the grief in his voice. After all, it had been ten years, not ten days since her supposed death.

Cord had been her favorite, and she'd believed she was his favorite sibling. It was Cord who nicknamed her Princess when she was only two, and Cord who had always gotten her out of trouble with her parents as she grew older. He'd taught her to shoot, to hunt, to hide. He'd tried to teach her how to lie, but that lesson had been much harder to learn. If it hadn't been for him she never would have survived the night her mother was killed until Gunny got to her.

God, this wasn't supposed to happen. Cord wasn't supposed to check her background to the extent he had, and Jazz shouldn't have had friends capable of linking her mother to Gunny, and Gunny to the missing Kendra "Kenni" Maddox.

The fact that it had happened had her off balance,

teetering between the need to run and the need to fight. Ten years of her life were gone, she couldn't get those back, but the thought of running, of being someone's prey for another ten years, was too much to bear.

She wished with all her heart she could believe the grief she'd heard in Cord's voice when he'd told Jessie that the person who once told him to "mind your manners please," was the best of all of them.

Her desperation, her own grief at losing her family, had her searching for reasons, excuses, anything that could allow her to trust in her family again.

That trust was gone, destroyed in a single night, she reminded herself. Until she found out who had been sending Kin to kill her, then she didn't dare trust any of them.

After Cord drove away from the house, Kenni returned to the kitchen and listened to the plans Jazz and his friends were putting together to reveal who wanted her dead.

Kate and Lara had driven out several minutes after Cord's departure, leaving only Zack, Slade, and Jessie to discuss who could be suspects and who couldn't. The fact that her brothers weren't on that list but her father was sent agony piercing her heart.

"Why Dad and Luce and not Cord, Deacon, or Sawyer?" she asked, her voice low as she pulled Jessie's list to her and began going over it.

"There was no reason for your brothers to strike out against you or your mother, Kenni. But your father married within eight months of your mother's death," Jessie answered gently. "Luce's name is on there because she stood to inherit the maternal trust that passes down from eldest daughter to eldest daughter—the trust your mother's great-great-grandmother set up. With your mother's death, Luce and her daughter Grace moved up to inherit. I believe it passes to them at the end of this year?" Jessie asked curiously.

Kenni could only shrug. "It's not really a big thing, though. Some profits from real estate mostly. According to Mother it didn't add up to much."

"The rumors that your father and Luce were slipping around behind your mother's back can't be discounted, either. Was there any merit to them?" Slade spoke up, the compassion in his voice noted, but ineffective against the pain radiating inside her.

"Mom knew about the rumors before her death," she breathed out wearily. "She and Luce argued over it before we left, but Momma didn't believe Dad was actually having an affair with her."

Her mother had loved her father, though. Loved him desperately, with everything inside her. The thought that her father may have betrayed that love had helped to destroy the foundation of everything she had believed in as a child.

Her mother may not have believed it, but her father's marriage to Luce had certainly given others reason to believe it.

As for Luce, she'd always been such a quiet, easily led personality, but her loyalty to her mother had never been questioned. Then again, Vinny Maddox's loyalty to his wife hadn't been questioned, either—just his fidelity.

She pushed the list back to Jessie before turning to Jazz. "I need to go home and get my things at least," she told him, lifting her gaze to his and meeting the blue fire in it unflinchingly.

His brows lowered broodingly. "It's too dangerous, Kenni."

"I really don't give a damn, Jazz." The retort was delivered without anger. "You're pushing too hard, too fast. Don't do this right now."

The tension in the room ratcheted up by several degrees, and as she stared into his gaze she could see he had every intention of refusing. As though she were a child too weak to defend herself, too stupid to know she was in danger.

"You know—" Rising to her feet, she faced the men coolly. "—I'm still alive, ten years after the order went out to kill me. I believe I can survive a trip home to collect my things. Or." A mocking smile tipped her lips. "You will find out exactly what a bitch I can be." Her gaze locked with Jazz's again. "Is that what you really want?"

"It's too dangerous, Kenni . . ."

She didn't give him a chance to finish. Turning on her heel she stalked from the kitchen. She wasn't some damned china doll he could set on a shelf and expect to stay there. Gunny had taught her to take care of herself if he'd taught her nothing else.

She couldn't afford to leave the little house she rented unprotected for long while her laptop and the DVR for her cameras were still hidden there. She couldn't take the chance that someone would search the house and find either. She needed to get to them first.

It was a damned good thing she knew where Jazz kept the spare set of truck keys.

She'd found them by accident the day before, taped beneath the drawer of his nightstand. Okay, so it wasn't so much by accident as it was by snooping. She'd actually been searching for a weapon when she'd found the keys.

She wasn't exactly dressed for what she was planning. Sandals weren't the most desirable footwear for climbing from a balcony, but she'd had to run with greater vulnerabilities before, she was certain. She just couldn't think of a particular instance at the moment.

She didn't give him and his friends time to consider what she might do. Going straight to the bedroom, Kenni moved to the balcony. There was a very narrow portion of the balcony invisible from the television room—and hopefully from Marcus and Essie's sight.

Sliding over the side she balanced for a moment on the edge before turning, gripping a rail, and lowering herself as far as possible. Wrapping her legs around the support post and working herself to the edge of the patio, she dropped to the ground, flattened herself against the side of the house for a moment, then ran for the front drive.

Jazz's truck was still parked where he'd left it. The door was unlocked and the motor running, thanks to the remote, before she reached it. She jumped in, adjusted the seat for her shorter stature with hurried movements, and within seconds was speeding along the gravel road. She'd warned him she could turn into a bitch, and he hadn't listened. Maybe next time he'd shut his mouth and open his ears.

After hitting the main road, Kenni didn't stay on it long. A quick turn along a hidden path and within minutes she'd reached one of the spots she'd chosen to hide a survival pack. Weapons, especially several of the survival knives she preferred, along with snug black pants, T-shirt, and boots that laced to her ankles were packed inside the old army backpack.

Within moments she was dressed and back behind the wheel of the truck. The wide path wound along a parallel course to the main road without coming within sight of it. Several miles from town she hit a shortcut. If Slade and Jazz were following her, and no doubt they were, she'd still manage to beat them to the house by several minutes.

Easing the truck into the alley behind the house, Kenni cut the engine then jumped from the cab and worked her way along the border of brush and miniature trees that grew along the privacy fencing between her rental and the neighbor's home.

She was in the back door within a minute and staring around the shadowed kitchen in disbelief.

It was trashed.

Fuck.

She had the laptop and DVR carefully hidden, but that didn't mean they hadn't been found. She had to have both to access the recorded feed and learn who had accessed the house and what they had done.

Small handguns were tucked at the small of her back and her ankle, obvious places to search. A six-shot derringer was tucked in the upper cup of her bra, a KA-BAR between her shoulders, and a mini bowie knife in the bottom of her boot.

She slid the baby Glock at the small of her back free. Moving across the room, careful to avoid the scattered cereal thrown over the floor. Just in case whoever had trashed the house was still there. The early-warning crunch of cereal against the floor would alert anyone who might be there waiting for her.

Holding the weapon close to her thigh, Kenni made her way across the kitchen to the doorway.

The house was laid out with no hallways; it was one of the reasons she'd chosen this particular rental. Looking from the kitchen doorway into the large living room also afforded her a view of the open bedroom door.

The living room was completely demolished, more so than the kitchen. There went her security deposit. Holes had been punched into the living room wall, following the camera wires through the room.

Dammit.

Slipping along the wall, careful not to brush against it, she made her way to the bedroom. Pausing, she lifted the weapon to her shoulder, bent low, and slid into the room.

It was empty. Except for the holes punched into the walls, wires pulled free, and clothes strewn around the floor. Clothes that were sliced, ripped, then dropped carelessly to the hardwood.

Moving to the largest hole in the wall she stared at it with narrowed eyes. The decoy DVR was gone, but the copper clip leading from the crawl space beneath the floor to the decoy was intact. The main DVR was still in place.

A faint, almost imperceptible crunch of dry cereal had her moving. Rolling beneath the bed, the Glock held ready, nearly holding her breath, Kenni waited.

"Fuck, Cord, either Jazz's little teacher forgot to clean house—for about six months—or some asshole came calling." Amused, Deacon didn't bother lowering his voice.

Kenni wanted to close her eyes, wanted to let that voice take her back to a time when fear hadn't been her constant companion and her brothers had been larger than life.

"My guess, some asshole came calling," Sawyer replied. His voice was so serious, so somber.

She didn't remember a day Sawyer had been somber when she was younger. Like the others, he was once carefree and so filled with fun.

"Do we know who the asshole is and why he felt the need to throw her cereal all over the floor?" Deacon asked at the sound of more cereal crunching beneath careless feet.

"It's a damned good thing we weren't trying to sneak in," Cord growled at that point. "Would the two of you shut up for a minute and let me think?"

"I don't know, Cord, that would be a hell of a long minute if you asked me," Deacon informed him. "We might bust waiting."

"I might bust both your damned heads if you don't shut the fuck up anyway," Cord snapped as he stepped into the bedroom.

Dark, scarred leather boots and frayed denim filled her gaze as he paused at the bottom of the bed. Behind him moved two similar pairs of boots and denim.

"She had cameras," Sawyer stated, his voice lower now.

"*Had* being the operative word," Deacon inserted.

"What the hell was she up to that she had the entire fucking house wired for video and audio?"

"She was scared," Sawyer said softly, almost too soft for her to hear, and the compassion in his voice had her throat tightening.

Cord moved then.

Following the sight of his boots as he moved around the bed to the other side of the room, she mouthed silent curses. Dammit. Dammit.

Hunching next to the wall where the decoy DVR had been torn from it, he remained silent. She couldn't see what he was doing, had no idea what he was seeing.

Sawyer left the room quickly a second later, followed by Deacon. The sight of them departing left her with a very bad feeling.

A very bad feeling. One she didn't like at all.

Slowly, he turned, the boots shifting by a few inches. He was staring at the bed, she could feel it.

Son of a bitch, he knew she was there.

Silently, just in case he looked, she slid the weapon into a tear in the box spring's lining and continued to wait. The silence was tense, filled with her fear and his patience.

"You coming out, or do I have to drag your ass out?"

She remained quiet and completely still. Maybe, if she was lucky, he wouldn't look.

"I saw the other cable," he said softly. "Sawyer and Deacon have gone after the DVR, Ms. Mayes. What will we find when we watch the video on it?"

Fuck!

"Cord." Jazz entered the room, his voice filled with anger.

Oh God, he would tell Cord, just as he'd threatened. He'd warned her not to run. He'd warned her he'd tell her brothers, and Jazz didn't make threats he wasn't prepared to carry out.

Kenni's head turned quickly, eyes widening at the sight of Deacon and Sawyer's boots scuffling just a bit in front of Jazz's.

Cord rose slowly, remaining silent for long moments. No doubt giving Sawyer and Deacon one of those disappointed looks he gave them whenever they were caught doing something they shouldn't be doing.

"She's under the bed," Cord said then. "I was just inviting her out."

"Yeah, I bet you were." Jazz didn't sound in the least pleasant.

"Jazz, we're going to have to talk about this," Cord stated coolly.

"I have nearly two more weeks, Maddox," he growled. "Get off my ass, will ya?"

Two more weeks? Someone had Jazz on a deadline? That was shocking.

"After this, you think I'm giving you two more weeks?" Cord's bark of laughter had Kenni wincing. She knew that sound, and it had never boded well.

"Fuck off," Jazz ordered, the hint of anger that escaped in his voice had her tensing more than Cord's knowledge of her presence. "You and these brothers of yours."

This wasn't going to be good. Three against one? Where were Slade and Zack?

"They didn't find what they were looking for, either," Jazz promised him. "But I'd say Zack has."

Kenni laid her head against the floor and shook it slowly. Having Zack find it was much better; at least then Cord wouldn't see or hear anything he shouldn't. But still, dammit, it belonged to her and she bet dollars to doughnuts she wouldn't be watching it first.

"Ms. Mayes." The voice was no longer way above her. It was floor-level with her.

Kenni lifted her head slowly, eyes narrowing to meet the dark emerald green of the eldest Maddox brother.

For a second, time fell away. She was ten again, staring back at him from beneath his bed after searching for the birthday present she was certain he must have bought her.

Smiling back at him nervously she forced herself not to speak, certain anything she said would only give her away.

"Would you like to come out and join us?" The gentleness in his voice was frightening. Cord wasn't a gentle-voiced type of person.

"Now." It was Jazz's tone that spurred her to move.

Rolling from beneath the bed she rose to her feet and kept her gaze on the floor. She didn't dare look up at her brothers. It had been too many years. Too many lost years spent never knowing if they wanted her home or wanted her dead.

Besides, the color of her eyes would be an immediate giveaway. If she didn't get out of there, she was dead meat, one way or the other. Because if he didn't kill her—which she doubted he would actually—Cord would no doubt strip her flesh from her bones with his fury.

"I'm ready to leave now." Clearing her throat, she lifted her gaze to Jazz.

He was furious. The blue of his eyes was brighter than ever, his expression so hard it could be stone as he stared back at her.

"That all you came for?" he asked, nodding to the location where the dummy DVR had sat.

"Yes. If Zack has the main device then I'm ready." She nodded, tucking her hair behind her ear as it fell free. She'd get the rest of it later.

"Go to the truck, Slade's waiting for you," he told her, his gaze moving back to her brothers.

"Without you?" Oh, she just didn't think so. She wasn't giving him a chance to talk privately to her brothers for anything.

His brows lowered, his expression warning now. "Pretty much."

She smiled sweetly. "No."

For a moment she was certain he would retaliate, that he would tell her brothers who she was and destroy any chance she had of learning who had killed her mother and hunted her for ten years. At the very least she expected him to attempt to force her to leave or to call in Slade and Zack to carry her out.

Instead his gaze narrowed, those heavy lashes shielding whatever emotion might linger in his eyes.

"Sure this is how you want to handle this?" he murmured softly.

"What's there to handle?" She shrugged as though nothing were riding on the answer. "I simply prefer to know what's going on rather than sitting in your truck wondering what's being said."

If he was going to tell them who she was, then she

would be there to at least glimpse any guilt that might flash in their eyes.

"We're going to talk later." The slightest quirk at the side of his lips paired with a flash of aroused anticipation sent a rush of warmth speeding through her body.

Damn him, he just had to go and get all sexy and remind her of what it had felt like to be possessed by him. She wished she'd thought of it first; maybe she could have rendered him speechless for a moment instead of the other way around.

"You can talk all you like, that doesn't mean I'm going to listen," she shot back, flipping her hand toward him as her chin lifted just enough to shoot him a killing look.

Cord shifted at her periphery, and it was all she could do not to turn and watch him.

She wanted to see his face, wanted to look in his eyes long enough to see if he was her brother or her would-be-assassin.

"Cord," Sawyer murmured, demanding his attention, the dark somberness of his tone nearly pulling her gaze to him.

She had to get out of there before she ended up giving in to the need her heart ached for rather than the caution her head demanded.

"Hurry and discuss whatever the hell it is you need to discuss with them. I'll wait in the kitchen, how's that?" She pushed past him, aware of his gaze on her until she turned into the kitchen doorway and slid to the side where she couldn't be seen.

God, her hands were shaking.

Staring at them, she tried to tell herself no one else had noticed it. She'd kept her hands pushed into her jeans, her fingers out of sight, just as she'd been very careful not to let them see her eyes.

She'd always been terrible at keeping anything from her brothers. They could tell when she was hiding something the moment they saw her. She'd never figured out how they managed that one, and they hadn't revealed their secret, either.

She was older now, she told herself. She was a much better liar than she'd been as a teenager. She'd had to learn to lie, or she would have died a long time ago.

Now she just had to wait for Jazz and his little discussion. He surely wouldn't tell them who she was while she was standing there. He knew how desperately she feared them knowing the truth.

He wouldn't betray her. She had to believe that, because anything else would destroy her trust in him. A fragile, cautionary trust her heart was clinging to with a strength that refused to let go. With a hope that refused to diminish.

Jazz watched the Maddox brothers. Cord, Deacon, and Sawyer were no man's fools. Or woman's. Not for a second had Cord taken his eyes off Kenni, but not until she informed him that he could talk all he liked, she wasn't going to listen, did he see a reaction in them.

Cord had actually flinched, while Deacon and Sawyer's eyes had widened in some surprise, or disbelief. If suspicion hadn't been there before, it was now.

When Sawyer had tried to get his brother's attention, Cord had shot him a look so hard, so filled with a demand for silence that Sawyer had immediately backed down.

"Why are you here, Cord?" Jazz asked him softly, hoping to keep the confrontation he feared the other man would instigate from Kenni's hearing.

Cord shook his head. Propping his hands at his hips for one long second he looked at the floor, his gaze so intense that Jazz actually had a moment's concern as he wondered what the other man was thinking.

When Cord lifted his head his face was carefully blank, his emerald eyes cool and without emotion.

"I had two of my men watching her house." The information came as a surprise to Jazz. "They reported seeing two men slip inside about dawn. They were dressed in black with their faces covered. Before my men were in position to find out who it was, they left. One of them was carrying a pack at his shoulder, though, and I wondered what they'd found."

"You didn't tell me anyone was watching the house." Jazz had known there would be, though. Cord wasn't sloppy and once he realized Kenni's identity was false, he'd have covered his bases.

"Yeah, my bad," Cord drawled, the icy tone of his voice causing Jazz to watch him warily. "I'll make sure it doesn't happen again."

Damn, they were all in trouble now. He would have been amused if he weren't certain it would get him killed at the moment.

"You do that." Jazz nodded. "And while you're at it, whoever's watching my house better disappear, too. Right fast."

If Cord could have tensed further, then he did, while his brothers watched in surprise.

"No one's watching your house." That was a hint of anger in Cord's green eyes now. "Yet."

"The watcher's fair game then?" Jazz pushed. He wanted to be certain. When he took the watcher out, he didn't want to chance killing one of Cord's men.

"Like I said, *yet*," Cord assured him. "If you'll excuse us, we'll be going now." His eyes narrowed on Jazz, though. "You and I will talk later, I believe."

Jazz stepped back from the doorway, watching the three men more closely now. Something wasn't right, but he couldn't quite put his finger on what.

Following the Maddox brothers to the kitchen he watched them pause, their gazes moving to Kenni as she deliberately avoided their looks. Leaning against the wall, she stared at the toes of her boots, arms crossed over her breasts, silent and obviously guilty of something.

He almost grinned. He would have, but he was aware of Cord watching from the corner of his eye, tracking every reaction Jazz might have. He was obviously suspicious, but evidently he wasn't suspicious of the right thing yet. Because if he had even a second's thought that his sister was standing in that kitchen, then World War Three would look like a picnic compared with his rage.

Without another word Cord left the house, followed by his brothers. Tension filled the three men, as well as anger. Whatever they'd come there to find had eluded them, and they weren't happy about it.

As the door closed Kenni moved quickly past him,

brushing against his chest and sending a rush of hunger straight to his already hard cock. If she was going to keep up that attitude, he'd end up fucking her before they left the house.

She was rolling beneath the bed again as he returned to the bedroom doorway. Jazz waited. The sound of material ripping had his brows lifting. The only thing it could be was the thin cover beneath the box springs.

Moments later she rolled into sight once again, clutching the small, tablet-sized laptop, a leather bag hanging from her arm. Jumping to her feet, she tossed him an imperious little look before brushing past him again and heading for the back door.

"Kenni, you're pushing," he warned her before she made it to the door her brothers had passed through minutes before. "That's not a good idea, sweetheart."

Jerking the door open she stomped outside and he could have sworn he heard "Bite me" before she stepped past the threshold.

Watching that cute little ass twitch with feminine ire had his cock throbbing as he pulled the door closed and followed her to the truck. It was so damned cute, he just might have to give her what she was asking for when he got her home. He was going to bite her.

"Why did we leave? Goddammit, Cord . . ."

"Don't take His name in vain," Cord murmured as he watched the girl stalk from the house, her rounded little nose lifted disdainfully. Like a princess with the scent of a peasant far too close to her delicate senses.

That profile, the jut of her chin, the expression on her face. They were eerily familiar. Too familiar, even though he knew better, knew he had to be imagining the resemblance.

He wiped his hands over his face. It couldn't be. It wasn't possible.

"Then answer me," Sawyer demanded. "Why?"

"It can't be her," he whispered. "You know it can't be."

The silence behind him was heavy, filled with certainty and fury. They were certain, but he couldn't allow them the luxury. He'd learned the hard way that it wasn't possible.

"You know better," Sawyer retorted, the low, dark undertone a warning that his youngest brother wasn't accepting the truth Cord needed him to believe. "You saw it as well as I did. You knew her as well as we did, Cord."

He shook his head. No, he'd known her better than anyone else. She'd been his shadow, as dear to him as his own child would be, he imagined.

And because he knew her, for a second, one grief-stricken, horrified second, he wondered . . .

"She would have come to us. If she was alive and here in Loudoun, she would have come to us, Sawyer. If she was alive period, she would have come home." She wouldn't have left him wondering, searching in vain, if she had been alive.

It wasn't possible.

Neither Deacon nor Sawyer said anything further, but that didn't mean they'd taken his word. Suspicion was a horrible thing in a Maddox. It made them stubborn, determined to find the truth.

They'd searched for her for years. Based on one homeless drunk's certainty he'd seen someone shoot the pretty little blond girl who escaped with the man wearing a marine's uniform, they'd searched for her.

Cord had almost driven himself insane with that search, and Deacon and Sawyer hadn't returned much better. They hadn't been there when Slade had needed their help. Cord hadn't been there when Jazz had tried to contact him for help. They'd come too close to losing control of the Kin because of their search for her and it had taken the better part of two years to regain it.

And now Annie Mayes with her eerie familiarity was throwing their lives into chaos again.

He wasn't going to allow it.

Putting the truck he'd driven into gear, he pulled out from the neighbor's hidden drive slowly. It didn't matter what he told them or how much he tried to make himself believe: He'd seen what Sawyer had seen and he had to force himself to leave.

Kenni had never been able to hide anything from them. The slightest secret and she couldn't even look them in the face. She could lie to anyone and everyone, even their parents, but when it came to her brothers, she gave herself away every time.

She couldn't look at them, she hid her hands, studied the tips of her shoes, tucked her hair back nervously with two fingers only.

Give her green eyes and soft, dark-blond hair, and their sister lived.

Or was she hiding as he'd suspected for so many years? Hiding and too scared to come home because someone told her she was being hunted by the Kin?

He'd come upon the rumor while in New York the

summer it had happened. The suspicion that the body found with his mother wasn't his sister. That rumor had sent him and his brothers on a quest that lasted nearly eight years.

He'd sworn to himself that his years of searching were over. He'd chased every rumor, followed every lead he could imagine, and hadn't even glimpsed her.

She was gone. It didn't matter the grief that shook him in acknowledging it. She'd had been taken from them in the same fire they'd lost their mother in and there was no changing that.

Or was there?

CHAPTER 14

Jazz didn't slam the door closed after entering behind her. He actually closed it so quietly that the snick of the lock had her swinging around in surprise, facing the brooding, heavily lashed glare he directed down at her.

He seemed so much taller when he had that look on his face. The one that indicated he was a hell of a lot angrier than he appeared.

"Do you have death wish?" he asked a little too calmly.

"Not really," she answered with a shrug as she turned and moved toward the kitchen, ignoring the increasing tension behind her. "Do you?"

She had only a heartbeat's warning before his fingers locked around her upper arm, swinging her around and lifting her to him.

"I'm beginning to believe that's exactly what I have," he growled just before his lips came over hers with a hunger and determination she wouldn't have expected.

Any resistance she may have had disintegrated as he carried her to the formal living room just off the entry.

Shadowed, the drapes drawn over the large windows, Kenni was only barely aware of the dark shapes of furniture. The wide couch he laid her on was perfect, though. And as his lips continued to ravage hers, he disposed of their clothes quickly and efficiently, dropping them to the floor beside the couch.

Powerful, experienced, his lips moved against hers, parting them and tasting her with his tongue. Like a fire pouring through her senses he burned away any thought of protest. Not that she wanted to protest.

Pleasure raced through her, gathering force and swirling in her senses until nothing else mattered. Until only his touch filled her reality, only his hunger sustained her.

Gripping his shoulders, Kenni lifted closer to him. Had it only been the night before that he had taken her? How had she survived without his touch since?

Her nails bit into his hard flesh, tested its strength as his callused palm gripped her hip, his fingers flexing against her touch-starved flesh. How had she lived without this? Without the hunger that poured over her whenever he touched her?

"Damn, you make me crazy. Fucking insane to have you . . ." His voice rasped with anger and lust as his lips moved to her neck, his fingers caressing from her hip to her stomach, trailing waves of fiery pleasure in their path.

His touch sensitized her flesh, had her lifting her hips, desperate for more.

"That's it, baby, come alive for me." His voice whispered over her as a light nip to her neck sent weakening flashes of sensation straight to the swollen bud of her clit and beyond.

Burying her hands in his hair, her fingers tightened in the strands as erotic, electric sensation pulsed in her vagina. Thighs tightening, hips arching, she moaned, sinking beneath the waves of swirling, aching rapture that pulsed through her nerve endings, building and growing with each touch.

Slick, heated moisture spilled from her vagina, the muscles clenching involuntarily, demanding touch there as well. Demanding the pleasure she knew he could give her. Adrenaline-laced and throbbing in excitement, blood poured through her veins, her heart pumping it through her body furiously as pleasure flooded her system. If the need tearing through her senses didn't abate soon, how would she survive it?

Fiery sensation wrapped around one hardened nipple then, so sharp, so sweet Kenni cried out, arching closer as Jazz's lips surrounded it. Drawing on it, suckling it with hungry demand while his palm cupped its mate, his fingers finding the stiff point.

"Oh God, yes. Jazz, please." It was more than good. It was a blazing path to rapture, to ecstasy. A path she raced along eagerly.

The heated, hungry suction eased. The lash of his tongue became lazy, tormenting licks.

And it wasn't enough.

Oh God, she needed more.

The callused warmth of his palm rasped against the flesh between her thighs, his fingers parting the swollen, bare folds he found there.

His thumb rolled against the sensitive bud of her clit, the caress causing lashing pinpoints of sensation to spread through her like torturous licks of static electricity.

Digging her heels into the cushions of the couch to lift herself closer, Kenni writhed beneath the caresses. Desperate, so needy, she ached for him. That fiery pleasure-pain, the explosions of rapture. The knowledge that she belonged to him.

"I love touching you," he murmured against her breast, "especially this pretty flesh." His fingers tucked into the narrow slit, caressing through it with slow, teasing strokes. "It's so pretty. All pink slick flesh, your honey clinging to the lips like a heavy, thick dew." His thumb eased lower, spreading the slick response as more rained from the clenched depths of her vagina.

"Did you really think I would let you run away from me, Kenni?" he crooned as his fingers found the snug entrance he sought and rimmed it gently. "That I would chance losing this?"

His fingers sank inside her before she guessed his intention. Two-wide, penetrating, parting her flesh as her hips arched violently, a moan escaping her lips, her senses shattering.

Her fingers fisted at her sides. Waves of ecstasy raced through her with the sudden release exploding through her with the force of a tidal wave.

Jazz caressed the spasming muscles of her inner flesh with the tips of his fingers. They rubbed and explored, turning what should have been a release into a rapid race back to that peak of desperation.

"What are you doing to me?" Hips arched, desperate, Kenni fought against the rising, burning lashes of agonizing need only to lose to the pleasure spearing the tight depths of her clenched vagina.

"That is so beautiful. Watching you come while my fingers bury inside you. Feeling you tighten around me and knowing I can push you back, make you explode all over again," he groaned as her hips jerked, burying him deeper. "That's it, baby, lift those pretty hips for me. Fuck my fingers."

The muscles surrounding his fingers spasmed furiously, flexing in response to the explicit demand.

"Jazz." The stimulation tore at her senses, wrapped around them and poured fuel on the lust burning inside her.

His fingers flexed again, rasping, caressing, pushing her to another peak until Kenni feared she would never survive intact.

"Are you close, baby?" His lips were at her nipple again, moving against the sensitive peak as her breathing became quicker, harder.

"Don't stop . . ." She could feel the rapture tightening in her womb. "Please, please don't . . . Oh God, Jazz . . . No."

He stopped.

Pulling his fingers free of her he turned her so quickly she barely registered the fact that she was on her knees before he moved behind her. Holding her hips in place Jazz pressed her knees farther apart, the head of his cock pressing against her, opening her.

"Slow and easy," he demanded, holding her still as she tried to push back, to take him with one of those quick, hard thrusts she knew would push her over the edge instantly. "Let me feel you, baby. Feel your sweet pussy milking me right in."

A cry escaped her lips, her breath locking in her throat for a second as she felt him pressing inside her.

Pleasure-pain erupted through the tender flesh, wrapped around her clit, and sent furious pulses of building hunger through the responsive depths.

The pleasure was so sharp and sweet she couldn't imagine never knowing it again as the fiery burn of the penetration attacked tissue unused to possession before him.

Slow and easy, just as he'd threatened. Kenni's back arched, her vagina clenching violently as she felt her juices spilling with rapid pulses to each fiery stretch of her flesh.

Jazz eased inside her, groaning as she tightened around each inch that burrowed through her flesh. His hips shifted, moved, pushing him deeper. His fingers flexed at her hip, tightened, holding her in place.

Desperate cries spilled from her lips with each hard stroke of his cock inside her, impaling her with a mix of pleasure and pain she found intoxicating. Then he eased back, slow, easy, teasing her with the retreat. Only to return, working her tender flesh open again, penetrating it with a fiery heat that burned through her senses.

She couldn't bear the pleasure. It tore at her, drove her higher on waves of building heat and shattering ecstasy.

"Hold on, baby," he groaned. "Ah hell, Kenni. You destroy me."

The next thrust drove him deeper, harder inside her. The sudden impalement, a shock to her senses, tore a cry from her lips and the control she'd been holding on to so desperately slipped out of her grip.

She needed him.

All of him.

Kenni whimpered with the loss when he retreated fully once again, but with his return she was waiting for him. Pushing back, taking him deeper, her inner muscles clenched and rippled around him. Tremors of building ecstasy worked up her spine, shuddered through her body. A band of tension began tightening through her womb, lashing at her clit and pushing her closer to the flames waiting to explode around her.

Jazz came over her, the heat and power that was so much a part of him surrounding her. One arm locked around her hips, holding her to him as he began thrusting inside her with a speed that drove her to the breaking point with a suddenness she wasn't expecting.

Explosions detonated through her senses, waves upon waves of such ecstasy they stole her breath, her reason, and what remained of her woman's spirit.

Muscles clenched, locked in place. As she shuddered beneath him, each successive detonation was more intense, driving through her. Behind her, Jazz thrust to the hilt, tensing, a groan tearing through him before spilling his release in furious, throbbing spurts that extended and deepened the orgasm rushing through her. Ecstasy raged through her senses, in waves that seemed never ending until she collapsed against the couch beneath him, exhausted.

Above her, Jazz's breathing was labored, the release he'd found coming only moments after hers. She remembered, distantly, the feel of his flesh throbbing harder, buried to the hilt as he groaned above her. But he hadn't spilled inside her as he had before.

He'd donned a condom.

Were those tears behind her eyes, threatening to spill? Tightening her throat, she swallowed against them. And why should that bother her anyway?

Before she could let that thought break the fragile control she had over her pain, she was aware of Jazz slowly easing from her, his breathing ragged as he collapsed beside her and drew her to his chest.

And where did they go from here? she wondered.

"Don't run like that again, Kenni," he warned her softly, pushing the remnants of pleasure from her senses with the order.

"Or what?" Pushing away from him she sat up, found her clothes lying on the floor, and picked them up wearily.

"You don't want to know *or what*. The next time I won't be nearly as understanding, count on that." The promise was delivered in a tone that had her swallowing tightly, wariness edging at her senses.

It was a wariness she ignored. She'd gone too far, had walked too close to the darkness to survive.

"I didn't turn into a china doll overnight and I won't pretend to be one so you can play the white knight," she informed him with a bite of anger.

Rising, she drew her clothes on quickly. She felt too vulnerable, too exposed to him now. The lack of clothing as he sprawled just as naked on the couch next to her had her too eager to submit to whatever he wanted.

Submission had never been her thing.

"So I can play the white knight? Where the hell do

you come up with these ideas? I never claimed to be a white knight, or to want to be one," he grunted at the accusation, rising and jerking his clothes from the floor.

She could feel his eyes on her as he dressed as well. Glowering and intense, he wasn't about to let the subject go and she knew it. And she didn't think her emotions could deal with it.

She felt too close to an edge she didn't understand or recognize. An edge where far too many emotions were teetering.

Dressed, she gathered up the leather pack she'd dropped to the floor and forced herself to leave the living room. Striding across the entry and television room to the kitchen, she was very well aware of Jazz following her.

The second she entered the puppies' territory Squirrel broke away from the others, bounding to her with a cheerful yip and bouncing around her in a bid to convince her to play with him.

Opening the gate, she gave Squirrel a gentle pet before shooing him over to his mother. Closing the gate behind her, Kenni ignored the fact that Jazz had paused at the entrance to the television room. He stopped there, silent, his arms crossed over his chest in an arrogant, demanding stance.

She set down the leather pack she'd collected along with her laptop from beneath the bed, opened the flap securing it, and began pulling free surveillance pictures she'd taken over the years as well as pictures taken in Loudoun after her arrival that matched up to the Kin she'd photographed over the years.

"I need the DVR Zack collected," she told him as she felt him moving closer. "Will he be here soon?"

She didn't hear him, but she could feel the tension behind her increasing, indicating he had finally followed her.

"He'll have it here soon," he growled, and it was an irritable sound.

She knew what they were doing. Slade and Zack, overbearing and arrogant, would of course try to go through it first to see if they could identify who had broken into the house.

Good luck to them. She doubted they were going to get past the encryption program Gunny had created for their security.

"It won't do him any good to check it first," she informed him, still fighting the languor that wanted to overtake her after the incredible pleasure he'd given her. "The encryption program is on my laptop and without the program, cracking it will take him far longer than simply bringing it over here would."

Gunny had made certain she learned the surveillance program and its encryption. The DVR, laptop, and cameras worked together. Having the DVR was useless without the laptop and its program to decrypt it.

"Have all the bases covered, don't you, Kenni?" he asked a little too gently. "Hidden clothes and weapons, encrypted cameras and DVRs. Yet you still have no idea who's trying to kill you. Why's that?"

She'd known he was going to be pissed and she'd known hard questions would come with her actions. She'd known it like she knew a bee sting stung; she just hadn't allowed herself to think about it.

"Survival. I was more concerned with hiding for a while longer, I guess," she finally answered him, trying to contain the emotions her brothers' presence had tempted free. "If Cord hadn't gotten so nosy, then I'd still be hiding."

And watching.

But why hadn't she done more to find out who had given the order to kill her mother, Gunny, and herself? Sometimes it had felt as though she were just drifting in a sea of questions and fears with no idea how to solve the problem.

"Why do I have a feeling you would have preferred being left alone to do just that?" The accusation struck home. The guilt, the anger, ten years of betrayal. Cousins who had shot her, tried to knife her. Years of running from the very people who should have been protecting her.

Ten years.

Ten years of fear and loss, and did he think that didn't bother her? That she didn't realize what had been taken from her?

"And how did it affect you, Jazz?" she demanded, swinging around and staring back at him in outrage. "You would have still managed to seduce me. I couldn't have held out for longer and we both know it. What did it matter if it was Annie's or Kenni's name you whispered as long as you achieved the end result?"

His jaw hardened, the muscle there ticking like a time bomb waiting to go off.

"You think the only thing that concerns me was whether or not I could get you in my bed? That was never a question, Kenni. I knew damned good and well you were going to end up in my bed. Keeping your ass alive does concern me, though," he informed her, his voice sharper than normal.

The ominous hardening of his tone had her watching him warily now. It wasn't just his voice. His expression looked carved from marble. It was his eyes that were truly disconcerting, though. They blazed, the sapphire blue roiling with an emotion she couldn't quite define.

Perhaps now, that wasn't all that concerned him. But had she just been some normal, run-of-the-mill kindergarten teacher?

"I think that's all you wanted from Annie Mayes," she whispered, rubbing at the chill chasing over her arms now. "What does it matter, Jazz? As you said, what you felt for me then was then. It's not now. I'm here now." Waving her hand to the house to indicate his life, she kept her gaze locked with his. "I'm endangering everyone I love, everyone I wanted to keep safe, and you think that doesn't bother me? That I could ever survive if anything happened to you because of me?" The bitterness she tried to keep banked thickened in her own voice now. "Do you think I ran for eight fucking years just to willingly let you take over and stand in front of me as though I were some simpering child?"

"I never accused you of being a child." Shooting her a withering look he let his arms drop, his hand lifting to stab a finger furiously in her direction. "But you've by God bitten off more than you can chew alone and you're too damned stubborn to see it."

Too stubborn to see it? Amazement lashed at her as

she threw back her head and placed her hands on her hips, the confrontation she'd been trying to avoid exploding within her.

"Why do you think I stayed hidden?" She clenched her teeth, her lips pulled back in furious contempt. "Why do you think I've fought you every damned inch since you learned who I was? Because I knew years ago what I was facing. But I didn't bite this chunk off, as you so charmingly call it. Someone's been force-feeding it to me and I've chewed it the best friggin' way possible. And by God I didn't just hide. I did my best."

She was yelling by time she finished.

Her temper, always unpredictable and hard to control, suddenly broke free of the restraints she kept on it.

How dare he? How dare he believe that because she hadn't known how to investigate who wanted her dead, she hadn't tried? That she hadn't cared?

"Here." Twisting around and grabbing the pictures she'd taken over the past two years, matched with those taken in the eight before, she threw them at him. "I matched killers sent after me in the past with faces from the present. Here." Picking up the flash cards she'd filled with notes, rumors, and gossip, she threw those at him as well. "That's all I have for two years of investigating the only way I knew how while keeping your fucking ass out of it. Keeping my brothers out of it. Keeping you alive because if I died, then—well hell. Fuck it. You already believed I was dead, what did it fucking matter?"

She was screaming.

She never screamed.

Rage was tearing at her senses.

"Ten years." She could barely speak now for the rioting fury ripping through every corner of her mind. "Ten years." A swipe of her arm and the laptop went flying from the table to crash to the floor. "You built my house, my pond, and my gazebo and I didn't even know." Holding her arms out toward the windows she fought to breathe, to pull back, to stop the flow of bitter rage. "You gave a dead girl her dream and then you let yourself die with her. Do you think that was what I wanted?"

Swinging to him once again she realized how much that had hurt as well.

"You let yourself die with me," she repeated. "My brothers get drunk every year on the date of Momma's funeral and Poppy grieves to the point that he calls Luce by Momma's name and her daughter by mine. And all that was supposed to make me suddenly stand up and declare to you I lived when I could be dead again in the next second? Oh-fuck-you-yes, I wanted to cause every damned one of you more pain. I wanted you, Slade, Jessie, Zack, and my brothers buried with me the second time around as well. Let's just make it a fucking party, why don't we?" Her eyes widened, sarcasm filling the rage. "Oh yeah, right, we'd all be fucking dead. Kinda hard to party then, isn't it?"

The sob that escaped her lips shocked her, but not enough to still the enraged agony washing through her.

Not that a single damned thing she said was making a difference. He was staring over her shoulder, his expression closed, distant.

"And every word I'm saying is going through one bullheaded ear and out the other," she flung out contemptuously.

"No, he's trying to figure out how he's going to save his own ass now that I know exactly what he's been hiding from us." The voice was steel-hard but vibrating with such agony, it dug hollow furrows of pain straight through her heart. "Turn around, let me see your eyes. You wouldn't let me see them earlier."

Kenni froze.

She could feel the blood leave her face as Jazz's gaze moved to hers, regret and resignation filling it as he stared down at her with a gentleness she simply couldn't comprehend.

"You should have known better than to try to fool your brothers, Kenni. They knew you far too well," he told her with weary resignation. "I think that's something we both forgot somehow."

She had forgotten.

She'd forgotten it wasn't possible for her to lie to her brothers in any way. Even by avoidance.

Her stomach began cramping with panic, a useless feeling she told herself. Panic wasn't going to aid her in any way.

Shooting Jazz a look that promised retaliation, Kenni turned slowly to meet the gazes of the three men she'd known not to reveal herself to.

"They'll just ground you for a few years. Well, a few decades maybe," Jazz murmured behind her. "They'll actually kill me."

He was kidding, right?

Her heart was ready to jump out of her chest, her stomach roiling and threatening to push its way past her throat, and he wanted to make jokes?

"Kenni . . ." Sawyer whispered her name, desperate,

disbelieving, as she stared at the floor and tried to tell herself there had to be a way to salvage the situation. To continue to hide.

"It doesn't surprise me that you can't look at us," Deacon said contemptuously. "Hell, there's no way you're Kenni. She knew how to face her own stupidity. And even she would have known how fucking stupid it was to try to hide from us, right here in Loudoun." He turned to Jazz then. "And you have the nerve to help her attempt it? Are you fucking crazy?"

She almost winced at the contempt in her brother's voice.

"Anything's possible, though I did advise her against it," Jazz stated, his tone bland as Kenni felt him lean against the kitchen door frame. "You know how damned stubborn she can be."

"She's right here!" The insult had her gaze lifting for one second, just long enough for the eldest, Cord to catch it, and hold it.

She was right there, and now there was no hiding from the brothers she'd adored as a teenager, and missed dreadfully in the past ten years.

Deep, heavy grooves of grief were dug into Cord's face, the emerald hue of his eyes dark, stark with pain.

"Why?" Quiet, vibrating with such agonizing disbelief, the single question stripped her bare. "Why, Kenni?"

He looked broken. He sounded broken and it was killing her.

To her soul, that one word laid her open, exposing emotions she hadn't dared face, hadn't dared to allow free.

"Why?" Lifting her chin, she faced him squarely now. The time to hide from these men was at an end now. If they were her enemies, if even one of them was an enemy, then it would be the end of her. Because she'd spent ten years determined to keep them out of the path of whatever madman haunted her life and destroyed her mother.

"Why?" She met him now as a woman, not the child she had been or the teenager he needed her to be once again. "Because I couldn't allow even one of you to be taken from me as well. I wouldn't have survived it."

"You call that an excuse? A fucking reason?" Cord snarled, the veins in his neck standing out in stark relief.

"I don't need an excuse or a reason—you taught me that, Cord," she retorted calmly, keeping a tight grip on her emotions, on the memories fighting to pour free, the rage, the agony of being separated from her family.

"Like hell . . ."

"Family," she told him softly. "They were hunting me, not you, or Deacon, or Sawyer. Me. Had I called you, who would have fought with you that you could trust besides Deacon and Sawyer, Slade, Jazz, and Zack? Six of you against an unknown number of Kin? Against a faceless, nameless enemy?" She shook her head slowly. "I didn't need a reason or an excuse," she repeated. "I wouldn't be the reason any of you died."

Silence filled the kitchen for long moments before a bark of laughter, filled with sarcastic disbelief, broke the tension.

Sawyer stepped forward, shaking his head, the shaggy dark blond of his hair brushing against his neck as he stared back at her as though he couldn't believe what he was seeing.

"Fucking superhero now, are you?" Deacon bit out furiously. "Son of a bitch, I wish I'd listened to Dad when you were younger and agreed to send you to a fucking convent."

Kenni blinked back at him before narrowing her eyes, cocking her hip and placing her hand negligently on the curve. "I never imagined I was a superhero, Deacon, but I never let myself believe that the three of you were, either. But I might start wondering why I've missed you so damned much if you keep up with the insults."

That was a horrible lie. There was nothing he could do to change how desperately she'd missed him or the others.

"My charming personality and the fact that I won't lie to you like that asshole behind you obviously has. Trust me, Kenni, not contacting us was really bad for his health." His chin jutted out pugnaciously, his lips thinning as the muscle at the side of his jaw ticked warningly.

"Lied to me about what, Deacon?" she questioned him in amazement. "Sorry, but I won't give you an excuse to hit him. Jazz hasn't lied to me about anything."

"He convinced you not to tell us you were alive," Deacon rasped. "Someone fucking convinced you not to let us know you were alive, or in Loudoun." Taking a step closer, his fingers curling into fists, his gaze locked with Jazz's. "Who else would have done so?"

"Kin."

Three pairs of differing shades of emerald turned on her with such intensity, it felt cutting. The sensation was distinctly uncomfortable.

She turned her gaze to Cord. She hated seeing the pain in his eyes increase, the grief and rage that hollowed his already savagely hewn expression.

"Kin," Cord repeated softly before breathing out heavily, rubbing at the back of his neck, and running his hand along the side of his face. "Fuck!"

The expletive didn't come close to expressing everything she knew that answer represented to him.

"Kin break into the house in town then?" Sawyer questioned, dragging her gaze back to him.

"I'm not sure yet." Turning, she stared at the mess she'd made during her confrontation with Jazz. She'd made a hell of a mess. "I'm waiting for Slade and Zack to realize they might need me to break the encryption on the DVR. The programs on my computer. Once I view the video I'll know more."

Cord moved slowly, heavily, to where the pictures littered the hard floor and stooped to pick a few up, studying them intently.

Many of the pictures were six to eight years old. She'd begun taking them with disposable cameras until Gunny had managed to procure a real one with a zoom lens.

"Kin." Holding one particular picture, he lifted his gaze to her. "David Mobley and Aaron Blake."

"Gunny killed Aaron, but David managed to get away. I have another picture of him in there somewhere. One I took last year at the school. I believe his youngest enters third grade this fall."

He nodded. "I'm her godfather."

She hadn't known that, but it didn't surprise her. David had been close to the family since they were children. A distant cousin, his father best friends from childhood with their father.

Slowly, Cord gathered the pictures together from the floor, straightened them, seemingly paying little attention to the individuals in them, but she knew him better than that. His memory was exceptional. He'd be able to name every person he saw in them years later.

"You can't strike at them, Cord," she told him softly when he straightened and set the stack of pictures on the table.

He stared at the stack of photos, his fingertips stroking over the table next to them for long moments.

"Dad threw this table out of the house just after the funeral," he said softly, still stroking the wood before he lifted his gaze to her once again. "Did you know it was the same kitchen set?"

She hadn't.

Swinging around she stared at Jazz where he leaned against the door frame, his arms crossed over his chest.

"You have a big mouth, Maddox," he growled.

Cord nodded to that as well. Lifting his hand he rubbed at the side of his face again, his expression so heavy Kenni's heart clenched in pain for him, as well as herself.

"I'm sorry, Kenni," he whispered, his gaze meeting hers squarely, the regret so heavy in his eyes she could only stare back at him silently. "I failed you."

"No, Cord . . ."

"You were seen the night of the fire escaping with a marine, still in uniform. An old homeless soldier saw you running and heard the gunshot that put a bullet in your shoulder, he said."

"Yes," she affirmed tightly.

"We looked for you," Deacon snapped, dragging her gaze to him. "For almost eight years, Kenni, we searched for you."

"I found out about our uncle Charles—Gunny, you called him." Cord's voice didn't change, but his expression grew heavier. "We met a few friends who were searching for him. They lost him in Chicago."

"He's dead," she said, answering the question in Cord's voice. "He sent me to collect a vehicle we were going to use to leave town. He was supposed to meet with someone who could tell him who was giving the orders and sending men out to kill me. When he didn't show up at the meeting place, I went back to the warehouse." Jazz moved then, shifting from the door frame, his arms coming around her comfortingly. A move that brought a glare to each of her brothers' faces. "I only found his blood . . ." Gripping Jazz's forearms tightly she broke off, her lips trembling despite her dry eyes. "I'd taken several pictures over that week of men that resembled those I'd known in Loudoun. I matched a couple once I arrived."

"Who?" The question was soft, the sound so nonthreatening Kenni watched Cord warily.

"Later, Cord," Jazz said as the sound of a vehicle coming up the drive could be heard. "Slade's here and I want to see that video. And I think the three of you need to do more than focus on who to kill. Focus on who's alive instead."

"They'll pay, sunshine," Cord promised, that too-soft, too-gentle voice sending a shudder racing up her spine. "I promise you, they'll pay."

CHAPTER 15

The DVR was still encrypted when Slade and Zack arrived.

"I want that program," Slade growled as he handed her the device, his gray eyes gleaming with amused irritation, his expression rueful. "Or I want to play with cracking it."

"Not hardly," Kenni drawled, turning back to the table where her laptop was waiting and taking the chair in front of it. "Gunny spent two years building the security encryption just for me. I think I'm rather possessive of it." Slanting a thoughtful sideways look for a second, she added, "I might give you a shot at cracking it, though." Just to see how long it would take him.

Turning to her brothers Slade nodded warily, obviously waiting for Kenni to pull up the video.

Deacon and Sawyer moved around the table to see the computer screen, arms crossed over their chests, their glowering expressions giving them a savage cast.

They were furious. Kenni could feel the waves of

rage pulsing around them. They were doing nothing to
hide it, but it was Cord's silent, icy expression that had
everyone's nerves on edge.

Even Kenni's.

Once that expression would have meant Kin arriving
from three different states then disappearing with Cord
for days at a time. She understood now that the groups
were more than just friends of her brothers or some or-
dinary hunting trip. No doubt, blood had been shed on
each of those excursions.

It took only seconds for the computer to recognize the
DVR's hard drive and pull it up. Clicking on the decryp-
tion program, she opened the video file within it then
sat back and watched the status bar as the file loaded. It
opened with a request to choose the file needed.

Motion-activated indoor cameras automatically recorded until all movement had stopped for five minutes. Choosing the first recorded file for that day she
watched as it opened, revealing the two black-garbed
figures entering the back door of the rental house.

They began there, systematically tearing it apart with
no regard for neatness, just as they began talking without considering who or what may be listening.

"Do you really think if she's that Maddox bitch, she
was stupid enough think she could stay hidden?" the
shorter of the two man team murmured.

She knew that voice.

Frowning, Kenni watched their movements, the shape
of their bodies, and their stride as they moved around
the kitchen.

"Oh, she's Kendra Maddox. The DNA tests confirmed it. Why do you think the boss is so desperate now?"

Kenni straightened in her chair. DNA?

A muted chuckle sounded then. "Wouldn't Colter be pissed to know we have his lab contact? She keeps telling him the results haven't come back yet. It's all I can do not to thank him whenever I see him, for being the nosy bastard he is."

Slade.

The blood she'd gotten on the kitchen towel at his house. Evidently Jazz hadn't rinsed and bleached it as he'd led her to believe.

Behind her, Slade cursed under his breath, the sound rife with anger. Served him right for stealing her damned blood. But it didn't serve her right, because his actions had been the catalyst for the renewed attempts against her.

"Before or after Cord let you know I wasn't really Annie Mayes?" she asked her friend's husband.

"After," he growled. The knowledge that his lab contact had sold him out must not be sitting well with him. "The background you came in with actually satisfied me," he added, the rueful irritation in his tone almost amusing.

"Marriage is making you lazy," Cord accused him disgustedly. "It didn't satisfy me for a minute."

But then Cord had been born suspicious.

"She has cameras," one of the men on the video stated as they entered the living room, staring at the picture she'd hidden the lens behind.

Striding across the room and reaching up, he jerked

the frame from the wall. Thankfully the camera on the other side of the room activated and began recording.

Bastards. They snapped the camera from its connection before following the wires through the wall, busting drywall and pulling them free as they went.

"Damned bitch," one of them breathed in irritation. "I have half a mind to feed her to my damned cat once she's dead."

Her eyes narrowed on the video. The way he'd spoken had triggered a memory not yet fully formed.

The silence behind her was deafening.

The threats continued as they traced the wires to the next camera in the bedroom, once again missing the backup there. Finding the decoy box they ripped it from the wall and packed it and the cameras into a black pack. Then they proceeded to destroy the bedroom.

"Don't forget to destroy the clothes." The order was given with an air of amusement. "Boss says it's about the worst thing we could do to her. I guess she likes her pretty clothes more than most women."

No, it wasn't that she liked her clothes more than most; she just wouldn't have had the cash to replace the quality of clothes she did have. Two years without being hunted like a rabbit and she'd managed to purchase a few of the more fashionable items she might have had if her world hadn't exploded on her ten years ago.

They took a lot of enjoyment in destroying them as well. As they ripped, tore, and cut the material, they also found a lot of enjoyment in discussing the "boss."

But what were they looking for?

Nothing in particular had been mentioned, though

they systematically went through every drawer, looked beneath them, tore at the carpeting, checked the vents.

"Nothing." The announcement was made as one of them exited the bathroom after destroying it as well. "She doesn't have anything."

"Boss says there's rumors she's been taking a lot of pictures," the other reminded him. "She should have at least had a camera."

"Or her cell phone?" the first retorted, scoffing at the idea of a camera. "You know what gossip is like around here. She probably said she wanted pictures and someone took it and ran with a camera."

That was always a possibility, Kenni thought in amusement. Gossip in small towns tended to be like that.

"They were after your files," Sawyer murmured then. "Any indication that you were investigating who was giving the orders or recognized anyone who'd been sent after you in the past."

"Where were they hidden?" Deacon question softly, indicating the pictures and hard copy of the few files she'd printed.

"Beneath her box springs." It was Cord who answered the question. "That's where she used to hide everything. Then she hid under the bed herself."

Well, one point for the older brother, she thought painfully. He'd paid attention when she was a child when she hadn't thought he had. Had he been even remotely involved in the attempts on her life, he would have told whoever was sent to search the house to be certain to check there.

"All kids hide under the bed," Deacon snorted doubtfully. "That doesn't mean anything."

"Not like Kenni. If there was something she valued she made a slit beneath the box springs and hid it inside there," Cord stated softly. "She would hide under the bed herself whenever she thought she was in trouble. We let her think she was pulling it off. She never learned she wasn't, evidently."

"She learned. She was just out of options when you stepped in with the boob squad." She nodded to Deacon and Sawyer. "I hope you at least use a muzzle whenever you take them out on jobs with you."

"Industrial-strength glue," Cord snorted.

"Yeah, I always said they were untrainable," she remembered, her voice softening at the insult she would throw at her brothers when she was younger.

Keeping her gaze on the video, she frowned as one of the black-garbed figures stood at the doorway and turned back to the room. His head tilted, his gaze circling with narrow-eyed intent.

He didn't even pause as his gaze swept over the hidden eye of the backup camera she'd placed next to a nail hole in the scratched, aged trim of the window. The lens blended in perfectly among the other blemishes, the trim replaced without so much as a scuff mark to indicate it had been removed at any time.

He sensed it, but he just wasn't good enough to know what it was he was sensing.

"Let's go, bro," the other urged. "Daylight's coming in."

Turning, the would-be assassin/burglar strode quickly

across the kitchen without disturbing the cereal thrown across the floor.

"I know them." Frowning at the video as the two left by the back door, Kenni could feel the answer to their identity teasing at her mind.

"So do I," Jazz murmured. "I just can't place it."

Her brothers didn't comment either way.

Closing the file she pulled up the file log, saw that the only recording remaining was the time she'd arrived at the house and disconnected the encryption program.

"Like Slade, I want a chance to crack that program." Sawyer was all but rubbing his large techie hands in excitement at the chance to get into Gunny's program.

"Gather your things, Kenni," Cord said then. "We'll leave as soon as I can discuss a few things with Slade."

The shocking statement had her head jerking up, her gaze meeting Jazz's as he came from behind her.

He stilled next to the table, his eyes meeting hers slowly.

"I'm not going anywhere, Cord." Setting the electronic lock on the laptop, she closed the lid and slid it aside with deliberate care. "I'm fine where I'm at."

"Like hell . . ."

She rose to her feet and turned to face him.

"Didn't Poppy tell you, this is home," she told him softly. "As long as Jazz allows me to stay, it's home."

A heavy frown creased his brow. "Think Poppy won't head straight here when we tell him?"

Kenni turned to Jazz with a mocking smile. "How many others will have to know, I wonder?"

"God, Kenni, Poppy's never recovered . . ." Sawyer

whispered in disbelief, his voice hardening at the
thought of keeping their father in the dark.

"There's no coming back from dead, Sawyer," she reminded him painfully, turning back to them. "Poppy
would be easier to get to than even the three of you. He's
cemented in those he trusts, and he trusts David. He always has. How many other Kin does he trust that far
who are aligned with whoever killed Momma?"

"Kenni, you need to come home," Cord growled despite the arguments as he glanced at Jazz. "Just because
Poppy gave him a few things he knew you loved and
Jazz built your dream house doesn't mean it's happily-
ever-after. That was then . . ."

"And this is now," she replied, her voice sharper
perhaps than she'd intended. "And I'm not going anywhere, Cord."

"Those are Maddox eyes, and Slade's lab contact
may have identified her DNA as Maddox, but I'm not
convinced she's Kenni," Deacon said then, his tone icy.
"Kenni wouldn't have hidden for ten years, she wouldn't
have denied her family the truth that she was alive, and
she wouldn't endanger the man she thought she was in
love with ten years ago."

"And Deacon would have known better than to
think I'm so easy to maneuver," she snorted as she began pushing the laptop, DVR, pictures, and files into
the leather bag. "The three of you need to figure that one
out now."

"You're not protected here, Kenni," Cord argued.
"Slade has his own family to think of, that just leaves
Zack to help . . ."

"She said she's not leaving." Jazz didn't raise his voice

or issue a threat, but the tension in the room intensified significantly.

She knew how the bone felt between two dogs now.

"Kenni's not one of your playthings, Jazz. It's been ten years since you asked Poppy to let you see her, don't try to convince us whatever you felt for her then still exists now," Deacon argued, his expression glowering.

Kenni didn't think she could bear to hear the answer to that accusation.

"Enough, all three of you." Slapping her hand to the table, she turned to her brothers and let them see the outrage surging through her.

"Kenni, you're still our sister," Cord bit out before she could say anything more. "Our baby sister. The thought of losing you again—"

"Is one of the reasons I didn't want you to know," she cried out. "Do you think I'm not aware of how the three of you and Poppy hurt? Did you think I wanted you to have to suffer any further?"

"Then come home," he demanded, his tone low. "Come home, Kenni."

But she was home. She could feel that truth in every fiber of her being. It wasn't just the house, the pool, or the gazebo. It was Jazz and part of her soul refused to let the dream of belonging to him go as so many other dreams had been lost.

It had to be her choice.

Jazz kept reminding himself that he couldn't make her stay, and he couldn't place his fist in any of her brothers' faces, unless they tried to hit him first. He rather doubted he could push them into hitting him first right now.

That didn't keep him from glaring at them.

Son of a bitch, he was almost scared they were going to talk her into leaving.

Cord would be the one to persuade her, he thought. She'd always been closer to him than the others. For years she'd been his shadow, trying to follow him everywhere he went.

"No, Cord." Her tone was firm, firm enough that she had her brothers looking at one another as though seeking answers. "I'm fine here. For now."

"And when this is over?" Deacon asked then, shooting Jazz a dark look. "When it's safe to go home, will you go? Or are you going to wait until he's finished with you? Until he's convinced you what great and wonderful friends the two of you can be while everyone's laughing at you behind your back?"

"Enough." Jazz stepped forward, placing himself at Kenni's back, ready to get her the hell out of there as both Slade and Zack moved to the ends of the table, bracketing the Maddox brothers. "Get the hell out of here, Deacon, before I end up pissing her off and teaching you a few manners."

Deacon's bark of sarcastic laughter loosened the leash Jazz normally kept on his temper. "Manners? Like yours, Lancing? The kind where you keep your damned mouth shut and don't tell us our sister is alive?" he snapped. "You should have contacted us immediately."

"Cord you should leave now," Jazz drawled with icy fury, lifting his hands to Kenni's shoulders as she started toward her brother, fists clenched, fine tremors racing over her body. "And get Deacon the hell out of my house until you can convince him to have a civil tongue while he's in it."

Deacon was getting madder by the minute, Jazz realized, and he didn't need that right now. Hell, Kenni didn't need that right now.

"You're making a mistake, Kenni." Deacon focused on his sister, his brows lowering as the anger raging through him darkened his gaze and hardened his expression. "You've been in Loudoun long enough to know what they say about his women."

"And what would that be, Maddox?" Jazz pushed Kenni behind him and stepped closer to the other man. "Go on, push some damned stupid insult out of your mouth about a single woman I've been linked to. Be that stupid man, so I have the excuse I need to kick your damned ass."

"Stop this." Kenni managed to push herself ahead of him again, moving to place herself between the two of them before Jazz pulled her back. "Deacon, this is enough. Right now."

The tension in her voice, the hurt was enough to send adrenaline pulsing through him. She'd been hurt enough in the past ten years; he'd be damned if he'd let her brothers hurt her further.

"Kenni, come on. Ten years and the man has never had a serious relationship." His bark of laughter was cutting. "Does that sound like a man you want to bet your heart on?"

"I bet my heart on him when I was sixteen and the three of you told me to stay away from him or you'd break his bones," she cried out then, surprising Jazz with that bit of information. "I didn't listen to you then, Deacon. I went to Poppy instead, and from what I've heard, he reined your asses in." Jerking from Jazz she stepped closer to her brothers, outrage and anger trembling through her. "Say one more nasty word to or about Jazz and I promise you, when I do go to Poppy, I'll tell why I won't be moving in, coming to visit him, or attending any holiday meal or party thrown in his home. Because my brothers are too possessive and too damned superior to accept that I have enough common sense to make a decision for myself, despite the fact that I did play a rather large part in keeping my own ass alive for ten years."

She didn't yell, she didn't have to. The minute she mentioned going to her father the three men backed down with their proverbial tails tucked and stayed there.

"Don't punish me," Sawyer muttered, giving Deacon a hard push to the door. "I didn't do anything."

"Poppy didn't care ten years ago if you were part of it or not. You let him open his big dumb mouth so you were just as culpable. Has his opinion on that changed?" she questioned them harshly, but even Jazz knew the answer to that one. Poppy hadn't changed one whit.

"Not hardly," Cord muttered, stomping to the back door before turning back to Jazz with a killing stare. "Don't let anything happen to her, Jazz. Nothing."

Jazz crossed his arms over his chest and met Cord's glare with one just as antagonistic. "Anyone will have to go through me, Marcus, and Essie to get to her," he informed her brother. "And you know yourself, trying to get through me isn't something that's considered advisable."

"The problem is, there's a lot of things about you that aren't considered advisable. Especially when it comes to women," Deacon snorted though he was already on his way out the door.

Tightening his jaw, Jazz forced himself not to follow the Maddox brother out the door and teach him the manners he'd obviously forgotten over the years. Instead, he turned back to Kenni.

Once again she lifted the pack containing her laptop and the DVR and headed for the doorway.

"Kenni, are you okay?" There was something about her expression, her eyes, that bothered him, that made his chest ache.

She did things to him no one ever had, made him feel things he hadn't realized he'd never felt before, and none of it made sense.

"I'm fine, Jazz." the assurance did nothing to relieve the tension building in his senses. "I'm just tired. I'd like to take a nap, I think."

He glanced at Slade and Zack as they, too, watched her, the curious concern in their expressions mirroring his own.

Hell, what had he done?

As she disappeared through the hall on the other side of the television room, he turned back to Slade.

"What did I do?" Hell if he knew, but damned if he didn't feel guilty all the same.

Slade just shook his head.

"Some things a man has to learn on his own, Jazz," he finally chuckled as he headed for the back door. "I think I'll go take a nap myself. I swear, you two are enough to make a man tired. Real tired."

Glancing at Zack, Jazz lifted his brow questioningly. The other man just shrugged as though to say it was hard damned telling when it came to Slade.

And that was the damned truth.

CHAPTER 16

He found her in the bedroom, the balcony doors now closed as she stood to the side and looked out on the edge of the valley as it met the slope of the mountain rising over it.

"Deacon and Sawyer left," she said as he moved across the room to stand several feet from her. "Cord's still out there, though, just above that table rock that looks out on the pool." Somber knowledge filled her gaze. "He thinks I didn't see him slip into the tree line."

Evidently her brother didn't have a lot of faith in his ability to protect her or in her ability to survive.

"Well, there go my plans for skinny-dipping."

The look she gave him was one of exaggerated disbelief. "Then you weren't intending to do so anyway. You wouldn't let Cord stop you."

His brow lifted. Shooting her a grin, he inclined his head in acknowledgment. "That's true," he agreed. "But if you want to skinny-dip, sweetheart, I'll make sure it happens for you."

He'd made certain she had her house, the gazebo with

the bed in it, the pool, and everything else she'd mentioned she would have on the property if it were hers and he'd never imagined for a moment she'd enjoy it in any way.

"Yes, you would," she whispered, and in her eyes he could see the knowledge of the same memories that drifted through his mind. "God, Jazz, you confuse me."

Of course he did. In the ten years she'd been running she'd known very little warmth or gentleness. It had been all about survival, about living one more day.

And Kenni was a survivor. As much as he hated it, as much as it enraged him that she'd been forced to learn the skills to survive, still, he respected the strength he saw in her.

It challenged him, though. It made him want to see how far he could push her personally, how deep that vein of independence and defiance went when it came to her lover.

"Because I'd make Cord lurk somewhere else so you could go skinny-dipping?" He lifted a brow curiously. "That's more self-preservation, sweetheart. You know I'd have to go and get me some of that." He nodded toward her with a wicked lift of his brows. "And that's not something we'd want him to witness."

She shook her head to that and he almost grinned. Of course, that gleam of future retaliation he saw in her eyes was something he was going to look forward to.

Moving away from the curtained doors, she stared around the bedroom for a long moment before turning back to him.

"What are we going to do now?" she asked, running

her hands through her hair and staring back at him with narrowed eyes.

"What do you want to do now?" he asked in return. "No doubt whoever went through the house was watching it after they left. That's what I would do anyway. They'll know who you're with and where you are. Cord knows that as well, that's one of the reasons he wanted to hustle you back home, where he believes you'll be more secure."

She was shaking her head even before he finished. She knew that wasn't her best bet.

No one had ever accused her of being a dummy. Confused perhaps, too damned stubborn and independent definitely. But she was smart. She always had been.

"That would be the worst thing I could do," she murmured before moving to her pack, lifting it to the bed, and loosening the leather flap while frowning thoughtfully.

"We've pushed and now someone's messing up." Leaning against the dresser behind him, he watched her unpack the clothes she'd had hidden somewhere. "We just need to push a little more."

"A little more push could find us in a sniper's sight," she warned him. "That's not a pleasant place to be."

And she would know. She'd been there more than once.

He had to take a careful hold of his control, something he could feel slipping, tugging at his determination to use caution now.

The hell she'd endured for the past ten years was

pissing him off more by the day. Facing her brothers had been incredibly difficult as well. So difficult she'd immediately distanced herself, pulling back and placing an invisible mental shield between herself and the three men she'd adored as a young girl.

"We're not going to figure it out right now," he warned her, coming to that realization himself. "What we can do, though, is see about getting something to eat and maybe going through the information you've pulled together so far." Straightening and dropping his arms from his chest, he gave her a hard look. "You shouldn't have waited to let me see the files and pictures you have, Kenni. You should have let me know you had the information."

"There's a lot of things I probably should have done over the years, Jazz," she stated wearily, moving past him. "Add that one to it."

Catching her arm Jazz pulled her to a stop and smiled down at her, carefully restraining the need to let the impulses rising inside him free.

"Are you learning from your mistakes, though?"

"Who said I made a mistake?" Soft, challenging, the dare in her voice had his body hardening as though he hadn't just taken her a few hours before.

Catching her free wrist before she could avoid him and securing it behind her back with the other, he stared down at her. The wildness reflected in her deep, emerald-green eyes was a match for the core of wildness that burned inside him.

Hell, he knew she was a match for him, in every way. He had a feeling she was too concerned with protecting those she loved than she was with understanding the emotions she didn't know how to deal with.

"I said you made one, cupcake." The assurance slipped past his lips before he could call it back, the need to force the emotions she kept so carefully contained, free, nearly overwhelming.

But that need had only been growing since the day he'd met her. Since he'd stared into hazel eyes and seen fear and mystery that were so much a part of her.

Her eyes narrowed. "Cupcake? Really, Jazz?"

"Soft, sweet, and so very edible," he assured her, his voice lowering as her lips parted, her subconscious sensuality peeking out, tempting him.

Lips trembling, her gaze flickered from his, though her body softened further. The contradictions in her would keep him guessing for years.

If he could keep her with him.

"Now, we have two choices considering you haven't eaten today. Dinner, or that bed over there with me between your thighs, riding us both to exhaustion. That won't take long for you, I'm guessing."

Shadows were already gathering beneath her eyes and her face was paler than it had been that morning. Her expression was strained with tension, with tiredness.

"Dinner," she snapped.

When she pulled against his hold again he let her go, slowly.

The need to touch her, to have her, was like a hunger he couldn't sate now. The need to take care of her was just as strong, he was realizing. To ensure she was safe, protected. Nothing else mattered, not even the lust that dug sharp little claws into his balls.

"Dinner," he agreed, stepping back from her before running his fingers restlessly through his hair. "Definitely dinner."

"How long before it's going to slip, Jazz?" she asked, carefully moving several feet out of his reach.

"Before what slips?" If he didn't get out of the bedroom and away from that bed, the image of her beneath him out of his mind, then there was no way she'd get dinner first.

"Whatever you're holding back," she retorted as though she knew what the hell she was talking about. "What are *you* hiding, Jazz, and how much longer can you actually keep it hidden?"

"You better hope I keep it hidden until I figure out how to leash it," he warned her. "Because trust me, darlin', that's an animal you just don't want to deal with right now. Not at all. Now, let's go see about dinner." He strode to the doorway before turning back to her. "Should I lay out a steak for that asshole brother of yours?"

Her eyes narrowed, lips thinning at the mockery in his tone.

"Might as well," she answered him, her sugary politeness when combined with the dare in her eyes almost more than he could resist.

"I'll do that then." Nodding shortly, he left the bedroom and the woman.

He really needed to feed her first. She was going to need her strength.

* * *

Who did he think he was fooling?

After eight years on the run with Gunny and meeting countless military types, she'd learned to recognize what one marine's outspoken girlfriend had called a vein of pure dominance in a class A sex machine.

The explanation that went with it had left her blushing for days. Now Kenni could well understand why the girlfriend had seemed so very smug.

That particular girlfriend hadn't been dealing with more than just the sex machine, though, while she was, Kenni thought morosely. She was dealing with a protective sex machine, something she'd never imagined coming up against.

The fact that he'd been incredibly aroused wasn't lost on her, either. She'd escaped, probably in the nick of time, though she didn't doubt for a moment it was because he'd let her go.

Moving into the kitchen behind him she watched his back carefully, left the gate opened just enough for Squirrel to slip in behind her, then moved to the table where she sat down. Lifting the puppy to her lap, she was amazed at how heavy he was, and the fact that hiding him wasn't really going to happen. He was too intent on giving puppy kisses to her cheek whenever she couldn't avoid him.

"That pup is going to think he's allowed out here," Jazz warned her as he moved to the back door.

"So?"

"So, it's not fair to the rest of them, and if the rest of them are out here then we'll have a mess you do not want to clean up, I promise." Before she could answer the charge he was out the back door, his deep voice booming. "Maddox, get your ass in here if you want a steak."

Kenni winced. No doubt his voice had echoed all across the valley. She could almost see Cord's irritated expression. If he was trying to actually catch someone who may be watching, those hopes had just been dashed to hell and back.

"There, he was invited." The door slapped closed behind him.

"It was your idea to invite him." Shrugging, she watched him with narrowed eyes as Squirrel finally curled up on her lap and settled down.

"I was being facetious," he informed her, his voice and his expression bland as he moved to the refrigerator.

He was not. He knew damned good and well Cord would have gone nuts when Jazz began grilling the steaks. Jazz wanted to irritate him with the bellowing invitation, nothing more. Come to think of it, those two had never really been able to get along despite the fact that she knew they were friends.

Kind of friends anyway.

"That's what you get for being facetious," she informed him as though he were serious. "Perhaps next time you'll forget the facetiousness."

He tossed the steaks to the counter as the back door opened with a firm push.

"Lancing, you have a big mouth," he snapped.

Jazz pretended to ignore him. Washing his hands quickly, he turned back to the steaks and began tearing them out of their white paper.

Her brother pulled a chair from beneath the table and

sprawled out in it before his hooded gaze slid in her direction.

"You have one of those damned pups at the table, don't you?" he asked as he crossed his arms over his chest, tucked his chin lower, and just stared back at her.

"Don't start, Cord. The pup isn't hurting you." He'd never let her have any fun, she remembered now. "Besides, Jazz knows where it's at so you're not really snitching."

"I don't snitch," he muttered as Squirrel began moving about restlessly at the sound of his voice.

She was definitely going to have to teach the dogs to bite Maddox men when they were being asses.

"Then leopards really do change their spots and Santa will be arriving via Jazz's fireplace this year." She shrugged before rising and moving to the gate, where she put Squirrel back in the television room.

"That fat bastard comes down my fireplace and I'll shoot him," Jazz snorted.

"No kidding." Of course Cord was in complete agreement.

"He wouldn't come see you two anyway," she promised them blithely. "You're on the bad list."

"Well, doesn't that just break my little heart," Cord stated with a definite lack of any such pain.

At one time, when she was younger, she would have told him he had to have a heart first. All in the spirit of sniping back at him. She couldn't do that now. All their hearts had been laid bare and left to wither.

Now she just rolled her eyes at him, unwilling to continue the game that had begun farther back than she could remember.

"Mom would have told us the kitchen table was the wrong place for ill words and insults," he said gently as he leaned forward to rest his arms against the tabletop. "But she would be laughing at us right along with Pop, wouldn't she?"

Kenni shook her head. She couldn't talk about her parents, not yet. She'd lost not just her mother that night, but Poppy and her brothers as well. She'd lost far too much to be able to discuss it until she knew that what was left, would be safe.

"You can't hide forever, Kenni," he warned her then, his voice resonating with tenderness, with heartache. "You can try, but it's not in your nature to isolate yourself to the point that you can't love or be loved in return."

"I've been hiding for ten years." Turning her head back to him she stared into his eyes, hoping he could see her determination as easily as she could see the arrogance in his face.

"Did you?" he asked softly. "No, baby sister, you weren't hiding, you were running—but you weren't alone. Once Gunny was gone, though, you came home to those you loved and who loved you, knowing damned good and well one of us would realize who was hiding behind the colored contacts and hair dye."

Had she?

Was that what she'd been doing, endangering them with her subconscious need for them?

"Kenni . . ."

"Cord, shut the fuck up and give her some space or take your ass back up that mountain." Jazz's hand descended on the table in a flat-handed blow that had her flinching violently.

Jerking her gaze from her brother, she stared up at the savage lines of his profile and the menacing look on his face.

Cord sat back slowly, his gaze on Jazz, narrowed and thoughtful for several heartbeats.

"You can't protect her feelings while trying to save her life, Jazz," he breathed out roughly. "You know it just doesn't work that way."

Jazz's head lowered, the menace on his face turning to outright intent backed by icy fury. "Test me again," he dared her brother. "Go ahead, Cord, keep testing me and I'll test my fist against your head. You understand?"

"Jazz," she whispered, hoping to dampen the air of violence beginning to pulse through the room.

"You understand me, Cord?" Jazz pushed, his voice only deepening, growing darker.

Two heartbeats later Cord nodded slowly, his lips quirking in acknowledgment that Jazz had won this round. For the moment. "I understand, Jazz," he assured him. "Now why don't you stop playing Kenni's shield and fix those steaks. You always were too damned testy when you were hungry."

The tension eased enough that she could breathe without the horrifying fear that these two men were going to try to kill each other across the kitchen table.

But the question Cord had raised still whispered through her mind, poking at her, prodding at her conscience. She'd told herself she'd come back to Loudoun to find the person who had killed her mother and destroyed her own life. Finding that person was beyond her abilities without help, though. Without the help of someone who knew and understood the Kin.

And more than once she'd wondered how she was going to face another day without her family and the man she loved.

The question now was, how would she face another day if she got one of them killed?

The steaks were grilled and eaten in silence, the anger coursing through Jazz finding no outlet, no way of discharging the tension thundering through him. And that was a first for him.

He'd learned how to control the fury that raged through his too-big body in his early teens when expending it meant possibly hurting someone without intending to.

The tricks he'd learned in those early years and had depended upon into adulthood weren't working now. Cord was pushing Kenni, trying to force from her what even Jazz refused to attempt to force from her. Cord would batter down the shield she'd placed between herself and those she loved. Jazz wanted her to release it willingly. Taking her heart wasn't what he wanted. There would be no satisfaction in stealing it, none in forcing her to give it to him. He wanted her to release it willingly. She had to come to him because she ached for him as desperately as he ached for her, because she couldn't face the next day without him.

Fuck.

He was in love with her.

He nearly dropped the wire brush he was using on the grill as the knowledge seeped into his senses.

He loved her. He'd loved her when she was sixteen and too damned young for the man he was becoming and he loved her even more now. Loved her until she was buried in his heart so deep that she filled his soul.

And there was a chance she would never release the distance she'd placed between herself and losing anyone she loved. The distance that ensured she held back the part of herself that would die with those she loved, if they died for her.

Pulling two beers from the cooler on the other side of the grill, he sat down on the bench built into the deck and unscrewed the cap with a violent jerk of his wrist. Tipping it to his lips he drained the bottle, tossed it to the trash, and opened a second with the same quick, angry twist.

Son of a bitch, he was going to kill the bastard who did this to her. To them. The gentle heart she'd once had wouldn't have known reserve or limits. She would have loved him without a thought to protecting any part of herself or holding anything back.

He'd lost that. Before he'd ever had it, he'd lost it.

"Babying her isn't going to fix her, Jazz." Cord moved slowly along the deck from the kitchen, a bottle of liquor in one hand, two glasses in the other.

"That's my best whiskey, Maddox," he sighed.

Cord snorted at the comment. "You think I was going to pick up that rotgut shit you keep for folks you don't like?" Sitting down heavily a few feet from him, the other man placed the glasses on the bench and filled them halfway before sliding Jazz's closer and placing the bottle between them. "Have a real drink, maybe it'll help clear your head."

"Or break yours," Jazz suggested instead. That actually seemed like a better alternative.

Cord chuckled. "Hell man, I think you've forgotten how damned stubborn that girl has always been. If she decided she was going to do something, then she did it. She wanted to learn to hunt when she was fucking five." Amazement still filled the other man, Jazz realized. "Five, Jazz. This pretty little princess who dressed in frills, lace, and ruffles, and she wanted to learn how to hunt." He shook his head. "The first time she tried to follow me she was wearing sneakers, striped tights, a black ruffled skirt, and some tiger-print little velvet jacket mom bought her for a party. I could hear her coming for a mile and she thought she was being quiet." Cord tossed back the drink and poured another. "She had her first buck that fall, even helped dress and skin it. She declared the whole process 'gross' and went back to her lace and ruffles until she was twelve and wanted to make sure she hadn't forgotten how to do it." His gaze met Jazz's, amusement lurking behind the pain that filled the green eyes. "She had her first buck before I did and before I got to her she'd nearly completed field-dressing it." He shook his head. "Dad had to teach her how to fish when she was three or four. Then when she was thirteen she was going to win that beauty pageant, remember?"

Jazz nodded, tossing back his own drink rather than think about the implications of what Cord was saying.

"She won, she was done," Cord whispered again. "Then she was gone. And I couldn't find her. I knew she was out there and I couldn't find her."

"And not once did you fucking tell me." Grabbing the liquor, Jazz refilled his glass then rose to his feet. "You didn't tell me she was alive. You never breathed a word that you were searching for her."

"She was my sister." Possession rang in his voice as Cord came to his feet, anger flashing in his face. "It was none of your business."

Jazz nearly staggered back at the declaration.

None of his business?

"She's a Maddox," Cord snarled. "You are not."

"Cord, go back up the mountain." Kenni stepped from the kitchen, her expression so fucking calm it made the bitterness in his stomach intensify.

"He's a big boy, Kenni," Cord drawled. "He can handle it."

"Go back home, up the mountain, hell, I don't fucking care, but take your attitude and your anger somewhere else. Now." Not once did her expression or her voice shift.

"And if I don't?" he challenged her.

The smile that curled her lips actually had her brother wincing.

"Then the next time you piss Jazz off I'm turning my back and letting him beat the shit out of you. How does that sound?"

Cord was silent for long moments before reaching back to rub at his neck while shooting Jazz a brooding look. "Is she serious?"

"If I'm lucky," Jazz promised him, wishing the other man would get cocky enough to warrant a fist to his dumb head. Kenni would forgive it then.

"Who says I won't beat the shit out of him?" Cord sneered.

"You might." She shrugged. "But he'll have the satisfaction of trying. Now, I'm going to shower and go to bed. I'm tired of refereeing for you tonight."

Turning, she moved back into the house, the weary droop of her shoulders a sign of the exhaustion he'd recognized earlier.

"Deacon and Sawyer will be here in a few hours to watch the house." Retrieving the drink he'd set on the banister, Cord tossed the remaining liquor back, grimaced, and stared at the empty doorway a moment longer. "That's not Kenni, Jazz," he said sadly. "Kenni's explosive, loving, she doesn't do anything halfway, and she doesn't hold back her heart. Is that really the woman you've waited on all these years? Really?"

"Whoever she is, Cord, she's the woman I've waited for," Jazz assured him.

Setting the liquor heavily on the small table next to the grill, Jazz stomped to the front door. "You owe me a bottle," he snapped before entering the house and locking the door behind him. Minutes later, the shades over the kitchen windows lowered. He set the alarm control for the house before heading to the bedroom and the woman still running.

And she would keep running, he realized, until something or someone stopped her.

CHAPTER 17

"Is there a reason you feel the need to wake me?" Scratchy, drowsy with sleep, Jazz's voice rumbled through the fog-shrouded morning light.

"Because I need you," she whispered, the hunger for him rising hotter, charged with needs and hungers she no longer tried to make sense of.

Thick, heavy black lashes eased open and electric-blue eyes peered back at her with a matching heat.

"How do you need me, Kenni?" he asked as she curled her fingers in the quilt and slowly began dragging it down his body. "You're overdressed, darlin'," he pointed out, callused fingers running up her arm to the narrow straps of the sleep shirt.

"I can remedy that," she promised.

She was going to remedy it as soon as she pulled the blanket free of his body. As it cleared his erection, though, she paused.

Good gracious.

Thick, heavy, a blunt spear of iron-hard flesh rose from between his thighs, lying nearly to his navel.

"Had I taken a moment to pay attention here, perhaps I would have had second thoughts," she murmured, running a finger down the heavy, throbbing vein that ran the length of the shaft.

"I would have convinced you." He grinned.

Oh, he was cocky, so very certain of himself. Jazz was like a force of nature, never changing course once his mind had been set and wearing away resistance as though it had never existed.

"Possibly," she agreed.

"Definitely," he promised her. "So, do you remove that very pretty article of clothing or do I tear it from you?"

A shiver raced up her back at the thought of him tearing it from her body. The image was completely sexy. But the thought of other alternatives, of being brave, of pushing her own boundaries, was sexy as well.

Easing to her knees, Kenni gripped the hem of the gown. Slowly, her eyes locked with his until the material blocked them as she eased the gown over her head and tossed it from the bed.

"Damn. How perfect," he sighed, a grin tugging at his lips. "Touch them for me."

Her brow arched. "Afraid you don't know how?"

"Oh, I know how," he promised wickedly. "I want to see how you do it. How do you pleasure yourself, Kenni?"

"How do you pleasure yourself, Jazz?" she asked then. "You show me and I'll show you."

Strong, broad fingers circled the base of his cock as his breathing grew harder, heavier.

"I pleasure myself with thoughts of you, darlin'," he

breathed out roughly. "Wondering if you're thinking of me. If you're pleasuring yourself with those thoughts and how damned sexy it would be to watch."

Oh, she had, many times.

Tipping her head back, she gave him what he asked for. Finding one of the hard, sensitive tips of her nipples, she slid her other hand from between her breasts, down her stomach, to the bare folds already growing slick with the heat spilling from her.

Watching him, watching lust galvanize his blue eyes as they followed the path, Kenni slid her fingers along the narrow slit leading to the aching depths of her vagina. Pausing at the swollen bud of her clit she circled the bundle of nerves before finding that spot at the side, barely covered by the thin separation of skin, and stroked it slowly.

"Fuck. Kenni." Tight, the sound low and achy, Jazz breathed out her name as her legs parted farther. "Ah, baby, those sweet juices are spillin' for me."

She was lost in the look on his face, the sound of his voice as he watched her. Then her body electrified as the fingers of his free hand moved between her parted legs, two fingers tucking against the clenched entrance of her vagina before pushing slowly inside her.

"Yes," she whispered, her fingers stroking, rubbing against the throbbing bud of her clit. "Oh, Jazz . . ."

His fingers stretched her, heating her flesh further as he penetrated it by slow degrees.

"That's it, baby," he whispered. "Let that pretty pussy milk at my fingers. Fuck, when it does that to my dick it's all I can do to hold back. To keep from coming so damned hard I swear I've lost the top of my head."

His voice joined the sensations racing through her body, drawing her muscles tight, lashing at her clit, the sensitive flesh of her vagina.

"Come for me, Kenni," he whispered. "Let me feel you suck at my fingers like that tight flesh sucks at my cock . . ."

That fast. His words, the images, the thought of him coming inside her, that heat ignited an orgasm she could never hold back, sent her spiraling into that chaotic storm of sensation with a suddenness that had her breath catching.

At the first strike of ecstasy his fingers pushed hard and fast inside her, throwing her higher, spreading apart as her muscles clenched harder, tighter, pushing the pleasure deeper through her body, spearing parts of her soul she knew would never forget it.

Crying his name, shuddering, her body shaking with the tempest tearing through her, she was only barely aware of Jazz moving until he was behind her, pushing her forward and in the next instant he was working his cock inside the clenched, milking muscles of her pussy.

"Jazz . . ." she cried out as the fierce, fiery lash of sensation began racing through her again.

Thick, hard flesh pushed inside her, working in by increments as the clenching, orgasming flesh parted hesitantly around his cock.

Each thrust inside, each burrowing impalement tore a cry from her lips until his cock was locked inside her full-length, throbbing, pulsing, pushing her back into the race for ecstasy.

"You make me crazy." Coming over her, one arm locking beneath her hips to keep them raised, his lips moved to her shoulder, her neck. "Feel how tight you are around me, Kenni. So tight and hot."

She moaned at the explicit words, her hips arching back, fingers curling into the blankets as his thrusts became harder, faster. Pounding into her as she cried out for more, begged for more as his mouth settled at her neck and his teeth raked the sensitive flesh.

As though it were a trigger the added stimulation set off an explosion that encompassed her entire body. Shuddering, quaking at the extremity of the pleasure raking over her senses, Kenni heard herself crying out to him as the explosions threw her back into the storm and left her wasted and exhausted beneath him as he found his own release.

Heat spilled inside her, jetting against her gripping flesh, sinking inside her as another shudder of pleasure tore through her.

If she lost this . . . When she lost Jazz, she would grieve for the pleasure he brought her. She hadn't shed tears in so many years, but Kenni had a feeling that losing Jazz would give birth to a river of tears.

"You are an addiction," he rumbled against her ear as he moved, easing his weight from her to collapse beside her on the bed. "Better than any drug I've heard of."

No, that was Jazz, not her.

He was the drug, and she was hopelessly addicted.

Curling against his side as he dragged her closer, Kenni opened her eyes and stared toward the balcony doors.

"Is Cord right?" That question had followed her into the night. "Did I deliberately endanger all of you because I'm too weak to fight?"

He stilled against her, his muscles tightening dangerously before he pushed her to her back and rose over her to stare into her eyes.

"That's not what he said, Kenni," he growled down at her. "That's what you're trying to tell yourself so you can keep holding back, protecting your heart from loving anyone too much. That's what Cord was trying to tell you. You can't keep running from those who love you, not when all that love is bottled up inside you, ready to explode free. You'll kill yourself keeping it locked up like that."

"But I'm not doing that, Jazz," she whispered.

Was she doing that? She couldn't see it. She admitted to loving them, to herself. Her brothers, Poppy, Jazz . . . God, she loved Jazz until her heart ached. He was her heart, he was so firmly entrenched in her woman's soul that she couldn't get him out if she wanted to.

"Think about it, Kenni," he advised, and though it was done gently that flash of dark dominance, of strength, flashed in his eyes before he glanced at the clock. "Hell, Cord's due here in an hour or so. He texted late last night that he wanted to show us something."

The irritability in his voice distracted her for a moment.

"Cord means well . . ."

"Hell, Kenni, I know that, or I would have already shot him." Rising, he pulled on the cotton pants next to the bed.

Following suit, Kenni retrieved her sleep shirt then a pair of light lounging pants that went with it.

"Go shower." She nodded to the bathroom. "I'll let

the dogs out. Marcus and Essie will let you know if I have any problems."

The puppies were dancing around, obviously trying out their new housebreaking skills. Squirrel stood before her, whining pitifully as Jazz's expression tightened warily.

"Go." She waved him to the bathroom door. "I'll let them out and I might even consider fixing your breakfast."

His brow arched. "You can cook?"

"I am an excellent cook," she informed him with mock offense. "If you're very lucky, you just may have perfectly fried eggs, bacon, and homemade biscuits waiting when you come down."

She could see the avarice in his gaze now. Pure, manly greed for a favorite meal. There was also concern though. Letting her go without him bothered him.

"Come on Jazz, Marcus and Essie would pitch a fit if I needed you. You know that," she promised solemnly, only barely holding back her laughter.

"Eggs, bacon, and homemade biscuits?" Evidently he wanted to be certain his hearing was in good working order.

"I said so, didn't I?" she pointed out in exasperation. "Now go, or Squirrel will wet your floor again, and that I do not clean up."

Jazz turned and moved quickly for the shower as Kenni moved for the bedroom door.

Hook. Line. Sinker.

Jazz stared at the closed bedroom door as he slipped

from the bathroom and moved to where he'd put his phone on its charger next to the bed.

Pulling the cord free he flipped it open, hit Slade's contact, and waited.

"'Bout time you called," Slade asked wryly as he answered the call on the first ring.

He'd been waiting for him, Jazz knew. Hell, he should have called the night before but he'd been too busy watching Kenni sleep. Hell, watching her breathe.

"Yeah, I've been trying to piece some of this crap together," he sighed. "I was going over Kenni's files yesterday and something's nagging the crap out of me. Evidently it's bothering Cord, too. He texted last night, he's going to be here in about an hour. I was hoping you and Zack could show up as well."

"Zack came around the mountain yesterday to see if anyone was watching. He said Deacon and Sawyer had their eyes on the house."

"Yeah, they've been taking turns with Cord," he snorted. "Guess they don't trust me with their baby sister, right?"

A chuckle came across the line. "That's possible. I have a feeling it's too late to worry about her virtue, though."

"Damned straight." He grinned. "She's mine."

"We'll be there in an hour or so then," Slade assured him. "Have some coffee ready."

"Will do." Hanging up the phone he reminded himself to make sure Kenni knew company might be there for breakfast and hurried toward the shower.

What pulled him up before he reached the door he wasn't certain. The balcony doors were closed so he couldn't hear the dogs barking. Glancing out into the side yard, he noticed Marcus and Essie weren't romping on the lawn like usual.

Sliding over Jazz opened the lock slowly, cracking the door just enough to hear Marcus's and Essie's furious growls.

Son of a bitch. That sound from their throats only meant one thing.

Grabbing the phone, he hit the SOS.

He was dressed in seconds. Pulling on his boots, he checked the concealed knife tucked under the heel. Pulling his Glock from a drawer, he chambered it swiftly before pushing it into a holster and tucking it at the small of his back. Another he didn't bother holstering; that one he gripped in both hands before moving to the door Kenni had left just slightly cracked.

The house was far too quiet—unnaturally so but for the muted sound of the dogs' snarls and growls. Moving silently down the stairs, careful to make certain he stayed in the carpeted areas, Jazz paused before moving into the foyer where he could be seen.

From where he stood he could see the television room. Marcus was at the dog door, digging at the metal barrier blocking it. Foam spilled from his mouth as he snarled and barked at his inability to force his way in.

Essie was pacing the fence line, looking for a way out of the yard. God help whoever was in the house, because Essie knew what she was doing. She just hadn't been able to do it since conceiving the pups.

Ten minutes, he thought. Fifteen at the most before the cavalry would crash this little party after he sent out the SOS.

Unless Essie and Marcus were able to clear a jump to the balcony without the smaller deck next to the pool that Jazz had removed to keep Essie from hurting herself or her babies while she was pregnant.

Maybe it was time to install steps after all.

Marcus and Essie both must have been forced to hold themselves too long, Kenni thought she heard them race to the dog door with enough force that the hard rubber flap cracked behind them. A second later Squirrel yelped painfully.

Kenni rushed from the kitchen expecting to soothe him from his indignation at having his nose tapped by the rubber. What she didn't expect to see was a full-grown male booting her baby out the dog door before sliding the metal partition back in place.

The real shock came when he turned to face her, though.

"Colby?" shock dulled her senses for a moment as betrayal knotted her stomach with a strangle hold.

Colby Weston? It had been years since she'd seen him and his twin, Phoenix. They were—once again—cousins. But these cousins were much closer; their mother was actually a Maddox.

Turning, she sprinted for the hallway and the safety of Jazz's bedroom. Phoenix stepped around the corner before she could reach it, a weapon in his hand pointing straight to her.

"Shower just turned on," he told his brother. "He'll be a few minutes."

Colby sneered at the comment, his gaze raking over her maliciously.

"Jazz will kill both of you." She backed away, moving into the kitchen again and the little corner shelf on the other side of the room.

If she moved toward the knives, they would stop her. She knew they weren't completely stupid, otherwise Marcus and Essie wouldn't have been fooled.

"We'll have our business finished and be gone before he's out of the shower," Phoenix assured her, narrowing his eyes gleefully as she bumped into the corner shelf, her hands going behind her back to steady herself against it, and to grip the handle of the antique corkscrew lying on it.

She hoped Jazz wouldn't be upset if she bloodied it a little.

Or a lot.

Her fingers curled around the handle of the corkscrew as Colby advanced on her.

"And what the hell do the two of you think you're doing?" she snapped, so furious that the bastard had hurt Squirrel that holding on to her control was next to impossible.

"Come on, Kenni, you're not completely stupid," Colby drawled. "You know why we're here."

"If I knew I wouldn't ask," she bit out, hoping, praying to delay them long enough for Jazz to get downstairs.

"That fucking marine that was there the night your mother was killed?" he reminded her. "He had something we want. I assume you have it now?"

He actually sounded convinced that she had whatever it was he was talking about. This was the first she'd heard of Gunny having anything her mother gave him, though.

"He would have told me if he had anything," she snapped. "Mom was dead before he arrived that night."

"And she didn't have it," Colby snapped, growing angry, his expression turning cruel. "She gave it to him and you know it. So just hand it over."

"I'm telling you, Gunny didn't have anything."

Colby sneered again.

"Killing him was fun, Kenni. Almost as much fun as killing you will be if you don't have that SD card your mother stole and slipped to her bastard brother."

Gunny? They had killed Gunny? How? Gunny was so much stronger, more intelligent. It made no sense that they'd been able to do such a thing. Colby and Phoenix were far weaker in strength and intelligence than any who'd been sent after her.

"I don't know what you're talking about. If Gunny had anything he would have told me," she snapped, waiting.

Colby was close, moving slowly closer as Phoenix kept watch from the doorway.

"Come on, Kenni," Colby mocked her cruelly. "Give us the card and we won't hurt you like we had to hurt Gunny."

Kenni stared back at him, ice moving through her veins now, a calm settling over her as he moved closer. Almost close enough.

"You didn't kill Gunny. You're not capable of it." She was certain of it.

Colby laughed at the response. "He should have never returned to the warehouse alone. That was the mistake he made."

He smiled and stepped closer. That was where he made his second mistake. The first was breaking into Jazz's house to begin with.

When he was close enough to actually touch her, to lift his hand and strike her, Kenni struck. Gripping the wooden handle of the corkscrew she brought it from behind her back, slamming it in beneath the sternum on an upward angle. Feeling the twisted metal crunch through tissue before entering the heart with a hollow *pop*, she gave a quick little turn, watching his eyes widen as his heart ripped open.

Blood spilled around her hand as Kenni gritted her teeth, forcing herself to hold his gaze.

"Colby?" Phoenix called his name from the doorway.

Life bled from Colby's eyes just as Phoenix jumped forward. Pushing the lax body weight to the side Kenni moved quickly, sliding out of the way as the twin caught his brother's body in time to keep it from collapsing to the floor.

As satisfying as that was, she now had no weapon and Phoenix moved fast once he realized what happened. Though she was desperate to avoid the blow she saw coming, Phoenix still managed to deliver a fist to the side of her face, sending her to the floor as pain dazed her senses.

Damn, she hated this part. She'd never been able to take a blow to her face and come back easily. It was one part of the self-defense training Gunny had never been able to condition her to.

"Son of a bitch, you killed him." Phoenix sounded dazed. "He's dead."

Corkscrewing the heart seemed to have that effect, Kenni thought, pushing herself into a sitting position as she searched desperately for a weapon.

A cry dragged from her when hard hands latched in her hair, dragging her to her feet as her stomach lurched sickeningly from the agony.

Oh God, she was going to vomit!

"You fucking whore," Phoenix hissed in her face. "I'll kill you now." The barrel of the gun went to her temple. "You killed Colby."

"You're next," she promised, feral rage ripping through her. "Jazz won't let you live after this. And if he does, Cord sure as hell won't. Did you think I wouldn't tell them who I was after you killed Gunny? That I was in danger?"

"You're lying. Cord would have told me. We're best friends. He would have let me know if your bitch ass was alive," he snarled.

Kenni smiled back at him with icy disdain. "Are you sure about that, Phoenix? Or do you just want to be sure of it?"

If he didn't shoot her she would damned sure carry a bruise from the barrel digging into her head.

"You're dead."

"You don't have the fucking ball . . ."

"Kenni, those biscuits done?" Jazz called out from somewhere between the hall and his bedroom. "I'm a hungry man."

He was furious; Kenni could hear it in his voice. He'd really be mad once he saw how Colby was staining his nice tile floor.

She was whirled around, the gun barrel digging into her head as Phoenix gripped the hair at the other side to hold her in place.

"I want that card," he snarled at her ear. "Or you can watch Jazz Lancing bleed, too."

Something exploded in her senses then. See Jazz die? No. She couldn't. She'd seen her momma die; she'd had to walk away from Gunny's lifeless body. She couldn't see Jazz taken from her. She couldn't bear it.

"Hey, Kenni, did you lock the dogs out again?" Jazz called out as he stepped into the television room.

The puppies were howling at the door. Marcus was watching Essie as she jumped, only to miss her mark.

"Kenni?" he called out again, the weight of the Glock at his back tempting him to pull the weapon.

Kenni wasn't answering but he could hear the scuffle in the kitchen and terror lanced his soul.

Moving to the kitchen he stepped inside before coming to a hard stop and feigning surprise at the sight that met his eyes.

He took one look at Kenni's face before directing Phoenix Weston a hard look. The bruise already marring her creamy flesh was a killing offense. Phoenix Weston was a dead man.

"You know, I'm getting really tired of men thinking they can abuse my woman," he told Phoenix softly.

Kenni's lip was bleeding, her eye swelling. And she was favoring her right ankle. But she was alive.

"Fuck you, Lancing. She killed Colby. We weren't going to kill the bitch. But she'll die now." There was no small amount of panic in Phoenix's voice.

That panic wasn't a good thing.

"Who killed Colby?" He just wanted confirmation, but the bloodthirsty look in Kenni's eyes assured him he didn't need it.

"This fucking bitch." He jerked Kenni's head back by her hair as she struggled against him. "Stay still, you fucking cunt."

Jazz winced at the insult and the fury flickering in Kenni's gaze.

Jazz tsked softly. "Colby's staining my floor, Kenni. Blood is damned hard to scrub out of stone."

"It will give it character," she snarled. "The bastard kicked Squirrel. He deserved it." Then her eyes narrowed. "What took you so fucking long anyway?"

"I had to get dressed," he murmured, meeting her eyes and hoping she saw the warning in his.

"Primp," she snapped.

"Both of you shut the fuck up," Phoenix cried out. Damn, pressure really brought the bitch out in the other man.

"What do you want, Phoenix?" Jazz didn't waste any more time. Phoenix was becoming unpredictable.

Phoenix snarled back at him, his hand tightening in Kenni's hair.

"We were going to be nice and just collect the information her mother gave her," he spat out. "But she had to go and kill Colby."

"I don't have it." She followed the grating denial by swiftly striking an elbow into Phoenix's kidney, just as Jazz heard Marcus and Essie bounding behind him.

Jazz stepped aside, lifted his brows, and watched Essie take a leap for the kitchen table and throw herself at Kenni. Marcus was right on her heels, his object the gun in Phoenix's hand.

Powerful jaws locked on tender flesh as Kenni's assailant screamed out his horror, but Essie had grabbed a mouthful of Kenni's shirt and pulled her from his hold with enough strength that Kenni went to the floor.

"Hold!" Jazz ordered before the male could take Phoenix's throat out.

Marcus turned a growl on Jazz at the order, his teeth poised at a horrified Phoenix's throat as saliva dripped from razor sharp-teeth. Marcus was prone to show Jazz his displeasure with his teeth.

"Do it and your ass goes to the barn," Jazz growled right back at him.

Marcus let his teeth graze tender flesh over a throbbing vein as the scent of human urine brought a grimace to Jazz's lips. Dammit, the kitchen tile was going to be impossible to clean.

Marcus was satisfied, though. He moved back, only to jump for Jazz when the kitchen door slammed inward and Slade then Zack rolled into the room. Jazz only shook his head, pushing Marcus aside and moving quickly for Kenni as she grabbed Phoenix's gun and came to her feet with a graceful, well-trained twist of her body.

"Kenni." He moved between her and Phoenix."We need someone to question," he reminded her as he read the bloodthirsty anger in her eyes.

"He kicked Squirrel." There was no fear, no hesitancy in her. "Colby said they killed Gunny. They don't deserve to live."

"If that's true, then he'll die by my hand. I was the one who trusted him." Cord Maddox stood at the back door, flanked by his second-in-command, Banyon Maddox, and three Kin lieutenants.

Kenni stared at him icily. "See why I didn't want to tell you a damned thing," she charged as she threw her hand out to indicate Banyon and the three men Cord had served with in the military. "You can't keep your damned mouth shut." Jazz turned to Cord slowly, furiously.

Before he could speak Cord shot Kenni a dark frown. "Men die when they fight alone, squirt, Gunny should have taught you that. So do women." Then he turned to Jazz, his gaze narrowing. "Why doesn't it surprise me that once again you didn't even bruise your knuckles?"

Cord might have been giving the appearance of a man who didn't give a damn, but the raging pain and fury building in his eyes told another story. Still, it was no excuse, and Jazz wouldn't let it go. Cord should have never betrayed her then dared to walk into her home and say something so ignorant to her.

"The day isn't over yet, Cord," Jazz promised him as Kenni's expression paled and pain darkened her green eyes. "Not by a long shot."

CHAPTER 18

Getting Kenni to sit down and actually sit still long enough to check the swelling in her face wasn't easy. For some reason she felt the need to pace. As she'd done so, she'd glared at her brother and cousin, as well as the two men Cord had brought into the Kin from the team he'd fought with in the military.

John T and Axe, and that was all most people knew them by. Reserved, loners for the most part, but pure hell in a fight and they watched Cord's back whenever needed. Jazz knew he should have expected Cord to bring them in. That was a serious oversight on his part.

"You okay?" Jazz touched the bruise rapidly darkening and swelling further on the side of Kenni's face.

"I'm fine," she muttered, throwing a glare over his shoulder at Cord. "He just had to tell them, didn't he?"

The betrayal she felt wouldn't be easily wiped away. He'd figured that out in the beginning. That one piece of information, her identity, she felt endangered her family too much to reveal until her mother's killer was

found. By revealing it and bringing the men he'd revealed it to into the house, he'd sliced at her sense of
security, the small amount of safety she'd tried to find
in Jazz's arms.

Gently, he pressed the ice pack he had with him to
her face. "He trusts them with his life, Kenni. And unfortunately, he's right. You and Gunny against the Kin
going out after you, over and over again, made both of
you weak. Neither of you was to blame, though, I promise you that."

Uncertainty shadowed her eyes, haunted them. The
tears she kept trapped in her soul darkened the emerald color and filled them with a pain so deep, it went far
beyond what she obviously revealed in her face.

"He should have at least asked first." The betrayal
refused to abate, and Jazz couldn't blame her a bit. He
just understood it.

That didn't mean he was going to forgive it, just that
he understood it.

Kenni didn't much care at the moment, though. Slade
and Zack had taken Phoenix to the basement and that
left no one to expend her anger on.

She tried to rise from her seat again.

"Come on, Kenni, sit here with me for a minute," he
told her firmly, placing the ice pack on the side of her
face again. "Let's see if we can help the swelling here."

"I need to check on Squirrel . . ." She actually made
it to her feet this time.

"Squirrel is fine." Rising, he looped his arm around
her waist as she tried to move past him. "You're going
to sit right down here." He pushed her back into the

chair. "And let all that lovely adrenaline racing through you begin to crash so we can contain it."

Kneeling in front of her again, he watched her closely as Cord's men moved around the kitchen.

"What are they still doing here?" She glared at them. "He needs to take them and leave."

"And you need to sit still and hold that ice pack to your face," he ordered, wondering if anything could get through to her and her need to release the fury pounding through her.

Rising, he turned to drag another chair over to the side of the table when he felt her move again.

"I've had enough of this!" Jumping from her chair Kenni stalked to the steel barrier holding the puppies outside.

Squirrel was howling in outrage at the sight of her, his head tilted back like a wolf as he formed a perfect little O with canine lips. It would have been cute under other circumstances.

"Not yet, Kenni." Jazz caught her before she reached the barrier. "There are too many strangers here for Marcus and Essie to be comfortable with the babies romping around them."

She hadn't considered that. The remorse on her face was as clear as the shock and pain.

"I have to get out of here, Jazz." She rubbed at her arms, her pale face almost white now as she stared up at him beseechingly. "I can't just sit here."

She was going to explode at this rate, he knew.

"Come on, I'll take you upstairs then." Maybe a few minutes alone, without strangers moving around her, would help settle her down. God knew he could use a few minutes himself.

"Escaping, is she?" Cord drawled from behind them then. "I should have known that one was coming."

Jazz almost cursed as Kenni froze for a second before turning to face her brother and cousin.

"You know how he gets, Kenni," Banyon said with a grimace. "He's worse than a damned kid at a candy store when blood is spilling."

"Don't waste your time, Banyon. Kenni doesn't believe in letting family in any more. She's going to protect us all, ya know," Cord drawled from the kitchen doorway.

Lifting the cup of coffee he'd helped himself to he sipped at it lazily before tilting it in her direction in mock acknowledgment.

"And you're a moron," she snapped. "Someone should have neutered you at birth to halt the testosterone development."

A mocking smile tilted his lips. "Too late now."

"Like hell. One day someone's gonna show you different with the sharp edge of a good knife," she guessed. "I want to be there when they do."

"Little girl, that's not a day you'll ever see," he assured her, still laughing. "Hell, Kenni, you're so damned good at running I don't expect you to stick around past fall now."

She smirked back at him. "Oh, I'll still be here, Cord Maddox, if for no other reason than to prove you wrong."

He sipped at his coffee again, his expression thoughtful.

"Don't do it, Cord," Banyon muttered. "Jazz will retaliate."

"Come on, Banyon, what's there to retaliate over?" Cord mocked. "A sister who cut us out of her life ten years ago? I should have figured out why I couldn't find her all those years. It was because she didn't want to be found."

"Finally figured that out, did you?" she asked painfully, rising from the chair as Jazz straightened in front of her. "Took you a while, didn't it, Cord."

As she turned her back on them and left the kitchen, she would have been surprised had she seen Banyon's and Deacon's expressions, Jazz thought. Not that either of them said a word.

And honestly, Jazz had had enough of it. This picking and poking at Kenni by Cord, Deacon, or whoever else decided they didn't agree with her decisions was going to stop.

And it was stopping right here.

Turning to where Slade and Zack stepped from the basement, Jazz waved them out to the back porch. Cord would know better than to accept an invitation outside by Jazz. That left good old-fashioned trickery.

Not that Slade or Zack stupid. But whether they agreed or not, they would still help.

As Jazz moved to the back porch, Slade and Zack moved to each side of him.

The screen door hadn't even closed when Cord pushed out of it, glaring at Jazz when he moved around him to face him.

"Trying to hide something, Lancing?" he snarled.

Jazz smiled complacently before delivering an upper-
cut that lifted the other man from his feet, throwing
him back over the steps and to the grass in the yard.

And he wasn't finished with Cord Maddox, either.

Fuck!

What just exploded in his head?

And why the hell were rainbows twisting and screwing one another across his vision. Those freaky lights
were scaring the shit out of him. Especially as he felt
himself being hauled to his feet.

Swaying, Cord gave what he hoped was a hard shake
of his head.

Okay, they were going away now. No more weird
rainbows.

Reaching up and gripping his jaw, he worked it slowly
as he focused on the man in front of him.

"Jazz?" He stumbled just a little before Jazz caught
him. "Thanks, man," he muttered, shook his head again,
then frowned up at him. "Jazz, did you just fucking hit
me?" He had to blink again to chase away more rainbows.

Amazement filled Jazz's features.

"Cord, I just helped you up, man." He sounded pleasant enough. "Here, let me see what you've done to your
face."

Cord dropped his hand from his jaw.

Hell exploded in his abdomen then. His stomach was
shoved clear to his throat with a whole lot of help from
Jazz's fist. Before he could catch his breath Jazz delivered another iron-bitch fist to his jaw and Cord was sure
something broke this time.

He slammed into the side of the porch.

Ah fuck.

Shit. Dammit.

His legs went limp. Cord felt himself slide down the wall supporting the porch until his ass hit grass.

Fuck.

Jazz's fists had only gotten harder over the years.

He might actually puke. Maybe Jazz ruptured his stomach?

"Get up!" Jazz demanded furiously.

Hell no. That shit wasn't happening. Those freaky-ass rainbows scared him.

"Tell Kenni some bullshit like that again now," Jazz snapped. "Next time I'll break your face."

"It's the truth. She has to stop running." Cord coughed, barely managing to hold his breakfast down.

"Maddox, you wouldn't know the truth if it dry-fucked your ass," Jazz sneered. "You stupid fucker. You're so damned blind it amazes me you're still able to walk."

Cord stumbled to his feet, wondering where the hell Banyon had run off to.

"You're too blinded by lust to see what's right in front of you." Cord stumbled against the porch, keeping a wary eye on Jazz. "You're going to lose her if you keep babying her."

Jazz took a step closer.

"Dammit, Jazz, you hit me again and we're going to have problems," Cord warned him, slurring a bit.

Damn, his face hurt.

"Get off my property and stay off!" The order sounded serious.

Hell, Jazz sounded serious. Jazz had never thrown

Kin off his property, no matter their disagreements. And there had been a few over the years. Pop would be pissed over it, but once he found out it happened after Cord learned Kenni was alive and living with Jazz, then he just might throw Cord out of the clan for a while as he'd threatened ten years ago.

That just wouldn't do. Not at all.

Cord tried to laugh but shit, it hurt. "Come on, Jazz, we're going to figure out what the hell is going on here and then we're going to kick some ass. Kenni's going to be fine."

Jazz moved for him again.

"Hit me again, Jazz, and I swear to God I'll turn into the best brother she's ever imagined having and talk her home before you've realized what happened," he swore. "Go ahead, test me on it."

Jazz paused.

The problem was, he was pretty certain Cord could do it. He wasn't nearly so confident that she belonged to him totally yet.

"When you two are finished posturing, we might need to talk." Slade broke the stare-off he and Cord were having.

Turning his head, Jazz met the other man's gaze, frowning at the icy rage in Slade's eyes.

"Phoenix talk already?" Jazz questioned him. He hadn't expected that.

"You and Cord need to come to the basement," Slade informed him. "We came upstairs to get the two of you before you decided to try your fists out on his face. Phoenix is refusing to talk unless Cord's willing to make a deal with him first."

The Maddox Clan was notorious for not making deals. What Phoenix had done was a killing offense and one that no order had to go out on. Every Kin, in every state, would be gunning for him if he was seen.

"I'm always willing to talk." Cord shrugged.

He knew what Jazz knew. It wouldn't matter what Cord promised, the Kin would carry out the sentence. It was a check-and-balance system designed to ensure that certain laws within the Clan were never broken. The murder of a Clan member being rather high on the list. Phoenix should be aware of that and if he wasn't, then Cord wasn't required to inform him of it.

Moving stiffly, the elder Maddox limped back to the porch, and Jazz couldn't help but let a mocking smile tug at his lips. He may act as though the fight hadn't fazed him but his face looked like a bull had kicked it and he wasn't moving easily. It would be a while before he forgot what it meant to piss Jazz off now.

Moving through the house, Jazz paused long enough to give Marcus and Essie the order to join Kenni in the bedroom.

A heavy steel door secured the basement from the upstairs while another secured it from the outside entrance. Locking both doors ensured Phoenix stayed where Slade and Zack had left him. Of course, the hard nylon wrist and ankle restraints helped ensure he didn't escape.

Slouched in a hardwood chair, he sat morosely between the shelves of camping supplies on one side and several antique desks and sideboards on the other. In front of him Slade and Zack had pulled two chairs over to old wooden worktable Jazz sometimes used when repairing household appliances or lamps.

Moving to the table, Cord perched on a corner and stared back at Phoenix through one bloodshot eye. The other had already swollen closed.

"Jazz hits hard, huh?" Phoenix remarked despondently, more for something to say than anything else.

"What kind of deal do you want, Phoenix?" Cord wasn't wasting any time on the other man.

Phoenix must have expected that, though, because he didn't protest, just gave a small nod of his head before breathing in roughly.

"I know I'm dying as soon as I'm off Lancing's property," he stated without inflection. "I just want you to make sure I'm buried next to Colby. He was my twin. We've never been separated. I don't want to be separated from him now."

Cord just stared at him. Evidently, such sentiment from a man willing to kill another's sister was a little hard to take in. Jazz knew it had shocked the crap out of him.

"Fine, I'll bury both of you in the same hole, how's that, Weston?" he finally snapped. "If you know who's behind this and you have proof. Otherwise, I'll have you buried on opposite ends of the planet. You got it?"

"I have proof," he promised. "I told Colby we couldn't trust her and he wouldn't listen, but he helped me get proof, just in case. I have several meetings recorded and pictures of her killing Kin herself. I have everything you need. I swear."

"Where is it?" Cord wasn't taking chances.

"On the chain." He lifted his neck to display a heavy gold chain with a small silver-and-black pendant. "The pendant slides open on the back. There's a computer chip there. It has everything."

"Convenient," Cord murmured as Jazz moved to the other man and with a quick jerk of his hand snapped the chain from his neck.

Turning the pendant backward he saw the small catch that held the back on and released it. In it lay a small black micro SD card.

"Get Kenni," Cord suggested. "Have her bring the laptop. She has a right to hear this."

Turning, Jazz nodded to Slade to go after Kenni.

As Slade turned and moved quickly to the stairs, he turned back to Phoenix. "How did you get past my security?"

"She had one of the devices that overrides the security codes," he answered, his voice thick with the tears that dripped down his face now. "She gave it to Colby and told him to make sure he returned it by this evening. She'll be waiting for him."

"Where?" Cord rasped, the rough tone of his voice a sound that assured a man death was coming soon.

Phoenix flinched.

"You'll know once Kenni brings the laptop. You'll know where to go."

Glancing over at Jazz, Cord gave a brief nod as they waited.

Minutes later Slade escorted Kenni down the steps, laptop in tow, and led her to the table.

Her face was still far too swollen, but the ice she'd

taken up with her seemed to have helped. Her eye wasn't totally swollen shut, and the bruising seemed to have stopped at the mottled-blue stage.

Bastards.

"Are you sure about this?" she asked, opening the computer and powering it up.

He gave a brief nod as he stepped to her. When the screen came up he handed her the micro SD to slide into the reader.

"Wait." Phoenix's voice had them pausing and looking back at him.

"You might want to have her wait to see it," he suggested. "Warn her first."

"I don't need a warning," she told him softly then activated the reader as she stared at the screen.

Maybe she had needed a warning.

Maintaining her composure would have been impossible if Jazz hadn't been there. His arm slid around her back, giving her the support she needed to keep from falling when the first video began playing.

"Are you sure this is what you want?" Colby asked the slender, dark-haired woman.

Tiny almost to the point of being frail, her long dark hair trailing down her back, her composed features belying what she was ordering the men to do.

"Aren't I always sure?" She smiled complacently. "I was sure when I ordered my sister's death and I'm sure now that we know where that bitch daughter of hers is. Kill the marine too, Colby, we can't afford to have him looking for vengeance."

Colby sat back in his chair and smiled back at her.

"I'll take care of it, Luce. Now take care of me . . ." He was undoing his pants.

She didn't need to see that. She couldn't watch it. There were three video files, and dozens of pictures. The proof that Sierra Maddox's sister had planned her death as well as her daughter's was irrefutable. The end result was her marriage to Vinny Maddox and ultimately taking over the upper sect of the Clan called the Kin, rather than just the lower ranks of soldiers the Kin often used for backup or support.

For power. For the gold it was rumored the Maddox Clan had hidden in case of a national catastrophe as well as locations of other Clans and planned defense measures should the worst happen and America be invaded for whatever reason.

The locations and plans she had sold the second they were found. The gold she intended to move and keep for herself.

"She's insane," Cord finally sighed as Kenni closed the laptop silently, her hands resting on the lid to keep from clawing at Phoenix in rage.

"If Colby and I aren't there in a few hours, she'll know something's happened," Phoenix told them. "She has an escape plan out of the house to a small private airfield where she keeps a plane. She'll fly out before you realize she's left the mountain."

"She's not going anywhere," Cord assured him. "You'll be buried with your brother as you asked. You have my word on it."

Phoenix nodded, tears still falling from his eyes as his head lowered and he sat silently, waiting. He'd just be released once they had Cord and Kenni's aunt in custody. He'd be driven to the county line but Jazz sincerely doubted he'd make it more than a few feet before he met the business end of a Kin bullet.

"Upstairs," Jazz growled, taking the laptop from the table and keeping his arm carefully around Kenni as he led her to the steps. "Let's figure out how we're going to handle it."

They weren't handling it without her.

Moving woodenly, Kenni told herself she was fine. She had everything in working order, and now that she knew the truth she could hold herself together. It was just a matter of a plan, and Cord was wonderful with plans.

But inside, deep inside, she knew the truth. When the break came, when the shield that had protected her since the night her mother had died shattered, the exposure of all she had lost and the pain she had pushed back might destroy her.

"Slade, you and the others go on to the kitchen. Show Deacon, Sawyer, and Cord's men the evidence. We'll be down in a few minutes," Jazz stated as he headed for the stairs, drawing her with him as she fought to keep from stumbling, to make her legs move correctly, to keep her body functioning.

Shock perhaps? She didn't think she'd been in shock since that first night, just after seeing her mother hanging in a murderer's hands. The bullet in her shoulder, the horrific feel of having it cut from her, unable to pass out from the pain or the mental fury that kept exploding through her senses.

Gunny had knocked her out. She wished someone would be that merciful now.

The bedroom door closed behind them before she realized they had entered the room and Jazz was pushing her into a chair before hunching down in front of her.

"Look at me." The growl in his voice was firm, too demanding to ignore.

It hurt to meet his gaze. Her throat was so tight that swallowing was nearly impossible as the band around her chest tightened further.

She'd lived with that band for so long. Like a restraint encasing her heart, her soul, and it let her know it was there by restricting her ability to breathe, reminding her that she couldn't let herself feel whatever she was feeling. But now she didn't know what she was feeling. It was clawing at her chest, raking over something exposed and raw as Kenni fought to breathe through the pain. That band across her chest restricted her ability to do that, though; it weakened her and stole some of the hard-won control she'd prided herself on.

"Momma loved Aunt Luce," she whispered, remembering many of the conversations they'd had on their shopping trips. "She said Luce was always sick when she was young. Momma stayed with her and looked after her. She thought they were so close. And she knew that last summer, didn't she? She knew her sister had betrayed her."

Her chest actually hurt. A heart attack perhaps, she wondered fatalistically. How very apt. How many times could a person's heart be broken before it was irreparable?

"Maybe she didn't," Jazz whispered, his fingertips whispering over her cheek. "Whatever she was supposed to have, she didn't give you, and neither did your uncle. If she had known, Kenni, she would have called your father, your brothers. Wouldn't she?"

That made sense. It made more sense than to believe that her mother knew and would have put them both in danger. Sierra Maddox had always placed her children above everyone else. Above everything else.

The band loosened enough to breathe. Staring into Jazz's eyes she could feel his strength enfolding her, wrapping around her like a soft, age-worn quilt.

"I'm going with you." Her voice sounded stronger now. She could do this. She could see it through. "I have to face her."

"Kenni . . ." He began shaking his head.

"You don't want to push me out of this, Jazz," she warned him, determination hardening inside her. "I'm the one she's hunted for ten years. It was my mother, my uncle, friends who wanted only to protect me, that were murdered on her orders. Push me out and I won't forgive you."

His expression tightened dangerously. "You want to be a part of it, then show me you can hold it together until we're finished. You break in the middle of it, Kenni, and you endanger not just the Kin that follow us, but your brothers . . ."

"Don't treat me like a child, I know who will be endangered," she snapped, glaring at him. "I'm not sixteen, Jazz. I have it together."

He stared back at her intently for long moments

before his expression eased enough that the savagery softened minutely.

"Yeah, you do," he finally agreed. "Let's get it done then."

Straightening, he held his hand out to her. Strong, broad, it was callused and roughened, but gentle when he touched. And the offer he was extending to her was one she didn't mistake. Even Gunny had never shared her protection with her. He'd always pushed her back; he'd never extended his hand to her in an offer to be a part of it.

Laying her palm in his, feeling his fingers close around her hand gave her more strength than it should have. It gave her hope. And hope, she realized, was something she'd been living without until she returned to Loudoun. Until she returned to Jazz.

Rising, she stood before him and placed her other hand against his chest, just above his heart.

"Jazz," she whispered.

"Yeah, Kenni?" His lips brushed against her hair before he leaned back to stare down at her.

"On the ride to New York, I told Momma you were all I could think about," she whispered. "She said if there was a more worthy young man to be fascinated with, then she couldn't think of him."

"Your momma was a good woman. A smart one." His lips quirked with his trademark smile.

She'd told her mother she wasn't just fascinated, but that could wait, she decided. It could wait until the past was resolved and she had a future to look forward to.

"Ready?"

She nodded, still staring up at him.

When his head lowered, his lips covered hers in a kiss that bonded any part of her soul that might have been free. She felt him, felt the hunger and the need fusing together in a heat that was always there, always ready to warm her.

Holding tight to his arm as the fingers of her other hand pressed against his chest, Kenni let that kiss have her. Her lips parted, her tongue meeting with his, tasting the passion and the power of his hunger and becoming intoxicated with it.

He was like a drug.

Irresistible, addicting.

There was nothing as filled with pleasure, heat, and solace as his kiss and his touch, his possession and his passion. She'd dreamed of it, fantasized about him, yet she'd never come close to the pleasure she'd found in his arms and in his bed.

She had fought for eight years to return to him, she finally admitted to herself. She'd fought to survive, to live, because in the back of her mind she knew that dying meant never seeing him again. Never having a chance to touch him, or be touched by him.

When his head lifted he still held her close, his arms wrapped securely around her.

"I have you, Kenni," he promised, his voice soft, filling her with the knowledge that she wasn't alone anymore. "I'll always have you, right here. Whether you stay or leave, no matter where you go or what you do, baby, I have you."

He had her.

Did he know, though, he'd always held her heart? Ragged, often broken and filled with all the tears she'd never been able to shed, but still, he'd always held it.

Whether she held his or not.

CHAPTER 19

They really didn't need a plan. They had all the evidence they would need, Cord informed them when they stepped into the kitchen. But to enact Kin justice on the wife of a Clan leader, that leader had to be in agreement.

It wasn't just Luce they had to face, but also Kenni's father. And no one knew what he may or may not feel for the young wife he'd taken mere months after his first wife's funeral. Though her brothers were all in agreement that it wasn't possible their father had been messing with his wife's sister before her death.

Cord, Deacon, and Sawyer would return to the house and make certain Luce was there. Once they had the house secure and any chance she had of escaping eliminated, then Jazz and Zack would bring Kenni in.

Kenni could feel the nervous tension filling her as she sat in the truck with Jazz a mile from the house. She could see the top of the roof peeking from above the trees as childhood memories rushed through her mind. Many of those memories included Jazz. He'd been riends with her brothers for as long as she could remember. He, Slade, and Zack had been three of her father's favorites, and he often joked that if he could have handled more boys, then he would have adopted them.

There were other memories, though. The time she'd fell from the swing and skinned her knees. Cord had paled so alarmingly even Kenni, only five at the time, had stared at his face in wonder. Then he'd ordered her to never get on that swing again and swore he was going to cut it down.

She'd run to Poppy and he'd made it all right. He'd kissed her skinned knee, bandaged it, and even though he'd been in the middle of a meeting, he'd given her his time and love.

There had been picnics in the backyard, family reunions that often filled the grassy acre of land next to the house.

There hadn't been a family reunion since her mother's death.

As time passed, the tension increased inside her, twisting its way through her stomach and tightening sickeningly every time she let herself wonder what his reaction would be.

Would he welcome her? Would he denounce her?

The man she had known as her father would never denounce her, she thought, but ten years was a long time when a heart felt betrayed. If he felt betrayed by her silence all those years, then he could turn her away.

"We're in place." Cord spoke through the small transmitters he'd passed out before they'd headed to the Maddox mansion.

The earbuds tucked securely into the ear canal, almost

invisible but strong enough to both send and receive every word. Though not a lot had been said once her brothers entered the house.

Putting the truck into gear, Jazz drove along the street then turned into the drive as Kenni listened to her brothers pull everyone into place. Poppy came from his office, Luce was drawn from her rooms, and Luce's daughter, Grace, sent to a neighbor supposedly to babysit.

Cord had wanted her out of the way while her mother was dealt with. Once Luce was contained then Grace would be brought home and everything would be explained.

Explanations wouldn't help, though, Kenni thought as Jazz put the truck in park and turned off the ignition. Nothing would ease the painful realizations Grace would have to endure.

"I'll come around and let you out," Jazz forestalled her as she moved to open the door. "Stay still."

He was still trying to protect her.

Loping around the truck, he pulled the door open and extended his hand to her again. Taking it, Kenni held on desperately as she stepped from the truck and he led her up the short walk to the porch where Deacon and Sawyer waited.

"Poppy?" she whispered, almost breathless at the thought of seeing him again.

"He's in the front room," Deacon nodded, his gaze heavy as they entered the foyer.

Breathing in slow and deep, her fingers holding tight to Jazz's hand, she moved toward the living room.

"Cord, what's going on?" Luce demanded, her stri

dent voice overly loud as Kenni neared the open double doors. "I have things to do."

"Like meeting with Colby and Phoenix?" The latent violence in her brother's voice was like a lash of fury. "That meeting's been canceled, Luce."

Silence met his announcement for long moments.

"What are you talking about?" Luce demanded, the icy confidence in her voice almost amusing.

"Colby's dead. A corkscrew to the heart by the woman you sent him after will do that. Phoenix spilled his guts, though. Know what I'm talking about now?"

"I won't tolerate this." There was the fear.

"Sit your ass down and shut your fucking mouth." Vinny Maddox didn't raise his voice; he didn't have to. Years of commanding strong, independent warriors had given him a tone no one dared to disobey. "Cord? Would you like to explain yourself?" His voice softened slightly for his firstborn.

"Let's see if Luce wants to explain her side of the story first," Cord suggested.

"You're crazy. I have no idea what you're talking about."

"Then I'll explain it," Cord promised. "Pop, Mother wasn't killed as a strike against you. It was Luce's attempt to make certain the evidence Mom had against her never saw the light of day. Evidence of collaboration with Clan family members to take over the Kin and to steal information and possible gold locations for her own gain. I have the proof, Luce. Want to keep protesting?"

Poppy was silent for long moments.

"She had your mom and sister killed?" Her father's voice hardened, turned stony, merciless.

"No, Pop, she managed to have Mom killed. But Kenni escaped with Charles Jones, the brother Mom called Gunny. Kenni's alive."

"Where?" Hoarse, filled with hope, her father's question was all she needed.

Kenni stepped into the room.

She didn't speak. Her gaze went instantly to the still-tall, still-powerful form of her father where he sat in his recliner, his expression quieting so suddenly Kenni felt her heart collapse.

She had no idea what Luce or Cord said from that moment. Clenching Jazz's hand with both of hers now, she stared at her Poppy with a desperation she couldn't contain.

His hands clenched on the arms of his chair and slowly, so slowly he rose from where he sat.

Dark blond and brown hair had turned gray in many places. His deep, emerald-green eyes flared with emotion, his expression becoming eagle-fierce.

She wanted to breathe, but her lungs didn't seem to work as well as they once had. Her knees were weak, her heart racing so hard she was breathless.

"Poppy," she finally managed to breathe out, the tightening in her throat returning, her voice hitching, pain resonating through every part of her body.

"Kenni?" He took one step forward then looked behind her at Jazz desperately, and she knew who he was looking for. She knew that agonizing hope that filled his eyes and for the first time since she was eighteen her eyes filled with tears.

"Poppy," she whispered. "They took her." She had to swallow but a sob ripped from her instead. "They killed Momma."

His expression collapsed. Tears filled his eyes as her own gaze blurred and burned.

"Kenni. Ah God, my sweet Kenni . . ." His arms opened and Kenni hesitated only a moment before releasing Jazz and racing to him.

Jazz let her go, the tension he'd felt since the moment he'd realized she was alive evaporating.

The woman he'd brought into the Maddox home wasn't the lover he'd held in his arms for the past weeks. This woman was the sixteen-year-old girl who had lost everything in her world in one tragic, pain-filled night.

As Vincent Maddox clasped his daughter in his arms, Luce actually thought it a moment of weakness. Turning to run she barreled into Jazz when he moved into her path, nearly falling on her ass before Cord caught her.

Nylon restraints were snapped expertly around her wrists as several Kin waiting for that moment entered the room. The two men who had arrived at the house with Cord earlier as well as several others positioned themselves around the room to ensure that Luce didn't escape justice.

Vinny was holding Kenni to him like a lifeline now, father and daughter weeping with a loss ten years past, yet never truly faced until this moment.

Jazz stepped back as Cord, Deacon, and Sawyer joined their surviving parent and the baby sister they could now realize as part of their lives again.

Swiping his hand through his hair, he looked around the room. He wasn't needed here now, he thought wearily. This was a time for Kenni to share with her family; with her father and her brothers. He had no place here.

Turning, he left the room slowly, glancing back when he reached the doorway and letting the scene sink inside him. Kenni was home, that was what mattered. When everything had settled and she'd shed her tears with her family, then he'd come back. Maybe talk to her father again. Vinny was big on tradition sometimes.

Until then, it was time to go.

"Jazz?" The sound of her voice as he slipped past the doors drew him back. "Jazz, you can't leave."

Tears covered her face, and that need for him that he'd longed to see in her eyes was there.

She'd stepped away from her father, from her brothers, and they all stared at him like the interloper he'd feared becoming. All of them but the one who mattered most, the Maddox Princess.

His Kenni.

She reached out her hand to him. "You can't leave . . ."

He shook his head slowly but went to her and took her hand to pull her against him and lay a kiss at the top of her head. "I'm not going anywhere, baby, just right outside with Slade and Zack. I'll be here when your Poppy's ready to let you go for a minute. How's that?"

"Thank you," she whispered as he pulled back and stared up at him, those tears still filling her eyes. "Thank you, Jazz."

He brushed one from her cheek with the pad of his

thumb. "Don't thank me, sweetheart. No thanks are needed. Just remember, I'm right outside the door."

"You won't let me go," she whispered. It wasn't a question.

"No, Kenni," he promised. "I won't let you go."

Releasing her to her father once more, he turned and left her with her family.

He had a chance, he told himself. A chance was all he needed to ensure she always ran back to him.

Where she belonged.

Joining Slade and Zack on the front steps he sat down slowly, glanced at them, and let out a hard breath.

"She'll be safe now." Once Luce was taken care of, once Kin justice took care of her, then Kenni's life would be hers again.

"Looks like it," Zack agreed.

"Tell her you love her yet?" Slade asked, the amusement in his voice pulling a frown to his brow.

Jazz frowned. "She knows." Didn't she?

"Bet she don't," Slade murmured.

"A hundred says she doesn't have a clue," Zack bet.

"Two hundred she moves in with Daddy within twenty-four hours."

"A thousand says there's not a chance in hell . . ." Jazz wouldn't allow it.

24 Hours Later

Jazz let her get as far as packing that single leather pack she'd brought from the house days before. Sitting back in the easy chair next to the balcony doors, he kept his mouth shut and just watched and listened.

"Everything is still so messed up," she was saying. "Daddy's really upset over Luce . . ."

No doubt, bitch had killed his wife and conspired to kill his daughter. What had Luce expected? Rather than turning her over to Clan justice, though, Vinny had turned her over to his bosses, a division of the Department of Justice. One that didn't look kindly on anyone attempting to sell their secrets.

"It won't be for long . . ." Kenni continued.

Jazz just waited.

"Sawyer and Deacon will feel more comfortable as well," she stated.

Fuckers, both of them, he thought furiously.

"You'll have your life back, Jazz." Her voice cracked when that slipped out of her mouth.

He stared back at her, his arm propped on the chair, one finger sliding back and forth over his chin.

Kenni's gaze flickered nervously. "Jazz?"

"I love you, Kenni," he said.

She seemed to freeze before her lips trembled in reaction. "What did you say?"

Jazz rose from the chair and moved to her slowly.

"Didn't you know, Kenni, that I love you?" How could she not have known?

Her gaze flickered hesitantly. "How would I know?" she asked, barely above a whisper. "You never told me, Jazz."

Fine, he hadn't said the *words*, but surely he'd showed her. Hell, he knew he had.

"So actions don't matter?" he questioned, stopping several feet from her.

"I didn't say that," she pointed out, frowning back at him now. "But the words are important too, Jazz. They're very important."

Yes they were, he admitted silently. They were very important. But some actions were just as important.

"You never protested that I didn't wear a condom," he said softly. "Are you on birth control?"

"No," she whispered, linking her fingers together when she could find nothing else to do with her hands.

"I could be carrying twenty different diseases, Kenni." He glared down at her in reproof.

To that, she shook her head slowly. "Jessie told me about sleeping with you," she admitted. "And how particular you were about condoms since you began having sex. I didn't fear diseases in the least, Jazz."

"And you didn't question why you were the only woman I've fucked without one?"

"I wondered." Naked, hungry need filled her face now.

"You told me you loved me." His dick was so hard he wondered if his zipper would survive it. "While I was coming inside you . . . How can you leave me, Kenni, if you love me?"

"Jazz . . ." she whispered breathlessly as he jerked his shirt off, then his hands moved to his jeans.

"Undress," he growled. "Take those damned clothes off before I tear them off you."

Stripping his jeans, he decided she was out of time.

"Kendra Maddox, I love you with every breath in my body."

Her lips parted on a gasp and Jazz took full advantage of it. Covering them, his tongue penetrated, found hers, and licked at it with hungry demand.

The little sleeveless T-shirt she wore was easy to tear from her. The material was that thin and fragile. The button popped from her shorts, the zipper might have torn, either way they slid down her legs to pool at the floor.

Her panties were easier than her shirt.

It barely took any effort at all to tear them off her ass. She wasn't wearing a bra.

Damned good thing, he decided, lifting his head.

"Pretty, sweet nipples," he whispered, lowering his head, suckling one of the tight, hard points between his lips.

Kenni arched against him.

It was so good. So wicked and hot.

Sharp pleasure exploded from the hard point, racing through her nervous system to stoke the flames heating her clit and the aching tissue of her vagina to a conflagration of need.

Her juices spilled from her, moist heat that made the ache sharper.

What was it about Jazz that made her feel drunk, intoxicated with the pleasure he could give her?

When his head rose Kenni whimpered at the loss of sensation, needing more. No matter how much or how often he touched her, she needed more.

"Your nipples are so hard," he crooned, stroking his

thumb over a sensitive tip. Kenni's breath caught as siz-
zling reaction raced through the tight bud.

"Like that, don't you, baby?" he whispered.

"You know I do." She could barely breathe for the fiery sensation streaking from her nipple to her clit, then
to the clenched depths of her vagina.

"I want to know everything you like, Kenni," he
whispered, his lips lowering to feather against hers as
he spoke. "Everything that makes your nipples hard.
Everything that makes your pussy wetter."

Her breath caught. Sensation flashed across her flesh
before whipping to her womb with clenching pleasure.

His hand lifted from her breast, threaded through her
hair, and tilted her head back for a hungry, mind-blowing
kiss.

At least it blew her little mind.

Parting her lips his tongue swept over hers, drawing
a ragged cry from her throat.

When his head lifted they were both breathless. And
Kenni was greedy. She was hungry, dying to feel him,
touch him—taste him. Because she knew no matter the
pleasure she gave him, he'd give her back far more.

When his head lifted her lips moved to his chest.
Broad, powerful muscles flexed beneath her lips and
tongue. As she moved lower, rasping her nails against
his side, her lips and tongue tasted more of his flesh.
Ached for more.

The broad, engorged head of his cock throbbed as she
curved her fingers beneath it, stroking down the shaft,
fascinated by the satin-over-iron feel of it. It wasn't just
the feel of him she needed, though. It was the taste of
him. The taste of his need, of his pleasure.

Swiping her tongue over the engorged crest, she didn't expect the taste of salt and male arousal to explode over her senses as it did. Lowering herself until she knelt in front of him, Kenni parted her lips over the swollen head, feeling it flex and throb against her tongue, filling her mouth as the explicit, erotic act had a slick rush of moisture rushing from her vagina.

"That's the way, baby," he groaned as her mouth tightened on the hard head of his cock, invading it. "That's it. Suck my cock sweet and tight."

The earthy words were almost as arousing as having the hard shaft working between her lips.

Stroking the heavy shaft from the base to just below her lips as it moved over the engorged head of his erection, Kenni sucked the wide flesh as deep as she dared.

Erotic hunger singed her senses, dazed her mind.

What had ever made her believe she could walk away from him? He was more essential to her than breathing.

His caressing fingers tightened in her hair as she lashed at the underside of his cock with her tongue. Rolling her tongue against the highly reactive spot, she was rewarded with another of those heavy male groans.

Shards of pleasure-pain exploded through her scalp as his fingers pulled at her hair, his hips flexing, shifting as he thrust against her suckling lips.

"Ah, Kenni, how fucking pretty," he groaned. "Hell, you're killing me."

Her lips tightened, drawing harder on his flesh as she became lost in the physical sensations. Waves of rapture so intense that she wondered for a moment if she should fear them washed over her, triggered by his pleasure rather than her own.

The heavy crest moved past her lips, shuttling against them, stroking over her tongue as Kenni fought to hold it in her mouth as long as possible. His hands tightened in her hair, his strokes shorter, harder.

"Ah fuck," he groaned, his cock head flexing in her mouth "Kenni, baby, move back." He released her hair, but she wasn't about to let him go.

"Kenni, if I spill in your mouth, you'll take it all," he growled, sexual dominance strengthening the words. "You hear me?"

He was close. She could hear it in his voice, feel it in the hard throb of the crest of his cock. Working her mouth over it, her tongue rubbing at it, her only thought to push him over that edge of release. She needed this. She needed all of him.

A hard groan was her only warning. The sound of it rasping from his throat. A second later the throbbing head buried deeper and the first pulse of his release erupted in the suckling depths of her mouth.

The salt-and-midnight taste of him was intoxicating. Each pulse of semen only made her hungrier, needier.

It wasn't just one ejaculation, there were multiple heavy pulses of the dark taste erupting in the suckling heat of her mouth. And she consumed them. She consumed him.

Seconds later he pulled free of her hold and before Kenni realized his intent he lifted her from her knees only to turn and toss her to the bed.

Pushing the tangled curls from her face Kenni stared

up at him, her gaze heavy-lidded at the sight of his rapidly hardening erection.

"I've kept a hard-on since I first laid eyes on you,"
he growled. "And I swear every time I look at you my
dick thinks it has to be hard."

"That's a good thing," she whispered breathlessly.

"Spread your legs. Let me see what you really think
about it."

Kenni spread her legs, slowly. As she did her hands
lifted to cup her swollen breasts, her fingers finding the
torturously hard tips of her nipples.

Jazz didn't know which sight was prettier, the plump,
honey-slick folds of her juice-laden pussy or those graceful fingers playing with her nipples. He knew what he
was dying to taste, though.

Moving to the bed he stretched out between her
thighs, licking his lips at the sweet, feminine scent drifting to him.

He pushed her thighs farther apart, watching as she
gripped her nipples firmly, her fingers rolling over them
faster.

She was close. The engorged, reddened bud of her clit
extended fully from its hood, seeking enough sensation
to flood her with ecstasy.

But not yet. He wanted to feel her orgasm exploding
around his dick as he pumped his release inside the snug
depths of her pussy.

Before that . . . Hell, he just wanted to taste her.

Kenni couldn't control the cry that tore from her lips at
the first lick of Jazz's tongue through the sensitive folds

of her pussy. She was certain that first lick would send her over the edge. She was primed, so ready for the explosion that when it didn't come her eyes jerked open, her gaze going immediately to meet Jazz's.

Wicked, erotic, his eyes were such an electric blue they almost glowed. And the intent she read there had a grin tugging at her lips.

"Afraid you can't make me come more than once?" she asked, her voice throaty to her own ears.

His brow lifted. "I have before."

"Purely by accident," she assured him, knowing better.

"Accident?" He had the audacity to laugh. "Baby, bad things happen to liars."

"Liar? How do I know it wasn't an accident? It's not like you actually let me know it was planned."

The opportunity was there and too perfect to resist.

"You're going to regret that tonight," he assured her.

"Promises, promises." She just wanted to come. He'd make her wait. Torture her if she let him.

He smiled. A slow, wicked, erotic smile that had her heart racing, her vagina clenching.

"Three orgasms before I fuck you," he predicted. "Two after that and the last one . . ." Wry amusement curled his lips. "The last one will probably kill us both."

"The first one now." She was at the point of begging.

Jazz only chuckled. "Not hardly, baby."

Instead of lowering his head to the aching flesh between her thighs, he rose over her.

Electric lust gleamed in his eyes as he brushed her fingers away from her nipples and lowered his lips to them instead.

"I was joking," she whimpered. Knowing the torture would be worse now. "Jazz . . ."

His lips surrounded a nipple, sucked it into his mouth, and his tongue began to play. With one hand lying low on her stomach, his teeth surrounded the tip with searing pleasure-pain for just a second before he suckled at it with firm, hot draws of his mouth.

When she was certain flames would engulf her entire body he repeated each lick, nip, and hungry draw to the other stiff peak. And each time she tried to touch him he pushed her hands aside until finally he captured both her wrists in one hand, stretched them above her head, and went back to killing her with pleasure.

Perspiration slicked her body. Heat licked over her flesh as he played with each hard tip. Until finally he captured one between his lips, drawing on it tighter, harder . . . The lashing pleasure shot straight to her womb, bowed her body instantly and exploded in a shower of exquisite pleasure.

No, he had not just done that.

But he had, and he proved it as he moved to her other nipple. With expert licks, nips, and draws of his hot mouth he had brilliant heat cascading through her in an orgasm that rocked her senses.

No sooner had she began catching her breath than she felt the leather shackling her wrists above her head. Tugging at the restraints, she stared up at the lust-tightened features watching her carefully.

"I can't touch you like this," she whispered desperately. She needed to touch him.

"You make me lose control," he whispered, his voice

rough, hungry. "Besides, this way all you have to do is feel good.

Feel good? This way he could torture her easier.

His lips lowered between her breasts, moving down her body as his hands stroked along an inner thigh. She was so wet, her juices spilling from her vagina, that her thighs were damp as well.

"Two down," he murmured. "One to go."

Okay, her clit, she thought, shocked at how quickly arousal rose inside her after her release.

Jazz didn't do anything quickly, though. With her restrained he had not just quick access, but full control. And he made use of it.

His tongue worked around her swollen clit, moving close but never actually creating the friction she needed to orgasm.

With her legs spread wide, knees bent, he devoured the swollen folds below, licking over them as his fingers eased along the narrow valley below the entrance to her vagina.

His fingertips found her rear entrance, pressing against it, entering as his mouth covered her clit.

Not enough.

Her head tossed, her hips arching forward to create the needed friction. Each push against his lips pushed his finger deeper past her anal entrance. When she was begging for it another finger joined the first and penetrated the tight ring of muscles.

Using the natural lubrication spilling from her vagina he was pumping his fingers inside her, fucking her rear with the same deep, bold thrusts he'd used when pushing inside her pussy.

His lips tightened on her clit, suckling it deep, harder. His tongue flicked at it, rubbed against it, then pressed . . .

"Oh God . . ." Like a trigger. His tongue pressed at the side of the swollen bud, rubbed and flicked and sent shocking, fiery explosions tearing through her.

Her muscles tightened, locked in place as his fingers moved along the incredible, nerve-laden ring tightening around them. Brilliant white light infused her senses and sent her hurtling into a release that had her sobbing his name.

Waves of ecstasy battered at her senses as she shuddered in his hold. Her body jerked, trembled until the aftershocks eased to a few little ripples racing up her spine.

And it wasn't enough.

She whimpered as her vagina clenched and flexed. The additional hunger almost torturous to her now over-sensitized body.

"This is the part I like." Jazz's voice was guttural and rough. "Every time you come it's like your pussy gets tighter. It's going to be so tight, baby, that the pleasure and pain will . . ."

The head of his cock moved into place, pressing against her then thrusting. Just as quickly he withdrew, only to push in again.

Three hard, agonizingly escalating thrusts and she was coming around the shuttling length of his cock as he buried it to the hilt inside her.

She was screaming his name as she felt her wrists release. Coming over her, Jazz gripped her hip and began moving against her. Even as her release rained around the head of his cock he was driving her higher, pushing her into a supernova she could feel reaching out for her.

"That's it, baby," he groaned at her ear. "Move with me just like that, Kenni . . . Ah hell yeah. Fuck me back, Kenni."

She couldn't control the arch of her hips. Jazz was thrusting into her fast and hard, pistoning strokes that ignited a torturous flame . . . It built. It seared her with pleasure, then when it exploded destroyed her with ecstasy, with a pleasure that drove her far beyond any previous concept of ecstasy.

Above her, Jazz called her name, his voice tight, strangled as the feel of his release throbbing inside her extended the rapture lashing at her, burning through her senses until she collapsed against the bed.

Boneless.

Exhausted.

She made a mental note though:

Never dare Jazz sexually again.

Not ever.

"I love you, honey-girl," he whispered drowsily. "With all my soul."

Okay, maybe she'd dare him occasionally.

EPILOGUE

Six weeks later

The funeral was a travesty. A joke Grace found little amusement in. But she was ordered to be there. Despite her objections, despite her arguments, still, she sat there beneath the summer sky at the edge of the Maddox family cemetery and kept her mouth shut as her mother was buried.

Lucia Maddox, widow of Benjamin Maddox, second wife to his brother Vincent Maddox, sister to Vincent's first wife, Sierra Maddox. Betrayer. Traitor. Murderer.

Her fists clenched in her lap, her nails biting into her palms at the knowledge of what Lucia had been and what she had ultimately gotten away with. She hadn't paid for her crimes. She hadn't suffered for what she'd done or served time without freedom for the crimes and the pain she'd inflicted on the Maddox family. Grace couldn't say she'd hurt those who loved her, because honestly, those who really knew her, hadn't loved her.

She'd played the poor unloved wife for nine years.

Poor little Lucia Maddox, the townspeople whispered. She'd married her sister's husband only to suffer with the knowledge that he'd only married her because she'd so resembled the woman he had loved. Then there were those who said Vincent and Lucia had been sleeping together long before Sierra's death. Grace knew better than that, just as she'd suspected it was Lucia who had begun the rumor.

What she hadn't known was that her mother had murdered her only sister and nearly murdered her niece, Kendra "Kenni" Maddox. For ten years Kenni had been on the run, often attacked by cousins she'd been raised with, men sent to kill her by Lucia and their demented belief that they could overthrow the Maddox family as commanders and overseers of the Kin. Lucia and the men following her, the men she'd whored herself to, had actually believed they could fool the Maddox men so effectively. Her uncle Vincent, his sons Cord, Deacon, and Sawyer, his nephews, loyal Maddox men and commanders of the mountain fighters known as Kin.

She'd destroyed so many lives—for what? Some demented belief that the Maddox family held stores of gold and top-secret government information?

Grace wanted to laugh at the thought.

She wanted to laugh as the reverend spoke so solemnly, so kindly of a woman who had fooled him as she had fooled so many others. She wanted to stand up and tell them all what fools they were. But how could she, because she had been the greatest fool of all. She'd loved her mother, despite her cold nature, her criticisms, and subtle cruelties. That was still her mother, until the day Kenni had returned to her home. Until Grace had stood outside the living room and heard her mother furiously admit to killing her sister. And she'd seen the pictures one of her mother's hit men had turned over to Jazz Lancing and his brothers. There were pictures and videos, reports of jobs and the low-level, weaker members of the Kin who had followed her.

Six weeks she'd kept the knowledge to herself that she'd gone through the information her uncle had thought was hidden on his computer now. Six weeks.

That day Lucia had been taken from the house by several government agents. Four days ago, her body had been returned, a report of an auto accident that killed her accompanying it.

Auto accident, her ass.

She had no proof, but she had no doubt that whoever had taken her back to DC had executed her. Knowledge of the Kin, of what they did, what they were a part of, couldn't be allowed to be revealed during a trial. She knew that. She'd known that when Lucia was taken away.

Heads bowed as the reverend solemnly recited prayers and asked that Lucia's soul be held in God's heart and everlasting light. Grace glared at the coffin. She remembered sitting there ten years before, sobbing, destroyed at the loss of a beloved aunt and cousin. Aunt Sierra and her cousin Kenni had been such an integral part of Grace's life that at times she'd felt as though she'd lost her mother instead.

God knew Lucia hadn't been much of a mother.

Finally, the prayers were finished, mourners dismissed, and it was over. The coffin would be lowered once everyone had left, dirt heaped on top of it, and Lucia Maddox's legacy would be buried with her. She would no longer torment, torture, or attempt to kill those who trusted her, those who would have loved her.

All that was left now was the fallout, and that fallout had once again destroyed her daughter. Lucia had ensured that the only dream Grace had held in her heart for so long was ripped apart.

"Grace, come on, sweetheart. Let's go home." Uncle Vinny laid his hand on her shoulder, pulling her from her musings as everyone began to drift away.

"Go home and host a wake she didn't deserve?" Grace sighed, ensuring her voice was too low for others to hear. "Pretend to grieve, Uncle Vinny?"

"Just for a little while," he promised. "Life will return to normal soon, I promise."

He promised.

It was a promise he couldn't keep.

As she turned to follow the others, a strong, broad set of shoulders drew her gaze.

He hadn't even spoken to her. She'd waited, hoping, believing he would, but he hadn't said a word since her mother had been taken. In the six weeks after Lucia had been taken away, she hadn't even glimpsed him. Before that, she'd seen him as often as once a week. He'd teased her, flirted with her, he'd looked at her with hooded gray eyes that grew darker, that grew hungry.

He didn't do that anymore either.

"It's time I move, Uncle Vinny." She held herself distant even as he offered her his arm.

"Not yet." There was no arguing with that tone, usually.

She steadied her voice and lifted her chin in determination. "Yes, it's time."

"Why?" The hard tone of command was simply impossible to ignore, but that didn't mean she had to obey.

"Because I need to think." She wouldn't lie to him, he deserved far better than that. "I need to learn how to live, Uncle Vinny. If I stay at the house with you, Cord, Deke, and Sawyer, then you'll just hover over me and try to protect me from what she's done. I have to deal with it, now."

He was silent for long moments and she actually expected him to argue. Instead, he breathed out heavily. "You're like a daughter to me, Gracie. Kenni returning hasn't changed that. When I thought she was gone . . ." He cleared his throat as emotion thickened his voice. "You were there, and you made me hold on when I didn't want to. Not Lucia, you. Because I knew you were grieving just as hard and just as deep as the rest of us were. I couldn't leave you alone. You didn't leave me alone."

Her eyes filled with tears. Had Lucia expected that? No doubt she had.

"No one blames you, Grace," he promised her. "Least of all that oblivious young man you have your heart set on."

She swung her gaze around, surprise surging through her at the statement.

Rueful amusement filled his gaze as he watched her affectionately.

"Think I didn't notice?" he asked her.

"He didn't." Turning, she stared back at that broad

back as the man she'd had her heart set on paused to talk to one of the women who stopped him.

She hated those women. Hated how they were so comfortable with him they could touch his arm or shoulder, smile up at him so confidently, so certain of their effect on men. Perhaps on him.

"He's a good man," Uncle Vinny said softly. "An honorable man. Sometimes, though, honor stands in a man's way when there's no reason that reaching out for what he wants would tarnish that honor. You're young, but he doesn't understand the quiet maturity that's so much a part of you. I have faith in him though. I think he'll get his head out of his ass soon enough."

She wanted to laugh at that. Six weeks ago, she would have laughed over it.

"Perhaps it was for the best that he hasn't done so before now," she decided. "He is honorable, Uncle Vinny. And a damned good man. He deserves far more than a traitor's daughter."

Before he could protest or make up any excuses his sons and the daughter he'd thought he'd lost were striding to him. Grace stepped back before slowly drifting away. She thought no one noticed either. She believed no one noticed that she walked to her car alone, and that she drove away alone. And she thought no one saw the tear she brushed from her cheek.

Most of her things were packed and waiting to be loaded in that car. If she was lucky, very lucky, she could take care of that before the family even arrived at the house. The question was, exactly where would she go?